Standing into Danger

DESMOND BRIGGS

Standing into Danger

SECKER & WARBURG
LONDON

First published in England 1985 by
Martin Secker & Warburg Limited
54 Poland Street, London W1V 3DF

British Library Cataloguing in Publication Data

Briggs, Desmond
Standing into danger
I. Title
823'.914[F]   PR6052.R443/

ISBN 0–436–06856–7

Photoset in Linotron 11/12pt Bembo
by Hewer Text Composition Services, Edinburgh
Printed in Great Britain by
Biddles Ltd., Guildford and King's Lynn

For
Patrick & Mary Salt

PROLOGUE

When the lighthouse on Duncansby Head came in sight, Captain Dougall left his cabin and went on the bridge. A Scot, he felt possessive about his home waters, and despite the presence, here on the bridge and in the adjoining radio room, of a battery of modern aids to navigation, everyone on watch that afternoon knew that while the *Katherina Vathos* steamed through the Pentland Firth, their captain would be dodging about with his ancient hand-bearing compass and crumpled chart, to pick out the lights and landmarks on either side of the strait.

The *Katherina Vathos* was a huge vessel – what the press called a super-tanker – and the pride of the Ithaki-Hellenic Line. She was outward-bound from Göteborg, in passage for Nigeria, and since this was only her third voyage since she had been commissioned, she was still in gleaming trim, from the red strake at her waterline, through the high, shining black topsides still untarnished by streaks of salt and rust, to the spanking white paintwork of her top-hamper. She was in ballast, her cavernous holds filled with enough sea water to keep the giant ship navigable and to give stability: even so, without a cargo, her hull rose out of the water almost sixty feet: she must look, thought the captain, like a smooth black cliff slicing through the choppy waves.

Captain Dougall had been gratified when his owner, Laertes Vathos, had appointed him to the command of the then still building tanker. He was, after all, the only master who held a British passport in the whole Ithaki-Hellenic fleet, and Vathos might with justification have selected a fellow Greek for the honour; but Captain Dougall was the senior skipper in the line, he had been with Ithaki-Hellenic for twenty years, and Vathos knew that he could count on the solitary Scotsman's complete, unquestioning loyalty: such a virtue deserved its reward.

Ben Dougall had served Vathos since the war. He had emerged in 1945 with a master's ticket, a row of medals and a commendation from the Royal Naval Reserve; but there hadn't been many commands open to merchant captains, who were a glut on the market, and Ben had been glad to join Ithaki-Hellenic, then nothing more than four rusty coasters plying the Eastern Mediterranean. Vathos had made it clear from the start that he had bigger things in mind, that he was pleased to have a British captain in his employ, and that if Captain Dougall served him well, the rewards would be substantial. Sometimes, Vathos had hinted delicately, his orders might be . . . unconventional.

Dougall understood perfectly. He considered himself a free agent; admittedly, he had acquired a wife while on shore leave during the war and, on the next leave, a daughter to match; but he considered his marital responsibilities discharged by the despatch, every month, of a modest sum for his family's maintenance, receiving in return a progression of photographs of the growing Alison, from baby in swaddling clothes through toothy schoolgirl to sulking teenager, which he dutifully displayed in the captain's cabin that he considered his real and only home.

As for Vathos' orders, he carried them out without question as to their rectitude. The ultimate destination of the cargoes, whether of contraband cigarettes and cognac, of heavy packing cases labelled agricultural machinery, or even, on more than one occasion, of scruffy and excitable Jewish immigrants, was of no concern to him. Vathos was lucky, and by the early Fifties, Ithaki-Hellenic had expanded into a fleet of well-chartered modern tankers reflecting their owner's early hunch that what the West would need most was oil: the most modern and by far the biggest was the *Katherina Vathos*.

2

Even here, on the bridge of the flagship of the fleet, rated as 100-AI at Lloyd's, Captain Dougall was in receipt of orders delivered verbally and in the privacy of Vathos' stateroom on his yacht off the South of France. Captain Dougall had accepted them with the same impassive obedience he had once shown to Admiralty orders to hunt down a killer submarine. As the huge vessel approached the narrows of the Pentland Firth, he felt stirring within him the wheels of excitement.

Captain Dougall left the bridge house and went out on to the wing. Here, high above the flat decks that seemed to stretch almost endlessly to the bows far ahead, he could feel the sea air on his face. Already, they had passed the Pentland light on Muckle Skerry and, away to the port beam, Duncansby, high on its headland – the northeasterly tip of the Scottish mainland – gleamed white in a sudden shaft of sun. He sniffed the air: there was little wind and the breeze he felt twitching at the brim of his cap was due to the ship's own motion. She was bowling along at a modest ten knots, an economical speed and a safe one in these narrowing waters. In any case, the engines weren't built for speed: they were puny in comparison with the vast bulk of the ship, and the captain grinned to himself as he recalled the mariner's tale of how the Japanese, when joining the rush to build leviathan tankers, had trained their skippers. According to the legend, they had placed in a lake a flotilla of forty-foot barges, each powered by a small engine of one-half horse power, and in this miniature ocean, like so many bumper cars at a fairground, the Japanese masters had been taught their new skills. There'd been no need for any puddling about in a pond for Captain Dougall: he knew he was capable of handling any ship, in any weather.

He went to the door of the bridge house and opened it.

'Mr Pissou, here if you please,' he called out.

A young Greek, the white tabs on his lapels proclaiming him to be a cadet, slipped off a stool on which he had been perched while writing up his log and came over, saying rapidly as he approached, 'Yes, sir, right away, sir.'

The captain frowned as he turned to face forrard. If only these damned Greeks didn't have to talk like damned dago waiters, he thought to himself. 'Put your cap straight, boy,' he said over his shoulder.

Pissou attended to his cap and waited, wondering what the captain wanted. The skipper's voice was soft and lilting, but this in no way diminished a formidable personality. Captain Dougall was tall and spare, with the clean skin and blue eyes that always seemed strange to his Greek colleagues: down each cheek were deep clefts, as of permanent disapproval, and the thin-lipped mouth turned sharply down, pursed in perennial distaste.

'This would be your first voyage in these waters, I'd be thinking, Mr Pissou,' the captain observed.

'Yes, sir.' The cadet pointed to the south, where a long line of dark, forbidding cliffs were fringed at their feet by the white of breaking seas. 'And that, sir, must be your homeland.'

'Aye,' said the captain.

'You must be sad, sir, to be sailing past the land of your birth. I know,' Pissou went on, aware that the captain seemed to be in a rare friendly mood, 'that whenever I sail past Ithaca, I feel sad.'

Dougall looked round at the cadet. 'So you're from Ithaca, are you, boy?'

'Oh yes, sir. My mother's cousin is sister-in-law to Mr Vathos,' he explained proudly.

'I see. That explains everything,' said the captain gravely.

The irony was lost on the cadet, who took him aback with his next question. 'And when you retire, you will return to live in the land of your fathers?'

'Retire?' The captain's voice was sharp: how could this lad have guessed his thoughts? Then, he reminded himself, while he was not yet fifty-five, to Pissou he must seem almost an old man; the question was natural. In any case, when the time came, he would indeed return to Scotland, to spend, for the sake of appearances, a year or so at his wife's cramped villa on the outskirts of Dumfries. It would give him a chance to get to know his daughter Alison, although, he suspected, she would turn out to be as dull as her mother.

'I've no time to talk about retirement, nor yet of what you call my homeland,' the captain went on. 'I called you out on

4

to the wing to let you have a look at this' – he gestured at the grey-green expanse of sea that lay before them. On the port side was the mainland of Scotland, where the brown moors, sullen under a lowering sky, were cut off suddenly at the cliff's edge, as if sliced off raggedly with a carving knife. To the north lay the islands of Orkney, with their rolling, whaleback hills. 'This is the Pentland Firth which, you should know, represents the most difficult navigational passage on the coasts of the United Kingdom. In there' – he nodded at the bridge house – 'you may find every modern gadget to make a sailor's life easy, but you've still got to know these waters as you know your own piss. Oh, it's calm enough now, for we've timed our passage for the slack of the tide, but when you get a westerly gale running against the ebb, you'll see a turbulence of the sea here that'd make Cape Horn look like your mother's bath water.'

'Is . . . dangerous, then?'

'Dangerous, lad? Of course it's dangerous. Especially at high water springs, when you'll have a ten-knot tide funnelling in from the Atlantic. And added to that, Pentland's a busy passage, so you have to keep a weather eye out for other shipping, and I mean out here, not just on the radar screen.'

Pissou looked around. Ahead of them steamed a large freighter, obviously heavily laden, for her gunwales were almost awash as she pitched into a long roller. Beyond her, smoke plumed from the funnels of two dirty coasters, and astern of the *Katherina Vathos* a flotilla of trawlers wallowed in her wake, a skirl of seagulls above them.

'Fishermen,' the captain commented, 'on their way to the herring grounds north of the Faeroes, I'll be bound. And that' – he pointed to a low and rocky island on their port beam – 'that's Stroma. It sits in the Pentland Firth and divides the tides, like a boulder in the middle of a mountain stream.'

As they steamed westwards, the islands of Orkney were opening up on their starboard beam to reveal a calm expanse of water within their encircling grasp. 'Scapa Flow,' said the captain. 'And that's odd.' His voice changed and he took out his binoculars to scan the anchorage. 'There's usually at least one or two salvage tugs in there, generally Dutch. The

5

carrion of the sea, I call 'em: they hover in there like vultures, waiting to prey on any poor bloody sailor who's got his ship into trouble. What is it, Nicky?'

They had been joined by the radio officer, a Corfiote named Nykiadopolou whose name had early been shortened by his master, and since accepted by the crew.

'I've been keeping watch, sir,' said the radio officer, 'and I intercepted a distress signal. It's from the *Dimitri Calypso* and I thought you ought to see it.' He handed over a clipboard, which the captain took and read.

'Request immediate assistance . . . engine trouble . . . cargo shifted, now listing 15° to port . . . position 64° North, 01° East. H'm.' He handed back the message.

'The *Dimitri Calypso*,' said the cadet. 'Wasn't she one of ours once?'

'That's right, lad. And when Mr Vathos sold her, Captain Velos decided to stay with his ship.'

'Shouldn't we go to help?'

'I don't think that necessary, sir,' the radio officer intervened. 'I overheard the salvage tugs: they must have been listening in to the radio traffic, for they're already on their way, without even waiting for confirmation from Lloyd's.'

'Then there's nothing we need do,' said Captain Dougall. 'The position is well north of the Shetlands, and the tugs will be there long before we could possibly put in an appearance. We'll maintain our course. Thank you, Nicky,' he dismissed the radio officer, 'and keep me informed.'

The *Katherina Vathos* had now left the narrows of the Pentland Firth and emerged into the open sea. Here, despite the calm weather, they could feel the length of the ship breasting the long seas reaching in from the North Atlantic. Over the Scottish coast lay a heavy grey bank of cloud and the horizon to the north was lost in a misty haze.

'We're lucky to have such an easy passage,' said the captain, 'although I reckon there'll be a bit of sea fog around before dawn.'

'Are there any seaports on this north coast of Scotland, sir?' asked the cadet, who was enjoying this spell away from his duties.

'Seaports? No, lad, not unless you'd count Scrabster, just

6

beyond Dunnet Head, and that's no more than a little bit of a harbour for an Orkney ferry and a few fishermen. After that, it's a bleak and desolate coast, bitten into by four sea lochs. The first is the Kyle of Tongue, and that's no place for a seaman, with its outlying islands and tricky shoals. Then you have the Kyle of Pogue; that's open to the sea, quite narrow and there's a nasty bar at the entrance. Round the next headland, Loch Eriboll is probably the safest if you ever have to find an anchorage in a hurry, for it has a lighthouse and deep water and even a large vessel could find shelter there without much difficulty. The last is very dangerous: the Kyle of Durness, and after that, there's Cape Wrath, the northwest tip of Scotland.'

'Cape . . . Rat, sir?'

'Wrath, boy, wrath, and that's what I'll vent on you unless you're back at your place on the bridge and catching up on your log within the next five seconds.'

Pissou realised that his odd interlude with his skipper was ended and hurried back to the bridge, followed by Captain Dougall.

In the bridge house, all was quiet, with only a faint hum from the air conditioning and an irregular, soft ping from the radar as it swept the seas around them.

'What course are we on?' the captain called over to the man at the Automatic Pilot.

'Two, seven, two degrees, sir,' the able seaman chanted slowly, having some difficulty with the English words.

Captain Dougall nodded and went to look over Pissou's shoulder at the log. The cadet had inscribed carefully in his stilted, upright hand the words March 22, 1965: below this were a serious of changes of course, as the ship passed through the Pentland Firth, and the entry upon which the cadet was now concentrating referred to the vessel in distress and the departure of the Dutch salvage tugs.

'Satisfactory,' the captain murmured, 'very satisfactory.' And as to whether his satisfaction was due to the neatness of the log, or to the absence of the salvage team, Mr Pissou had no idea.

During the late afternoon dog watch, Captain Dougall usually adjourned to his cabin. A mound of paperwork, always plentiful at the start of any voyage, awaited his attention on his desk; but, deciding that there was no point whatever in tackling it, instead he made straight for his bunk: he would need all his concentration later during the night, he reminded himself as he eased off his boots and was, at once, asleep.

He awoke to a single, sharp knock on the door. Instantly he was alert, swinging his stockinged feet to the deck as he called out, 'Come in.'

It was the chief engineer, a stocky, dark-visaged man in spotless blue overalls and a peaked cap. While, at the captain's invitation, he helped himself to a brandy, Dougall glanced at the chronometer high up on a bulkhead: 19.50, it read. His sea sense had already told him, from the faint rhythm of the engines that thrummed through the ship and from the easy motion, that the *Katherina Vathos* was still on her course; now he glanced through the porthole: outside it was quite black, with runnels of moisture trickling down the glass.

'As I thought, Chief,' he said, 'we'll be having a bit of fog later.'

'Any problem?' The chief cocked a thick black eyebrow at his skipper.

'None at all. On the contrary, it'll be a help: it will add to the confusion.'

'And you? How will you manage?'

'On the bridge, it will look as though I'll be navigating by dead reckoning; but in fact, I have my own RDF set tucked away in yon wardrobe. Come and have a look: you're the only one who knows I have it.'

The captain unlocked the cupboard. On a shelf, there stood what looked like a small portable wireless; but, as he now demonstrated, it was a battery-powered Radio Direction Finder, of a kind more normally found on pleasure yachts.

'It's very simple, Chief,' he explained. 'In these waters, there are three lighthouses equipped with radio beacons, each sending out a distinctive signal: one is to the east of us, on Stroma, there's another to the west on Cape Wrath and the third, away to the north, is on Sule Skerry. By tuning in to each and taking back bearings, I'll be able to plot our exact position at any time.'

'That's a comfort, at any rate. I must say, Captain, I don't like anything about tonight's operation . . .'

'No more,' barked the captain. He sat down at his desk and waved the chief into the chair opposite. 'We have both agreed to carry out our orders, and that's all we need to remember.'

He looked across the paper-littered desk at his chief engineer, whose face was shadowed from the harsh lamp by the peak of his cap. Ben Dougall and Ulysses Stavros had been at sea together for many years; both had joined Ithaki-Hellenic at the war's end, both enjoyed to an unusual extent the confidence of their owner and both had profited from it. There was comradeship between them, each knew and trusted the other's skills and above all, they liked each other. About the set of their shoulders, as the clock inched towards the hour, there was an air of nervous tension, and their voices, as they checked through the last details, were lowered, conspiratorial.

'At the next watch, the first officer will hand over to number two,' said the captain.

'That's when he'll go and have his dinner. He'll be off the scene when the action starts.'

'Aye. Hector Manises is a good seaman, for all his nit-picking ways, and he might easily cotton on to the fact that something odd was going on. And later on, you'll be taking care of him?'

'Oh, yes, Captain. I shall, as you say, take good care of him. Who'll be at the helm?'

'Able Seaman Privas.'

'A good choice: he'll obey your orders without question.'

'And, since his English is very limited, there's just a possibility of misunderstanding.' The captain's sardonic grimace was echoed by a more cheerful smile from the chief.

'Now let's see,' Captain Dougall went on, 'the weather's right – this fog is a bonus – and the tide is right, for it's the last of the high water springs; are you absolutely sure that everything on your side is prepared?'

'Certainly, Captain. Zero hour, as they say in the films, is at 20.24.'

'In that case, you'd better be away to the engine room, and I'll be off to the bridge.' The captain heaved himself into a heavy dark-blue overcoat, adjusted his cap, found some gloves, then, with his binoculars around his neck and his hand-bearing compass in his pocket, began the climb to the bridge.

He watched from his swinging chair as, at twenty hundred hours, the watch changed. Mr Manises handed over to George Enikos, the second officer; the navigation officer emerged to check the course and to report the ship's position to the master, all of which Mr Pissou, who was coming to regard himself as the captain's personal aide, noted down in his log.

The navigation officer looked curiously at the cadet, and the captain explained. 'It's Pissou's own log,' he said. 'I've told him to maintain it this voyage, for training, you'll understand. And I dare say,' he added drily, 'it'll make more seamanlike reading than yon battery of teletype machines you've got chattering away in the chart house.'

Besides, he had a shadowy inner thought that, whether or not the plans for the night went as expected, the cadet's jottings might just come in handy.

'Let's take a look at our neighbours,' he said, leading them over to the radar. On the screen the sweeping beam lit up a number of green blips; he pointed to one, almost on the edge. 'That'll be the big freighter ahead of us in the Firth, I'll be thinking?'

'Yes, sir. She's making good speed and is away to the northwest.'

'How many miles?'

'About twenty, sir.'

The captain nodded: well beyond the range of visibility, especially on a cloudy night like this. 'And these?' His finger hovered over a scattering of small blips close together.

'A fleet of trawlers, sir, out of Aberdeen. I heard them talking on the radio: they think they're on the track of herring.'

'A shoal of herring, eh?' said the captain happily. 'That'll keep them busy for the night. What happened to those two coasters ahead of us earlier?'

'They're off the screen, sir. They must have rounded Cape Wrath and headed south.'

'So we're pretty much on our own. That's how a seaman likes to be on the high seas, Pissou, and don't you forget it.' With that, the captain left the bridge and went out on to the wing.

With his gloved hands on the rail, he could feel, even up so high, the vibration of the engines as they drove the huge vessel through the seas at a steady ten knots. It was a dark, clammy night: under the glare of the masthead arc lamps, scarves of sea mist wreathed about the length of the deck before him: it was as if the ship was moving within a round wall that encircled her, a world of her own with only the sibilant, sempiternal swishing of the seas to break the solitude and the silence. On either beam, the glow of the navigation lights, one green, one red, threw on to the wall of darkness a ghostly hint of colour.

Captain Dougall was surprised to find within himself no particular affection for the ship under his command. For all his earlier vessels, even for the rusting coaster that had been his first, he had felt pride and a hint of love that deepened as he came to know their ways. But they had been proper ships, merchantmen; while the *Katherina Vathos*, for all her size and sophisticated equipment, was too new, too vast and too impersonal to be more than a slowly moving bulk storage container.

At twenty-four minutes past eight, Greenwich Mean Time, the first explosion came.

1

'Good morning, sir.' The tall man in a long scarlet coat did not actually touch his tall and shiny black top hat as Martin Coley mounted the steps of Lloyd's in the early summer of 1963, but the greeting was enough to give Martin a warm sense of belonging: it was akin to entering a club and it confirmed Martin's feeling that he was a small cog in the great financial machine known as the City of London.

Now Martin passed through an ante-hall, a high, sparse chamber with a marble floor. At one end was an insipid stained-glass window surmounting a war memorial and a Roll of Honour, lending a little of the atmosphere of a school chapel. Around the walls were austere grey benches, for the use of outsiders denied entry to the Room, where visitors might wait for their host under the eye of another scarlet-robed functionary. From him, too, Martin received a half-nod in salutation. Like a club or a school, Lloyd's had its own rules, traditions and shibboleths: it was typical, for instance, that the man he had just passed was called a 'waiter'; anywhere else, the title would have been commissionaire or doorman, but this was Lloyd's, Lloyd's of London as they sometimes emphasised to the ignorant (indicating thereby that there was no connection whatever with the younger bank of a similar name): Lloyd's was proud of its origins in a seventeenth-century City coffee house and it was for this reason that the attendants were still addressed as waiters.

Martin was heading for the heavy swing doors. Here a well calligraphed sign announced:

This Room is
PRIVATE
and for the use of
MEMBERS
SUBSCRIBERS
ASSOCIATES &
SUBSTITUTES
only.

Martin himself was only as yet a Substitute, but it was with his sense of fellowship enhanced that he pushed through the doors to enter the Room.

The Underwriting Room was no ordinary chamber. It was vast, over three hundred feet long, and slightly kinked half-way down, like a boomerang: all along the sides ran square columns encased in dark-green marble, as harshly structural as girders in a hanger: from floor to ceiling they must have measured forty feet, and from them was suspended a long, running gallery from whose balustrade one could look down on the full expanse of the floor below. Both floor and gallery were filled with rows of 'boxes', nearly five hundred of them, crammed together between broad aisles. Each box consisted of no more than two long wooden benches facing each other across a broad, blue baize-covered table: at one end was a standing bookcase containing the leather-bound ledgers and the reference books that were the tools of the underwriter's trade. At this time of day – for it was only twenty to nine – the blue baize was almost clear: the waiters had already been round, laying out fresh blotting paper, a neat stack of incoming post awaited the underwriter's paperknife, and clusters of telephones stood silent, but that was all.

There was a quiet air of expectancy about the Room, as if it were awaiting some command from the red-robed caller at his rostrum to leap into life. Later, when business was at its height, there would be a scrimmage of brokers around each box, queuing to show their risks to the underwriter; every table would be littered with opened ledgers, pencilled

13

scribbles of long division percentages on scraps of paper, re-insurance slips, telephone messages, notices and advices from brokers on such matters as alterations of cargo manifests or a new port of destination for some vessel on whose hull the box had written a line. Around each box would grow a rising tide of crumpled and discarded papers, like the foaming scum in some grimy dock, for it was the usage at Lloyd's that the floor was the waste-paper basket.

Martin Coley liked to be early at work. It gave him time to assume for the day his Lloyd's personality, quiet, deferential, on-the-spot. As he threaded his way through the boxes, passing the yet unchattering ticker tapes, the notice board festooned with intelligence reports of shipping activity from Lloyd's agents overseas and the huge leather-bound Loss Book where details of each foundered vessel were recorded in a tall copperplate hand, his appearance was much like any other young and ambitious man going to work in the City. A first impression of Martin Coley was one of neatness: from the well-polished black shoes, both laces tied in symmetrical bows, through the smoothly pressed grey worsted suit, its waistcoat pockets just revealing on one side the blue leather and gilded edges of his Lloyd's diary and on the other the clips of two fountain pens, to the stiff white collar with a blue knitted silk tie carefully knotted, Martin's turnout was impeccable. Only his hair, light-brown and wavy, showed signs of indiscipline above the ears and at the nape of his neck: at one time he had endeavoured to control it by the use of hair cream, but this he had soon learned not to do.

In one of the aisles beyond the caller's rostrum lay his destination, his place of employment, generally known as Mr Murchison's Box. Here he flung down his copy of *The Times*, automatically leant over to turn the date on the desk calendar to '5 June 1963', then picked up that morning's *Lloyd's List* – the daily journal of the shipping industry – and headed off downstairs for his customary ten minutes on the bog. Glancing at the headlines, concerning a new order for giant oil tankers placed with a Japanese yard, he reflected with relief that in discarding *The Times* he had left behind the more sensational outside world. In the Underground train that morning, glancing around, he had seen every front page

14

screaming the current scandal: 'Call Girl Scandal – Profumo Quits', 'War Minister "misled" the Commons', 'Russian Spy in Astor Love Nest?', each headline trumpeted in turn and even *The Times* had so far unbent as to illustrate its story with photographs of the girls concerned, albeit remaining careful to name them formally as Miss Keeler and Miss Rice-Davies.

The start to Martin's working day never varied. Every morning, at exactly seven o'clock, his mother would hammer on his bedroom door. By the time he was downstairs, she had his breakfast ready in the kitchen. At twenty to eight he would kiss his mother, still in her négligé and with her first cigarette of the day in her lips, pick up his newspaper, withdraw his rolled umbrella from the hatstand in the hall and, slamming the front door so that its stained-glass panel rattled, set off for the short walk to Ealing Broadway station.

For all his life, Martin had lived with his mother at 31 Oaklands Drive, London W5. It was one of a thousand such houses run up by a speculative builder in the Thirties, set back about twenty feet from the road, with a path of crazy paving running up to the porch and a short concrete drive to the lean-to garage. The frontage, too, was stereotyped for individuality, with panes of bottle glass in the lattice work of the bow windows and a few blackened beams applied almost at random to the gable. But for Martin it was, and always had been, home: the patch of brighter, newer tiles on the roof that showed where repairs had been effected after a landmine dropped in the next street during the Blitz, the crookedness of the lintel over a first-floor window that gave the house a dropsical air, almost as if it were winking at him, and the creak with which the front gate greeted his departures and returns, all these were signs that for him No. 31 was different, special.

By contrast, the rear façade was plain, almost gaunt. No excess of Tudor fancy here: just plain grey pebble-dash, against which a network of drainpipes stood out as ugly as varicose veins, their peeling paint spilling smears of rust down the walls. The long and narrow garden, however, was well tended; Mrs Coley had long since abandoned her efforts to make her son take an interest, though occasionally he

15

might be persuaded to mow the strip of lawn, so she contrived to make the time in her busy day to keep the garden as tidy as she maintained the house.

For Beryl Coley was very efficient. The only daughter of a newsagent in a modest way of business, she had hoped to rise in the world when she married Ted Coley, a clerk at Lloyd's. They moved into Oaklands Drive, with their baby son and a maid-of-all-work, on a mortgage, and Beryl assumed the life of a suburban housewife. The coming of the war changed Beryl's life for ever. The maid disappeared into the ATS, and Beryl soon found that keeping the house and preparing the meals herself presented no problem if she kept to a routine. Then Ted Coley enlisted: although this brought a burden of constant anxiety, she was gratified that at least her husband was serving in the Brigade of Guards and her pride increased when, after signal service at Dunkirk, Ted was made up to sergeant.

In 1944, the war came home to Beryl Coley. First, both her parents were killed, by one of the first 'doodlebugs', a flying bomb that came out of the blue to demolish a complete block of flats. Almost automatically, Beryl took over her father's shop, thinking to keep it warm until peace came, when she would be able to sell it for a nice nest-egg. Then came the telegram with the news that Ted Coley had been killed in the fighting around Falaise.

Beryl was tough, and although she grieved for Ted, she realised that now she was on her own: it was up to her to fend for herself and for Martin, by now a pupil at a nearby, fee-paying day school. Accordingly, she applied herself to the business: her bright cheerfulness attracted custom and, with increasing shortages of such items as cigarettes and a hard bargaining skill in after-dark, back-door deals in cash and no questions asked, she was able to make sure that her more prosperous customers never went without. To two, in particular, she was attentive: Mr Oulton, a local solicitor, and Mr Banks, the aptly named manager of the local branch of the National & Provincial. What with the doodlebugs and with talk of a newer and even more devastating rocket on its way, property was cheap in West London at the time, and by the end of the war, with the assistance of Mr Oulton

16

and Mr Banks, Beryl owned three corner shops, all with honest manageresses and doing good business.

In the austerity that followed peace, Beryl continued to prosper. People still wanted their cigarettes, which so many of them had taken to under the stress of wartime and now could not do without, and they craved the distraction of newspapers and magazines to take their minds away from the shortages and the daily deprivations. In the years after 1945, Beryl added two more shops to her little chain. Among the representatives of the wholesalers upon whom she depended, she became known as a good sort, always ready for a few rounds of rum or, if they could get it, gin, either in the little office above her father's old shop or at The Target, a roadhouse a mile or two away on the Oxford road. Here she would often be found at lunchtime, her cheery laugh ringing through the crowded Flare Path bar as, the only woman in a circle of males, she held court. In her tight, royal blue costume she was still an attractive woman: but she took her drink like a man and made sure that when her turn came, she stood her own round. Moreover, no matter how many gins or rums were passed across the bar counter, when the time came for business she still struck a hard bargain.

For all the occupation of her busy day, Beryl was always home by the time that Martin returned from school. He now attended Latymer Upper, an excellent grammar school in Hammersmith whose fees of £60 a year were well within his mother's means. Martin was a quiet, studious boy, not scholarly but with the kind of mind that coped well with examinations: he had taken School Certificate when he was only fourteen. He seemed to have few friends, and, disliking team games, only developed a certain ability at lawn tennis. He would come home at about six, by which time Beryl was sitting in the lounge with her first gin and Dubonnet of the evening; they would exchange news of the day and then, while Beryl prepared their evening meal, Martin would settle to his homework.

Much the same routine had obtained when Martin went to work. Lately, however, he had formed the habit of stopping off with some of his Lloyd's cronies at a smart pub off Knightsbridge for a few beers; often by the time he reached

17

home, he would find his mother in an odd, silent mood; but with the arrival of a television set in the corner of the lounge, there was little call for talk.

It was through Beryl that Martin had obtained his present position. When Ted Coley was killed, she had received a letter of sympathy from his commanding officer, a Major Murchison. She had written to thank him for his condolences – it was clear that the major had held Sergeant Coley in some esteem – and when the year ended, she followed up with a Christmas card 'from the Home Front'. Then Major Murchison, on leave in London, took the trouble to pay a visit to his sergeant's widow and her little boy; after that, Beryl was careful to maintain the Christmas card habit. By the time the major was married, Mrs Coley's name had crept on to some list and remained there: every year the Lloyd's card, with the crest and motto 'Fidentia' on thick plain white board and inside a printed message of greetings from Ivor & Ursula Murchison, held pride of place on her mantelpiece.

When Martin was seventeen, she gave some thought to his future. She was ambitious for him, eager that he should be out of trade and make his way in the City, like his father; but for Martin, she would not be content with a modest, clerkly job. Still, she realised that he would have to start at the bottom and, bolstering her courage, she wrote to Mr Murchison, as he now was again despite a deserved MC for gallantry, seeking advice about Martin's career.

Mr Murchison had replied at once, in his own hand, with its use of the Greek 'e' betraying his classical education. He would be glad to see Sergeant Coley's boy, he said; but he considered it best that this interview should be deferred until Martin had undergone his National Service.

Conscripted into the Royal Corps of Signals, Martin had been marked down as Potential Officer material. In due course, he passed through WOSB and OCTU: Beryl felt very proud when she watched his company slow-march up the steps in the Passing Out ceremony: he looked so smart and manly in his uniform, with his peaked cap and white epaulettes that, for a moment, she wished he had been destined for a military career. Martin served out his term in Cyprus; when he was demobilised, he was grown into a

18

man. And not just physically, with his straight, broadened shoulders and a healthy tan in place of his schoolboy pallor: he was still quiet, but behind his reserve there lay a new confidence in himself, something he had perhaps learnt from the command of his own men.

Martin had only dim memories of his first interview with Mr Murchison. It had taken place when Lloyd's was still in the Old Building, and he had had some difficulty in finding the discreet entrance in Leadenhall Street. At last, he had sent in his name by the god-like figure in a red coat who guarded the door and soon Murchison emerged from the Room to sweep Martin off to a cramped and bare little office under the attics. Martin had by now quite forgotten what was said at the interview, but he must have given satisfaction, for it became apparent that he was being offered a position.

'If you'd come to me six months ago, I couldn't have done anything for you myself,' Murchison said. 'But I'm planning to expand some of our underwriting lines soon and we'll be needing more hands on the box. I took on another young man about six months ago: Toby Blackett. I'll ask him to show you the ropes.'

Martin could do no more than nod: he was too full of excitement to speak. He just grasped that he was to be paid in the region of £7 a week, with the hope of some bonus on the annual profits; but he had no clue as to what his duties might be. Nor was Murchison more positive.

'We're only a small box,' he explained, 'so you'll have to pick up things as you go along. Once you've settled in, we'll begin to have an idea where your talents lie.'

It was all very offhand, very gentlemanly. This, Martin was to learn, was Murchison's style: just as his dress – dark suit, stiff collar, watch-chain across his waistcoat, bowler hat, rolled umbrella and gloves for use outside – and his slim, upright figure, with sandy hair brushed flat on either side of a ribbon-straight parting, were those of an officer of the Brigade of Guards, so he treated his young men as if they were his subalterns: on easy, first-name terms off-duty, but with more than a hint of steel when they were at work.

'I'll take you down and introduce you to the box,' Martin was now told. 'We'll be a bit crowded, I'm afraid, but once we move into the New Building across the road in Lime Street, we'll all have more space to breathe.'

At the entrance to the Room, they paused. Martin had a vague impression of yellowish marble and touches of fading gilt, over which reached a shallow glass dome, through which grey daylight filtered down. It was like a mixture of a railway terminus and a very large bank, with the crowds of ever-moving humanity and the grime of the one and the portentous dignity of the other. The floor was crammed with what he was to learn were boxes and in their direction Murchison made a gesture.

'So this, sir, is Lloyd's.' Martin made the remark half in awe and half because he felt that some observation, however banal, was expected of him.

'Indeed, Martin, indeed.' Murchison cleared his throat. 'Here is the greatest, I think one can say the only, free marketplace in the world of insurance. Each underwriter has, as it were, set up his booth to trade, often in competition with his peers, with the brokers who bring with them risks from every corner of the earth. Individually, each box is a separate underwriter; but, collectively, we are Lloyd's.'

There was an air of pronouncement about Murchison's last sentence, as if it was in quotation marks and a part of the lore of Lloyd's: Martin had made a note of it and often found it of use when himself escorting visitors around the Room.

It was some years now since they had moved into the New Building. With its air conditioning, modern lighting and wider aisles, it was vastly more comfortable; and on this June morning, as Martin returned from the cloakroom and made his way to the box, the air was fresh, soft and cool and would remain so all day until 4.30, when smoking was permitted.

Remembering his own initial confusion in his first days with Mr Murchison, Martin sympathised with strangers who found it difficult to grasp just what the box represented. For these two wooden benches, this table and a few leather-bound ledgers were the only physical manifestation of an enterprise handling a premium income – what in an ordinary business would be a turnover – approaching three million pounds a year. Yet here there were none of the apparatus of big business: no receptionists or secretaries, no lavish offices, no conference rooms or cocktail cabinets: just three men and the underwriter, facing each other across the blue baize.

The box was made up of several elements. First and foremost, it was a syndicate of individual 'names', some fifty of them. Most of these were 'outside' names, men of substance who, having demonstrated that they possessed wealth in excess of £75,000, pledged themselves without limit upon their liability to back Ivor Murchison's skill as their underwriter, as the man who accepted risks on their behalf. As in a club, prospective members were proposed and seconded from within: they then had to appear before a Rota Committee of senior working members, to satisfy Lloyd's that they were the sort of men who would be suitable, that they were indeed possessed of the qualifying means and, most important of all, that each candidate was fully aware that, in the event of catastrophe striking and of Murchison failing to balance his books, they were liable to lose everything they owned, down to their bed-linen and their gold watches.

Upon election, outside names paid a hefty membership fee and put up a substantial deposit. At one time, only the security of gilt-edged Government stock had been acceptable, but nowadays ordinary equities were permitted, in addition to a minimum of gilts. These were registered jointly in the names of the Corporation of Lloyd's and the individual name; the member received the income from them, but the existence of these deposits formed an additional buttress for the protection of policy-holders.

'Working' names – those who earned their living at Lloyd's, either with underwriters or brokers – had certain advantages. Both their show of wealth and the scale of their deposits were subject to much lower limits: moreover, their profits were treated by the Inland Revenue as earned income and therefore liable to a lower scale of taxation.

It was Martin's ambition to become a working name. To accumulate the necessary capital was, of course, the main problem. Already, he had taken out a life assurance policy, but its growth was slow, and there was a limit on the amount he could afford to lay aside from his still modest salary. His opposite number on the box, his friend Toby Blackett, had, he knew, already put out feelers to Mr Murchison about joining; but Toby came from a background of family money, a different matter from Mrs Coley's little chain of shops.

Another and separate business also had its being at the box. This was the underwriting agency formed by Murchison's father and still known as Alfred Murchison & Son Ltd. This, unlike the syndicate, was a limited liability company controlled by Ivor Murchison and his wife; it played no part in the writing of risks and existed to run the affairs of his names within Lloyd's. Since Murchison's were marine underwriters, he farmed out, through the agency, his names onto other syndicates in the aviation, motor and non-marine fields, and in the same way he took in names from other agencies wanting his marine experience. This was all in the cause of spreading the risks; but it brought into the agency useful commission.

A stranger to Lloyd's often found it strange that, by contrast with most enterprises of their scale, the box had no accountant, let alone anyone to whom letters might be dictated. But the flow of moneys between the underwriters and the brokers, both in the form of premiums and accepted claims, was handled by Lloyd's own Central Accounting, which had recently been computerised; for other matters, Murchison had the benefit of advice from a large firm of Lloyd's accountants, who also dealt with routine correspondence with the members of the syndicate. If Murchison himself had occasion to write to a name, it would be in his own elegant hand.

Officially, the box was known to the Corporation of Lloyd's as I. P. Murchison & Ors: less formally, it was called 'Mr Murchison's Box' and it was thus that Martin would answer the telephone. Colloquially, however, they were often referred to, with schoolboy ribaldry, as 'the bat-buggers', a usage which sprang from an instance of underwriter's initiative.

For several years, Ivor Murchison had been in the habit of taking a salmon-fishing holiday in Norway. There he had made the acquaintance of a Norwegian shipbuilder named Apallson. One evening at the lodge, Herr Apallson, on learning that his new friend was a member of Lloyd's of London, mentioned a difficulty he was experiencing over his insurances: in brief, he did not think it just that while his ships were still in course of building, or lying in the water while being fitted out, he should be charged almost as much as if they were sailing the high seas. When Ivor Murchison returned to London, he raised Apallson's problem with his brother-in-law Andrew Draycott, a director of the large Lloyd's brokers Draycott, Parsloe & Co.

Draycott saw the potential at once. He embarked on a tour of shipyards both in Europe and the Far East; back in London, he formulated a new kind of policy to suit the needs of the market he had discovered. Since his brother-in-law had made the initial introduction, Murchison's became involved both in the development of the policy and in the setting of an appropriate and lower rate of premium for the shipbuilders. For some time, Ivor Murchison had been looking for a marine line where he could become the 'lead' underwriter: he too visited several yards, and now Murchison's led the slip, his scribbled initials at the top signalling to other under-writers who would follow that he judged the risk and the premium acceptable. The Norwegian for shipbuilding is 'batbyggeri', and it was not long before 'the bat-buggers' became the nickname of Murchison's box. At first, the soubriquet was viewed by Murchison with distaste; but now, with both Toby and Martin using it without thought, he had accepted it, realising that its use showed only a bantering affection and implied no lack of respect.

Martin had joined Murchison's when this line of busi-ness was just beginning to take off. From the start, Ivor Murchison had encouraged him to further knowledge of the ways of shipbuilders' yards and always consulted with Martin when a broker presented a new risk. The market had grown steadily and this year they expected it to account for a fifth of their total premium income.

Reaching the box on the stroke of nine, Martin saw that another early arrival had made his appearance, settling into his usual place opposite Mr Murchison's seat.

'Good morning, Mr Wells,' Martin greeted him formally, handing over *Lloyd's List*.

'Hullo there, Martin, on time again, I'm glad to see.' The remark was invariable. Mr Wells – for no one, not even Mr Murchison, ever addressed him by anything other than his surname – was a desiccated little man in his late fifties. He had thin grey hair, a pale dry complexion; and with his pursed lips and small cold eyes behind thin gold-rimmed spectacles, he could reduce a babbling cub broker to a stammering silence. He had been with Murchison's for many years, having started as a boy with 'old Mr Alfie'. Although, officially, he was deputy underwriter, he disliked taking any decision should Ivor Murchison be absent: a straightforward renewal was within his capacities, after subjecting the broker's slip to close scrutiny and checking his ledger to see if there were black marks against the owner or a history of previous claims. The clan of brokers knew his ways, however, and increasingly they would wait until Wells left for his morning coffee or his early lunch: then they would slide up to broach their business, either with Martin if it were a marine or shipbuilding risk, or with Toby should it concern cargo or cover against Excess Loss.

Still, Wells was part of the furniture of the box. He had never nourished ambitions to become a member and appeared content with his clerkly status, knowing that in a year or two he could retire with a generous pension. His attitude to the two young men was detached: he realised that in due course one, but not both, would succeed him as deputy, and that his duties would then be executed in a more enterprising manner, but it was not his place to show either favour. Only in petty matters of routine was he strict: he seemed to derive a remote pleasure in detecting a failure, say, on Martin's part to record the fullest details of a claim, or on Toby's of mislaying an alteration in a cargo manifest.

'Ahem.' Wells glanced at his watch and cleared his throat. 'It appears that our young friend is going to be late again this morning. It is becoming a habit with Toby and he should know by now that Mr Murchison does not approve of unpunctuality.'

2

'Christ, I'm going to be late again.' Toby Blackett came into the sitting room of his flat, scratching his backside. He was wearing nothing except a pair of bright red underpants; his thick black hair was tousled, under his eyes were purple shadows and his chin was dark, unshaven. His figure was good, with a broad, flat chest and white, almost luminous skin: only on his long, well-shaped legs was there a faint haze of hair. He went to the mantelpiece and took his first French cigarette of the day, coughing violently as he lit up. On the shelf was a line of invitation cards, many of them out of date, and above this there hung a gilt-framed mirror. Toby peered into the fly-blown glass, examined his reflection and shuddered; then he stumbled to the door, past a coffee table laden with an empty bottle of hock, two smeared glasses and a brimming ashtray, picking his way over some cushions scattered on the floor among a litter of empty record sleeves – Bert Kaempfert, Frank Sinatra, and Noël Coward's *Sail Away*, which had recently opened at the Savoy Theatre. All this detritus Toby ignored: he was intent only on his need for black coffee.

In answer to his craving, a voice came from the kitchen. 'I've put the coffee on.' This was Paul Blackett, Toby's younger brother. As Toby slumped into a stool, Paul added, 'You look as if you need it. And you're going to be late again: do you know it's ten past nine? I thought you said Ivor

25

Murchison was getting a bit shirty about your non-appearance in the mornings?'

'Bugger Ivor bloody Murchison,' Toby muttered, his long nose deep in his mug of steaming coffee. 'I'll earn my miserable keep when I get to Lloyd's.'

When they started work, both brothers had lived at their mother's house in Hanbury-on-Thames, about twenty miles from London. There they had been leaders of a group of free-and-easy young men and women, ranging in a noisy pack through the neighbourhood with its Thames Valley pubs, its weekly cocktail parties on Saturday nights and its almost weekly weddings.

Molly Blackett was a widow, comfortably well off. Even so, she had made it clear to both boys that they would have to earn their own livings. She was, financially, no fool. Her father had died early in the war; his estate had seemed very ample at the time, but after the ravages of the estate duty office, it had been reduced by more than half. On the advice of her cautious solicitor she had not settled capital on her sons but had set up a discretionary settlement, with a capital sum of £25,000. In theory, the trustees would be given very wide powers to do what they liked with the money. 'In practice,' the solicitor had explained, 'the trustees will regard half the capital as Toby's and half as Paul's and will mandate the dividends direct to them.'

Molly Blackett's dispositions had occurred about three years ago, and it was not long before they had their effect on the household at Hanbury. With a private income each of about £400 a year, Toby and Paul became restless. London beckoned: the social round of Hanbury-on-Thames, once their hub, began to seem narrow and provincial. The brothers had found themselves a cramped flat in Belgravia with a good address, and it was here that they were taking what passed as their breakfast.

Toby refused to hurry: for one thing, he had a hangover, and for another, the work that awaited him at Lloyd's, being routine and clerkly, was no spur to punctuality. His salary was meagre and it irritated him always to be short of cash; of course he'd get a decent raise when he succeeded as deputy on the box – a position he considered as good as his, for after all he had been longer with Murchison's than Martin Coley.

There was, he admitted, a certain kudos in being able to say airily that he was 'at Lloyd's' when asked where he worked; but kudos didn't equal cash. Even if he managed to become a working name soon, he wouldn't be anywhere near the real money, and he'd been long enough in the City to realise that there was plenty of real money around, if you had the right contacts and the right ideas.

Toby stood up to brew himself another mug of coffee.

'What did you get up to last night?' he asked. 'I lost sight of you in the crowd and when we came to leave, you'd already disappeared.'

The brothers often went to the same parties, hunting in pairs, each one passing on to the other discarded girlfriends.

'I took that model, Kerry something, off to the Blue Angel. But what about you? Where did you go? And who was she?'

Paul was curious: the big-boned, fair-haired young woman in a blue satin cocktail dress had seemed out of place at the noisy gathering, and he had been surprised to see his brother so attentive.

'She's called Hilary – Hilary Parsloe.' Toby reached for another French cigarette. 'And if you must know, we ended up at Annabel's.'

Paul whistled. The new nightclub in Berkeley Square was known to be very smart and very expensive.

'I know,' Toby agreed, 'but Hilary wanted to show off her "Madison" and insisted on Annabel's.' The Madison was the latest dance craze, a cross between country dancing and the twist.

'Well, I hope she was worth it,' Paul commented.

'She will be, she will be,' Toby muttered; then, glancing at his watch, he leaped to his feet. 'Is that the time? I'm going to be bloody late – I'll have to blame the Eleven bus again.' He hurried across the landing to the bathroom.

'By the way,' Paul shouted through the open door, 'you won't forget you owe me that fiver you borrowed last night?'

'You'll have to wait until the end of the month,' Toby called back, his mouth full of shaving lather. 'I'm skint until then. And I'll be skint for ever if I'm sacked for being late,' he

27

added gloomily. 'I'd better put on a stiff collar today: that'll put Ivor bloody Murchison in a good mood.'

On the 8.12 from Essex to Liverpool Street station, Ivor Murchison sat in his customary corner seat in his customary first-class compartment. On his lap *The Times* crossword, completed in nine minutes; and he had already skimmed through the Births, Marriages and Deaths, checked the closing prices on one or two shares in which he had a special interest, and with a shudder of distaste cast his eye over the Leader, a portentous piece about the political morality of the war minister's resignation. Now, as the train rattled over the points at South Woodford, he turned his thoughts away from the current scandal with relief, turning over what the day was to bring forth.

There was, he remembered, a prospective name visiting Lloyd's that morning. Introduced by a friend from school, he should present no difficulties; and the box needed a few more names, up to a dozen even, if he was to have the margin of cover he needed for a significant increase in his underwriting premiums. Then he must make sure he ran into a friend working at the powerful brokers, Willis, Faber: he'd heard on the grapevine that they were about to show the market a good risk with a large premium attached, a fleet of freighters of Greek ownership but under the Panamanian flag of convenience: normally, he wasn't too keen on owners who made use of such flags, and was suspicious of Greeks, especially those bearing handsome premiums; but this owner had a spotless reputation, and he wanted to make sure that Murchison's secured a good line on the slip. Meanwhile, at the back of his mind was a nagging worry about a risk he had written some weeks ago: he had accepted a larger line than he liked on a cargo of goatskins outward-bound from Smyrna, and although he couldn't give a reason for his unease, he decided to take another look at the risk this morning and to re-insure the lot elsewhere.

Thus, as on every weekday morning, Ivor Murchison tuned up his mind for the market place that lay ahead. The pattern seldom varied: a deliberately leisurely breakfast with his wife at Tickton, then into the old Ford Consul for the ten-minute drive to Elsenham station. He didn't believe in ostentatious motorcars: the old Ford was quite sufficient for the station run, although in a year or two he might hand it over to his son Giles, while his wife needed the larger Ford shooting brake for her country activities.

Ivor Murchison had met Ursula Draycott on one leave during the war, and had married her on the next, three months later. He had never had cause to regret it: the first flush of wartime passion had deepened into a real love, fortified by a complete community of interest, for Ursula was a Draycott, of Draycott, Parsloe, and with her grandfather, her father and now her brother the chairman of that broking firm, Lloyd's was as much in her blood as her husband's. From that source she was also, independently, well endowed. Their home, Tickton House on the edge of Tickton Green, was in her name, and even if the unthinkable ever occurred, some cataclysm that shattered the foundations of the world of insurance and drained away every name's private resources, their finances were so arranged that, short of revolution, the Murchisons should never want.

Their life was comfortable, without ostentation. Tickton House was a plain East Anglian farmhouse, its stucco walls painted a deep ochre: its age was indeterminate, much added to over the years, but the high, spiralling red brick chimneys betrayed its sixteenth-century origin. Ursula Murchison ran the house and garden efficiently, with the aid of two dailies and half a gardener, and still had time, especially during term, for their local branch of St John's Ambulance Brigade and at least one dinner party a month.

Their daughter Lucinda, now aged nineteen, had grown out of the pony stage. With Heathfield behind her, she had spent some months in France, learning the language. During the summer, there were plenty of small dances in the neighbourhood – no need for the pretension of a London season – and in the autumn he hoped she would go to a cookery school in London and share a flat with a girl cousin. As for Giles, Ivor Murchison admitted to himself that he doted on him.

Ivor had his son's future well mapped out. It was in a way a pity that there was no longer National Service, for a year or two in the army might have knocked a few corners off the

29

boy, but instead he planned a spell abroad, probably working in one of Draycott, Parsloe's overseas offices: then back and into the box, to learn the business from the bottom, just as he himself had learned it from his father, the well-remembered Alfie Murchison. And the timing was good: when Mr Wells retired, he would choose either Blackett or Coley as Deputy, but also as heir presumptive to his own place; then, in a year or so, he would start to take things a little easier. In due course, the new deputy would be promoted into the underwriter's seat, to keep it warm until such time as he judged Giles qualified to take over.

A decision would soon have to be taken about the new deputy, for there was no room on the box for two young men of roughly the same calibre. When he had taken on Coley, he had marked him down as no more than a probable successor to Wells; but increasingly Martin was showing both the quick wits and the feeling for the market that were required of an underwriter. He wasn't as gregarious as Toby Blackett, and his modest background would, ten years ago, have ruled out any question that he might be in the running; but, Murchison reflected, an underwriter must move with the times, and a successor like Martin Coley might be no bad thing.

Toby Blackett's background was perfectly acceptable; and he had a wide acquaintance among his contemporaries at Lloyd's which in the years to come and as they achieved promotion might prove most valuable to the box. Toby's manner with the brokers was good, too, and, personally, Murchison liked him as a young man. Against that, his approach to his work was a little casual, and, unlike Martin, he didn't seem to have much sense of all that Lloyd's stood for.

As the train drew up under the grimy glass roof of Liverpool Street station, Murchison reached up to the rack to take down his umbrella and bowler hat. It would be as well, he decided, to take a look at both young men away from Lloyd's itself, to judge them from a different angle before he made up his mind. Walking past London Wall and across Leadenhall Street, he decided to have them both down to Tickton for a weekend. Apart from anything else, he'd be interested to have his wife's opinion of both candidates.

3

At the same time that Murchison arrived at the box, important decisions were being taken within Ithaki-Hellenic. It was in no formal sense a board meeting: no officers of the company were present, except Laertes Vathos himself and Mme Vathos, no minutes were kept, there was no agreed agenda. Ithaki-Hellenic had, of course, many directors, and each of the subsidiary companies in Athens, London, New York and Zurich many more; but they all knew that they took their orders from Vathos: what he decided they implemented. Power was in his hand, and wherever he was, that was the seat of power.

On this June morning in 1963, Vathos was in the main saloon of his yacht *Thermopylae*. The vessel had arrived the night before at Cannes, after a voyage under sail from Sardinia, and was now berthed, stern to quay, in the yacht harbour Porto Canto while her crew, in white tee shirts with their ship's name across their chests, busied themselves making her ship-shape after the voyage, carefully refurling the canvas and tying it in neatly along the spars, polishing away the salt from the brasswork, holystoning the teak-laid decks. Outside the saloon, a white awning had been spread above the afterdeck, wicker chairs and tables set out and by the passerelle, the gangway that led to the quayside, the deck steward had arranged a huge vase of scarlet gladioli – this last a signal to informed onlookers that the yacht intended to stay at her berth for some time to come.

31

Laertes Vathos was at his most content on board the *Thermopylae*. Here, if anywhere, he considered himself at home. When he could spare the time to take her to sea, he worked as hard as any member of the crew, dressing like them, working the sails, scrambling about the rigging and standing his watch just as they did. When, as now, she was in harbour, the ship became his floating office. Ashore, a few hundred yards away in a small apartment just behind the Croisette, there was a small bureau, manned by a multilingual secretary with two telephones and a telex; along the coast at Monte Carlo there was a more elaborate équipe, managed by his two most loyal personal assistants; and in the other cities, he made use of his subsidiaries' offices there. But all major decisions he reached when on board the *Thermopylae*.

The yacht's Greek name was no passing fancy. As a boy, Vathos had been fascinated by the stories of the China tea clippers, the fastest vessels under sail then built, which, a hundred years ago, had vied with each other to be the first to bring the annual cargo of tea from the Orient to London. The old *Thermopylae* had been the fastest: so when his wealth grew to the stage when he could afford to indulge his whim, he caused to be built a yacht as like a clipper as Thornycrofts could manage. With her raked masts, her creamy canvas and her sleek hull, the new *Thermopylae* was a beauty, and a working ship under sail, unlike the floating palaces of his shipowning compatriots with their swimming pools and their French Impressionists.

Vathos liked his comforts, however, and his yacht was no mere museum piece. She possessed powerful engines, radio and a ship-to-shore telephone, plenty of lavish bathrooms and an excellent galley; while in port, air conditioning kept her interior comfortable. Despite all these attractions, Mme Vathos did not much care for shipboard life; generally, she remained in their apartment in Paris, where their two stolid daughters were at school, and when her husband made the South of France his base, she installed herself in the comfort of a suite at the Majestic, from which she had just arrived, stepping carefully up the passerelle in her high-heeled crocodile shoes.

Her appearance was defiantly un-nautical. She was short

32

and dumpy, her plumpness emphasised by her clothes, a close-fitting coat and skirt in cream silk; her hair was smooth and black, eyebrows elaborately plucked and arched, lips bright red against her pale cheeks: only her small eyes, black as olives, gave a hint of her native shrewdness.

Catherine Vathos came from a family of Greek Alexandrines in the cotton business. Wealthy enough to ride out the war in comfort, her mother's only cares had been to make sure that everything about her was what she considered chic, and to have her two daughters married suitably. In this, Catherine had been a disappointment: her mother could not approve of the tough, coarse young sea-master who came ashore in Alexandria in 1945 and began to pay court to her daughter: the man had no manners, he did not even speak French: Mr Vathos was, beyond doubt, not *comme il faut*. By contrast with the handsome English major who was paying court to Catherine's sister Hélène at the same time, M. Vathos seemed quite uncivilised; whereas Major Villiers, in his dashing Sam Browne and with the gloss of victory about him, had delightful manners and was eminently *sortable*.

Catherine ignored her mother. Laertes Vathos was not only refreshingly different from the dandified and scented young Greeks who frequented her mother's salon; but she detected within him, behind his blunt air and his dark, beetle-browed features, a driving force, a determination to have his own way. Nor did her father altogether disapprove; while he could not provide a dowry in the face of his wife's hostility, on the quiet he gave his new son-in-law financial support towards the purchase of a rusting Liberty ship that lay idle in the harbour and on which Vathos had had his eye for some time.

It was an investment that proved successful. For when Catherine's parents were forced to flee Egypt after Suez, suddenly penniless, it was Vathos who came to their rescue, providing them with a handsome apartment in Athens and a lavish income until their deaths.

Catherine's early married life had been hectic. Laertes Vathos soon came to realise that, aside from her physical attractions, his wife possessed a good business brain. He formed the habit of having her present whenever he faced a major decision or, in the first years, a daunting crisis: Mme Vathos seldom said much when there were others present, unless she knew them well; but when they were alone, her advice was cunning, to the point; like him, her nerve never faltered, and her deeper subtlety was a potent counterweight to his forcefulness. It was Mme Vathos, for instance, who had suggested the advantages of placing a British captain in command of some of their more unconventional cargoes; and while Vathos had, early on, opened her eyes to the potential of the dependence of the industrial West upon the oil wells of the Middle East, it had been Mme Vathos who, in her turn, foresaw that in time the Egyptians would tire of being a client state of the British and, to a lesser extent, of the French: they would throw out their fat king, she told him, and then they would, with the Suez Canal in their hands, have a stranglehold on the gullet of the West. A shipowner with foresight could prepare to take advantage of the ensuing panic.

In the aftermath of Suez, Ithaki-Hellenic became respectable. Not only were enormous profits made, but the major international companies, which had hitherto shunned Vathos as being perhaps a little shady, now sought him out with lucrative charters. By the end of the 1950s he was established as an important shipowner in world terms; though well behind the giants like Niarchos, Onassis or Livanos, he was much less prone to publicity than they. The Sixties, however, produced a new threat: the arrival on the scene of the super-tanker, capable of transporting as much crude as three of Ithaki-Hellenic's largest vessels, and it was this that Vathos had summoned his wife from Paris to discuss.

'. . . so you're proceeding with this super-tanker, then?' Mme Vathos was seated on a sofa in the air-conditioned saloon, behind a tray laden with the sweet, heavy Turkish coffee to which she was addicted.

'I am, my dear, I am. We cannot afford to be left behind.' They spoke in English, the tongue they favoured for business. Vathos possessed a strong American accent, while his wife's was heavily French.

'But the investment will be enormous, $12 million, you say. Can we afford it? Have we enough *liquide*?' Mme Vathos

34

had a bourgeois love of liquid assets, of readily accessible cash, and it went against her instincts to dissipate so much upon the building of one vast vessel.

'Don't worry, my dear, we won't be paying for it. The banks will: they're falling over each other in the rush to lend us the money and we just have to choose the best deal for us.'

'Perhaps. But I do not like to owe so much.' Mme Vathos set down her coffee cup, now smeared with crimson lipstick at its rim. 'And who are these so generous bankers?'

'I think we'll get the best deal from London. That's a good thing in itself, for I think the time has come when we must build up our presence in Britain. It's sound politically, and for all their spendthrift governments, their incompetent managers and their idle workers, London is still one of the great financial centres of the world. It will be good for Ithaki-Hellenic to be seen to have rather more than a post box in the City of London.'

'More work for Algie? I wonder how he will take to that?'

The small London office was in the charge of Mme Vathos' brother-in-law, Major Algernon Villiers. He was paid a substantial salary, more than enough to keep Mrs Hélène Villiers in a penthouse overlooking Cadogan Gardens: hitherto, his duties had been less than arduous, being mainly concerned with securing hotel suites at Claridge's or the Dorchester for his employers, the placing of a small amount of insurance in the London market and some routine attendance at the Baltic Exchange.

'Algie?' Mr Vathos pronounced the name with a hard 'g', as though it was some kind of green and slimy waterweed, which was close to the opinion he held of the husband of his wife's sister. 'Algie will do as he's damned well told. In any case,' he continued, lighting his first cigar of the day, 'he'll have help. I want him to find us a bright young man, very English, with a swell tie and a swell accent.'

'And what will this so bright young man do that you, Laertes Vathos, cannot do?'

'He'll be able to persuade those powerful men in the City of London that I am a good guy, that I'm respectable. Look at me! What do you see?'

Mme Vathos gave him a steady stare. 'I see my husband,'

35

she said quietly, taking in the broad, strong shoulders under the blue reefer jacket, the deep chest straining the white tee shirt, the craggy, heavy-browed face, 'and I like what I see.'

'Thank you, Catherine. But what these English see is a Greek; and Greeks, they know, are shifty, unreliable, liable to do them down, not to be trusted. But if they are assured that Laertes Vathos is not like other Greeks, and if they hear this from a clean young man who speaks in their own terms, then I shall be accepted and then I shall be in a position to use all that the famous City of London has to offer.'

'And what might that be?' Mme Vathos arched her eyebrows and lit a fat white Egyptian cigarette.

'For example, preferential rates of insurance. We pay out a fortune in premiums at the moment: I want to place more of our risk in London, particularly at Lloyd's, but until the word goes around that Ithaki-Hellenic is a first-class risk, we'll still figure in their secret little black books and be charged too much. I intend to change that: and I mean to start with our new tanker. She will be built to the highest specification, and once we secure 100 A1 rating at Lloyd's, we will have broken in.'

'I'm still not convinced.' Mme Vathos exhaled, twin columns of blue smoke funnelling out from her delicately shaped nostrils. 'But if you've set your heart on your beloved super-tanker, and if you think it will advantage the future of Ithaki-Hellenic, then proceed. But remember what I say: the shipping market may be good now, but it can change very quickly; by the time your *navire monstre* embarks on her maiden voyage, it may be that super-tankers will be a glut on the market.'

'You think so?'

Mme Vathos shrugged. 'I do not know for certain. I only indicate the possibility. Still, we can afford one super-tanker. Where are you building her?'

'Apallson's in Norway. They weren't the lowest tender, but we'll be sure of the Lloyd's rating.'

'And who is to command this Leviathan of yours? I trust you will bear in mind my opinion that Captain Dougall is by far our best master.'

'Captain Dougall will have the appointment.' Vathos stood up and went to the aft door, leaving his cigar in an ashtray, where a twirl of smoke twisted upwards to be sucked into the air-conditioning vents. 'In fact, I have already sent for him, and he will come on board later this morning. I thought, my dear, that you would like to be present when we tell him the good news. Mind you' – he turned to face his wife – 'there may well be difficulties.'

'What difficulties?'

'Our new vessel will be Greek-owned, by a Greek shipping line. All our crews are Greek, and so are most of the officers. It will cause comment among them when we appoint a British captain to our flagship. For that reason, I intend to make Manises the first officer.'

'Hector Manises?' Mme Vathos was as familiar with the senior officers of Ithaki-Hellenic as her husband. 'But he's not even from Ithaca.' She knew well the esteem in which Mr Vathos held the seamen from his own native island: in fact, Ithaca was something of an obsession with him. His own name derived from the island's port Vathi and the only time that he insisted on his wife's presence on the *Thermopylae* was when they visited Ithaca, dropping anchor in the deep bay from which the town, with its circle of whitewashed houses crowded under the flanks of Mount Stephanos, took its name. There would be a kind of civic reception, with the town band playing on the quay, flags flying, and the Nomarch himself waiting to welcome home the island's most successful twentieth-century son.

'Manises is Corfiote, but he is a very good seaman. He's held his master's ticket for five years, and he's entitled to look forward to his own ship soon. It will make for less trouble if we make him first officer of the super-tanker, at the same time indicating that when we build another, he'll have command of her and his appointment is to give him the necessary experience.'

The deck steward opened the door to announce that the British captain was coming on board.

Ben Dougall had no idea why he had been summoned to Cannes, leaving his own ship unloading at Naples. He surmised that he would be receiving orders of significance –

such summonses had not been infrequent in his years with Ithaki-Hellenic – and Mme Vathos' presence confirmed his guess. He had stopped off at an hotel after the flight from Italy to change into his best tropical whites and now, instinctively, he came to attention in the cool saloon, with his gold-braided cap tucked under his arm.

'Captain Dougall coming on board, sir,' he reported formally.

'Good morning, Captain,' said Mme Vathos, 'I trust you had a pleasant journey from Capodichino?'

While Mme Vathos and the captain made polite conversation, Vathos ordered the deck steward to remove the coffee tray. 'I'll have a lager,' he said, 'and for my wife her usual concoction.' Mme Vathos favoured a bright pink drink, made from Punt e Mes and Grenadine. 'Bring the malt for the captain.'

Captain Dougall looked up. Another signal: when he was given malt whisky, it meant good news; when blended it told him to expect more unconventional orders.

Vathos seated himself at his desk. 'Now, Captain,' he began, 'I have to tell you that Ithaki-Hellenic have commissioned our first super-tanker. We want you to assume her command.'

'I'm very gratified, sir,' said the captain. 'Where will she be built?'

'Apallson's in Stavanger have the contract,' the owner replied. 'And I can tell you she will be 91,500 tons DWT.'

'That's one hell of a ship, sir. She'll be vast.'

'Her length overall will be 880 feet, with a beam of 120 feet. As you say, one hell of a ship, Captain.'

'And the engines?'

'Burmeister and Wain, two-stroke single-action diesel. They'll deliver 23,000 hp at 110 revs per minute, giving you a maximum speed of around 16 knots.'

Dougall did some quick calculations. 'That'll mean we would cover about 370 sea miles a day. Not bad for such puny engines, puny that is by comparison with the size of the vessel. What crew will she need?'

'The minimum,' said Vathos. 'She's designed to be worked with nine officers and not more than twenty-five hands.'

38

'Very economical,' the captain observed. 'Will I be permitted to select my own officers?'

'With one exception. Manises will be your first officer.'

Dougall frowned. He knew Manises as a competent officer and a good seaman, but personally there always seemed to be unspoken friction between them. The Greek resented the seniority of the British captain and he had the feeling, when on occasion they had served together, that Manises was always at his back, watching to note any slip Dougall might make – not that there were any, he thought to himself. He knew better, however, than to question out loud his owner's decision.

Vathos had noted the frown and he knew how his captain felt. As conciliation, he asked, 'And who would you like as your chief engineer?'

'Without doubt, sir, Ulysses Stavros. He's the best we have and,' the captain added slyly, 'he's Ithacan.'

They then embarked on a discussion of other dispositions, to be interrupted by Mme Vathos from the sofa.

'I have an appointment at the hairdresser's,' she said, 'but before I leave you, there's one thing I want to know. Have you decided what you are going to call this new monster of the seas?'

'She will be the star of our fleet and one of the largest vessels of her kind ever to sail the oceans,' her husband answered. 'There is no doubt in my mind: she shall be named after my beloved wife: the *Katherina Vathos*.'

4

By ten o'clock, the Room was busy. Around each box were gathered the brokers, standing in line to wait for the underwriter's attention; in the aisles were other little knots of men, exchanging the gossip of the market place, while waiters in livery hurried between them, distributing envelopes and circulars to the boxes; above the hubbub, a sharp ear could pick out the voice of the Caller, intoning the names and firms of brokers needed elsewhere: it was curious that, however much the hum of chatter filled the Room, a broker would always hear the chanting of his name, then hurry to the rostrum to pick up his message, or go to the nearest telephone.

Murchison's was a small syndicate. Sometimes, if the market was quiet, they found themselves alone; but this morning they too had a queue of brokers. Most were 'scratch boys' – young men sent out to obtain the underwriter's initials on a slip, for a risk which had already been agreed verbally. One was 'bat-buggery' business: a new supertanker being laid down at Apallson's in Norway. There was nothing untoward about the risk and Martin settled to write the slip when Ivor looked over his shoulder.

'Who are the owners?' he asked. 'Who's she being built for?'

'Ithaki-Hellenic,' said the broker, a young man from a small firm.

'Indeed? Rather ambitious for them, I'd have thought. I didn't know they were in the super-tanker class.'

'To be honest, sir, I don't know much about them,' the broker admitted. 'The risk came through people we work with in Piraeus.'

'Well, let's look them up.' Murchison reached out for the *Confidential Index*. 'Ah, yes, Laertes Vathos,' he said to himself. 'I seem to remember he had rather a murky history just after the war, but he looks like a clean enough risk now.' He looked up at the broker. 'We write a small line now, but when the time comes to show this tanker, once she's commissioned, don't forget to come and show it to us.'

'I'll make a note of it, sir,' said the broker, tucking the slip away.

Then came a lull, and Mr Wells looked up from the Risks Ledger and took off his spectacles.

'I think I'll take my coffee break now,' he announced, 'and answer the call of nature.'

Since Wells made much the same pronouncement at the same time every morning, no one paid undue attention; but Ivor Murchison glanced across at Martin and made a slight gesture of his head. Martin took the cue and said he'd be off for coffee too. He knew that the underwriter wanted to haul Toby over the coals for his lateness, and would have liked to stay and enter some defence of his friend, but he realised there was nothing he could say and the sooner the interview was over, the better.

Toby's dark head was bent over *Lloyd's Shipping Index*, checking the movements of some freighters, when Murchison addressed him.

'I shouldn't care to write a slip on the punctuality of the Number Eleven bus,' he remarked.

'I am most terribly sorry, sir,' said Toby in his best subaltern manner, 'and to be honest, it wasn't all London Transport's fault. I mean, I was late anyway.' To this confession, he added a hopeful, disarming grin.

'It's all very well, Blackett,' Murchison rapped back, 'but you're making a habit of being late and it simply won't do. We underwriters must be in our places by nine-fifteen at the latest, or goodness knows what business we might miss. And

41

if I can make it on time after coming thirty miles from Essex, then I don't think I'm asking too much by insisting that you are punctual. It's unfair to the other chaps and it suggests a sloppy attitude to Lloyd's and to your work, which I warn you I will not tolerate.'

'It won't happen again, sir, I promise.' Toby was very solemn. 'And I'll try coming in by the Underground, it's probably more reliable.'

Murchison would have liked to say more, but broke off when he saw Martin Coley hurrying back to the box. Martin had paused to glance down the casualty bulletins, and he had found some news which might distract his employer from Toby's derelictions.

'It's the *Queen of Izmir*, sir,' he said, 'there's notification posted that she has engine trouble off Qatar. She's signalled for a tow, so it must be serious.'

'Damn,' said Ivor Murchison, remembering his thoughts on the train that morning, 'I always was worried about that risk. Let's have a look.' He reached out for the Risks Ledger and thumbed through Wells' careful calligraphy. 'Just as I thought,' he announced, 'it's those blasted goatskins. I knew we should have re-insured them; as it is, stuck in the Persian Gulf in high summer, the whole bloody lot will rot.' He gave a dry laugh. 'Rather them than me,' he added. 'I wouldn't like to be on board in June in Qatar, sitting on top of a hold full of foetid goat.'

Both young men laughed, and Martin asked the pertinent question.

'How big is our line?'

'Bigger than it should be,' answered Murchison grimly. 'I remember that Draycott, Parsloe were having difficulty in completing their slip and they pressed me to write a bit more. But wait a second' – he peered at the ledger again – 'what in heaven's name was that rusting heap doing in the Gulf? We covered her cargo for a passage from Iskenderun to Casablanca, an easy run through the Med in temperate climes; but if she wandered off through the Suez Canal and down the Red Sea at this time of year, it's odds on that the whole cargo would rot anyway, and we had no business to be writing it.'

'Surely the brokers would have advised us of the change in destination?'

'They should have, Martin, they should have. But there's no note of it here against the risk, and that means we'll have to dispute the claim when it arrives. Who led the slip, do you remember?'

'I think it was Stuart-Holland, sir,' Martin replied.

'Oh.' Murchison's silence was eloquent. They all knew that underwriter's reputation: after a brilliant career in the golden days of the late Forties, he had taken to long and expansive lunches, and now most astute brokers were aware that, in the afternoons, Stuart-Holland was an easy sell.

'I'm sorry, but I'm afraid we won't be able to fight the claim.' Toby had been shuffling through some papers he had taken out from his belly drawer. 'It's my fault; I forgot all about it, but this arrived late one evening and I just shoved it away to deal with the next morning: then it slipped my mind.'

The paper Toby produced was a cyclostyled memorandum from Draycott, Parsloe, one of dozens that arrived on the box every day and all day, and it notified all the underwriters on the slip of the changed destination for the *Queen of Izmir.*

'I see.' Grimly, Murchison took the piece of paper. 'Well, Blackett, it looks as though your carelessness has cost our names ten thousand pounds.'

Toby was uncomfortably aware that he had put up the second black mark of the day; but, perhaps because of Martin's presence, Murchison made less of this error than of his unpunctuality.

The next broker to visit the box was, as it happened, from Draycott, Parsloe. In his twenties, he had thin, fair hair already receding into baldness and a rich red complexion, but his main feature was a wide mouth with teeth as pointed and sharp as a pike's. His name was Michael Pendragon, and he was, as Ivor Murchison recalled, a drinking companion of Toby Blackett. More to the point was the fact that Ivor's brother-in-law was Pendragon's employer.

'Good morning, sir.' Ivor Murchison affected the traditional, gentlemanly style of addressing all brokers, from

43

members of the Committee down to the most raw scratch boy, in formal fashion.

'Good morning, sir,' the broker replied, at the same time giving Toby a quick wink over the underwriter's shoulder. 'It's the Petronella renewal,' he explained, placing a slip on the table.

'Ah yes,' said Ivor, glancing down the initials of the underwriters who had already written the risk, 'I've been waiting for this. I was hoping you might be able to let us write a rather larger line this year.'

Petronella NV, a Dutch-owned fleet of tankers, was a most desirable risk. Well skippered and efficiently run, Petronella's record was clean, and there was no need to consult the *Confidential Index of Shipping* for details of any dubiety about ownership or losses: Petronella was proud that all its vessels were classified as '100-AI at Lloyd's' by *Lloyd's Register of Shipping* (an organisation independent of the Corporation of Lloyd's but one on which all underwriters relied).

'That might be a little tricky, sir.' There was a stubborn look on the broker's face: he was hoping not to waste much time at this box. In fact, he could easily fill the slip in a morning with the larger syndicates, and he was only here at Murchison's because Mr Draycott insisted that they be shown the risk. 'You already write a quarter of one per cent,' he pointed out, 'and I don't think we have any leeway to allow you more. How much extra did you have in mind?'

'I want one per cent,' said Murchison flatly. Martin, Toby and even Mr Wells looked up at this: the underwriter was asking to cover half a million pounds, a huge risk for their syndicate.

'Quite impossible, I'm afraid, sir.' There was a hint of patronage in Pendragon's light laugh.

'Just a moment.' Murchison leaned back to give the broker a very direct look. 'I would suggest that perhaps you owe us a favour. After all, you were keen enough to persuade me to complete your slip for that cargo of Turkish goatskins that will now be rotting in the Persian Gulf.'

'Oh, that.' Pendragon shrugged dismissively. 'Win some, lose some, that's the name of the game, isn't it, sir?'

Toby Blackett had followed the negotiation with interest. He didn't know what old Ivor was up to, but here, he saw, was a chance to redeem himself.

'Come along, Micky,' he said easily across the table, 'do us a favour. I'm sure you can spare us a little more on Petronella if you try.'

'Well . . .' The broker looked impatient. He was anxious to complete the slip that day; already he had wasted some valuable minutes at Murchison's and a lavish lunch date loomed. Still, Toby was by way of being a friend, and no fool: it could do no harm to oblige him, rather than that stuffed-shirt Murchison. 'I could let you have half a per cent, I suppose,' he conceded.

'Three-quarters,' snapped Murchison, driving the bargain.

'All right,' Pendragon agreed with a sigh, 'three-quarters it is.'

Mr Murchison scribbled on the slip, initialled it and added a rubber stamp before passing the slip over for Wells to enter the details.

There were no other brokers hovering, and it was Martin who asked the question in all their minds.

'That line on Petronella is a bit of a mouthful for us, isn't it?'

In order to ensure that no underwriter accepted risks in excess of the resources available to him, the Corporation of Lloyd's imposed a self-regulating limit on the amount of Premium Income that each syndicate might turn over in any year: this was reached by totalling up the sum of each individual name's own limit, and the amount of premium each name might write was related to his deposits.

'You're up to something, aren't you, sir?' Toby suggested with a grin.

'Apart from the fact that the Petronella line is an excellent risk and that the premium is not to be sniffed at, yes, I do admit an element of longer-term planning.' Murchison looked over his shoulder: there were no attendant brokers, nor any other bystanders who might eavesdrop.

'If we are to keep station with our competitors in the Room, then we must grow. Conditions for Lloyd's are not easy, and I don't see them getting any better. Our rates, which God knows are low enough anyway, face competition, not only from the Americans but from every newly independent country.'

'I was always told that ever since the San Francisco earthquake, the American market loved Lloyd's,' Martin observed.

'1906 was a long time ago. It cost Lloyd's over a hundred million dollars – an incredible sum for those days – and the fact that we paid up on the dot, while many American companies repudiated their liability, has indeed done us a lot of good. Not any more: and the rise of nationalism, chauvinism – call it what you like – means that apart from the Americans and the Japanese placing more of their insurance at home, each newly independent country wants to follow suit.'

'I know.' Toby laughed. 'As soon as they let the new president out of jug, he devises a new flag, creates a national airline and sets up his own insurance company.'

'That's about right,' Murchison agreed. 'So we must fight for a larger share of what's placed on the market here in the Room. Now we're writing a bigger percentage on Petronella, as the slip goes round the Room, people will notice. Word will soon be around that our underwriting has become more aggressive.'

'I see the sense of that,' said Martin, looking very serious, for he found these colloquies about underwriting policy most absorbing. 'But we'll have to be very careful about our limits, until we have more names and a broader base to work from.'

'As to the latter, I've already put out some feelers that we might welcome a few new names – in fact, one is coming to see me this morning. And I don't need reminding that, even apart from our underwriting limits, we'd be in the very devil of a mess if the unlikely happened and two of Petronella's spanking new tankers ran into each other off the Lizard. We'll have to reinsure a good whack of the risk as Total Loss Only.'

In the same way that a bookmaker balances his book by laying off with other bookies the bets which are more than he would like to lose, so an underwriter re-insures. Murchison would make up his mind how much of the Petronella risk his syndicate could stand: the balance he would then place elsewhere, the slip being broked around the market like any other proposal. Like so much at Lloyd's, this traffic was two-way: Murchison's often wrote re-insurance lines, not only from syndicates but also from the insurance companies. Thus, every big risk would be spread across all the resources of the London insurance market.

'It's a pity,' Toby remarked, 'that we have to wave good-bye to all that lovely premium.' His eyes were hooded, calculating, and Martin, looking across the box, realised that his friend was brewing some scheme. 'I mean,' he pursued, 'it's almost impossible that the whole of Petronella's fleet would go glug to the bottom at the same time.'

'Improbable, but not impossible,' said Murchison. 'What we have to face is the remote chance of some almost global disaster, as if, for instance, the San Andreas Fault split wide open and tumbled Los Angeles and San Francisco into the Pacific. It's against such eventualities that we re-insure.'

'And the re-insurers scoop all the lovely profits,' Toby pointed out.

Ivor Murchison shrugged. 'That's the way the market operates. Mind you, with the scale of risks growing more mammoth every year, there's a good case to be made for establishing some kind of catastrophe fund, as a reserve against some vast horror. I happen to know that a couple of members of the Committee have been negotiating with the Inland Revenue for months, but the tax boys simply won't have it.'

'Why not?' Toby was indignant.

'You have to remember that from a tax point of view, each name trades as an individual. The syndicate as such has no fiscal entity. And since there are strict and elaborate rules about the amount each name may take from his profits to form his own special reserve, the Inland Revenue don't see that they need make any further concessions. On our side, we don't like to press too hard, in case they tighten up on the special reserves.'

'But there are other ways.' Toby leaned across the table, his tone excited as he elaborated. 'A group of syndicates

47

could get together with a big broker and set up their own re-insurance outfit. If we based it in some cosy tax haven, like Bermuda or the Bahamas, it would be well beyond the reach of the tax vultures, and we could soon build up a handsome fund: we'd have the use of the money, we'd all benefit and no one would be the wiser.'

Ivor Murchison looked at Toby with amazement, his thin, fair eyebrows arched.

'I never thought to hear such an idea in my own box,' he exclaimed. 'Good heavens, man, you're proposing something close to tax evasion. Even apart from that, the thing's unthinkable. There would be a clear conflict of interest between our names and those who ran the offshore outfit.'

This judgment delivered, Ivor stood up. 'It's time I went to meet Gasper Grieve at the main entrance,' he told them. 'He's bringing a potential new name to lunch with me, but I'll bring them back here first.'

Sir Woodbine Bulkely-Grieve, Bt, was an old friend of Ivor Murchison. They had been at school and through the army together: it was at Eton that the baronet had acquired the obvious nickname 'Gasper': Woodbine had been a baptismal weakness of his family ever since the first baronet, Admiral Woodbine Bulkely, had done rather well in the matter of a Spanish prize ship captured off Barbados in the War of Jenkins' Ear. The admiral had settled in the Welsh Marches on the proceeds, and built the seemly red brick. family mansion still known simply as 'Beamish'.

Gasper Grieve was, Ivor reflected as he threaded his way across the Room, the ideal outside name. He wasn't dependent on Lloyd's, and the annual cheque was in the nature of a bonus: he perceived the value of making his capital work twice, he refrained from pestering the box when a major loss hit the headlines, but he knew the importance of having confidence in all his underwriters as well as his agent (Ivor) and always made a point of calling on their boxes when he found himself at Lloyd's.

When Ivor emerged through the swing doors, he saw that Sir Woodbine was already waiting for him under the War Memorial window.

48

'Good morning, Gasper,' he called, extending his hand, 'I hope I haven't kept you waiting.'

'On the contrary, I'm early. I wanted to have a word with you before Trevor Bleach arrives – I thought I ought to fill you in about him, so I've asked him to meet us here in ten minutes.'

'All I know is that Mr Bleach seems anxious to become a member. I hope you've told him that times here aren't as good as you've enjoyed in the past: it's not the ideal time to be joining.'

The two men began to pace up and down the marble floor, unconsciously falling into military step. Beside Ivor's slight figure, Sir Woodbine seemed large. With a big-boned frame and a thick neck set on wide shoulders, the hound's-tooth check suit that he wore in London seemed to cramp him; his face was smooth, his complexion highly polished and flushed with that ruddiness that goes with an outdoor life. Only his eyes belied the bluff and hearty appearance; pale and small, set very close, they flickered around constantly, as if suspicious of what they might find in the undergrowth.

'Trevor Bleach isn't the kind of chap you and I are accustomed to dealing with,' Gasper explained.

'Indeed.' Ivor cocked an eyebrow at his friend. 'I suppose by that you mean he's not out of the top drawer.' He laughed. 'Ten years ago, that might have mattered here; but now, I can assure you, we welcome all sorts – butchers and bakers, even boxers, provided they're possessed of the right money. Lloyd's is very democratic these days.' There was a dry irony in his voice, as if he didn't altogether relish the change.

'I was introduced to Bleach by a fellow at the Club,' Gasper went on, 'and I must say, he knows what's what financially. He calls himself a consultant and since I started taking his advice, I'm very pleased with what he's done.'

Ivor paid full attention. Gasper Grieve might look like a dim-witted squire but he was nobody's fool when it came to money; he had a sly instinct for a good deal and, as important, a shrewd eye for selecting men whose brains he could pick.

'Bleach says that while there's still a Conservative government, we must use every opportunity to . . . to rationalise my funds.' Sir Woodbine rolled the phrase around his tongue, as if it were a succulent oyster. 'Soon the socialist jackals will be in power again, and they are bound to move against us – wealth tax, another capital levy, God knows what horrors they have in store.'

'So what does Mr Bleach suggest you do?'

'I've done it.' Gasper looked very pleased with himself. 'In the last six months, I've given away a fortune!'

'I hope you've kept enough for yourself and Almina,' Ivor cautioned. 'I've known men in your place get into such a lather over the prospect of estate duty that they pass on far too much to their children.'

'Don't worry, I've plenty left. Bleach has been very clever. My first concern was for Beamish itself: it costs a fortune to keep up a place like that, and it would be good to know that it might still be safe when Bulky's grandchilden take over.' Bulky was Gasper's son and heir: the family favoured obvious nicknames.

'There's always the National Trust,' Ivor observed.

'I'd thought of them, but they want too bloody much in the form of an endowment. Bleach has a better wheeze: we've placed the house and the more important bits and pieces – a couple of Zoffanys, the Lawrence, the William Kent tables and the Chippendale in the Saloon – into a separate, non-profit-making company. I pay what is called a fair market rent, but it's peanuts; and to show willing, we have to open to the public from time to time. One Wednesday a month isn't much of a hardship, for we don't get many visitors in Herefordshire, and Almina rather enjoys dressing up as a guide – sometimes she even gets tipped!' Sir Woodbine gave a bellow of laughter and Ivor smiled: Lady Bulkely-Grieve, a faded, wispy blonde with a voice as soft as a whisper, was an unlikely tourist guide.

'Then I thought I should do something for Almina – she hasn't a penny of her own – so Bleach persuaded me to shovel a hundred grand's worth of equities into a trust for her, and then when she dies that can pass straight on to my daughter without the vultures getting their teeth into a penny.'

50

'And I imagine that while you have the chance, you've taken care of Bulky too?'

'Oh, yes, that's another discretionary trust – after all, the boy's not much more than twenty-one and one wouldn't want him to blue the lot at Asper's. He's copped half the estate – about 3,000 acres, all let, and another hundred grand. And, since I don't want to have my daughter hanging around waiting for her mother to drop off the peg, Alice has a small fund – about thirty thousand – to make her more marriageable.'

'You'll have to take care she doesn't fall into the clutches of the Chelsea heiress hunters.' Ivor warned him. 'One of those young men could spend his way through that in a year.'

'H'm, I don't think Alice would be such a fool.' Gasper frowned: he didn't like to be reminded that human frailty might disrupt his careful arrangements. 'For myself,' he pursued, 'I've kept all the forestry: when I hand in my dinner pail, it'll be scot free of duty, and the rest of the estate will only suffer minimal tax. All I have to do now is to shovel as much as I can overseas: Bleach is working on that now, but he hasn't yet come up with a watertight scheme. If it wasn't for all the exchange control regulations, I'd be home and dry.'

'I'm not sure I would be happy about that,' Ivor observed, pursing his lips. 'It smells a bit of tax evasion to me.'

'It's not evasion, my dear fellow, it's avoidance. Bleach is always laying it on about the difference. Don't you remember the judge who said something to the effect that it was every man's right to arrange his affairs so that the incidence of tax was reduced as much as legitimately possible?'

Gasper Grieve had always been frank about his financial affairs and Ivor calculated that, even after these dispositions, his friend must still possess something in the order of a quarter of a million in equities: to manipulate even half that sum overseas would need some dexterous and possibly dubious work on Bleach's part. Ivor was about to give a warning on these lines when Sir Woodbine grabbed his arm.

'There's Bleach, coming past the waiter now,' he said.

The figure approaching them gave an overwhelming impression of grey. The silk suit, the neatly knotted tie, the smooth hair, even the eyes, all were colourless. The face

51

itself was curiously unlined, contrasting oddly with the iron-coloured hair; and, as the visitor smiled at Gasper's greeting, his teeth showed brilliant, almost artificial white.

'Pleased to meet you, Mr Murchison,' said Trevor Bleach as they shook hands; then the three of them entered the Room and made their way back to the box. As Ivor Murchison went through his usual patter about the history of the Lutine Bell, the function of the Caller and the importance of the Loss Book, he reminded himself of what he had learned of Bleach's circumstances. Every prospective name was required to submit a full statement of his finances, certified by a chartered accountant, and Ivor had studied Trevor Bleach's with care. It was his duty as the underwriting agent concerned, of course, but Ivor possessed his share of curiosity about other men's money.

There was no house at all: an unusual circumstance, for with many prospective names, their residence was by far their biggest asset. Bleach's London address was an anonymous block of service apartments. But his statement showed a portfolio of blue-chip equities – Shell, ICI, Glaxo, Marks & Spencer – providing a good range of securities with a total value of more than £200,000. Then there was over £60,000 in short-dated government stock, an odd investment for a financial consultant, although one which would appeal to Lloyd's, since the funds were so accessible; Ivor suspected that this investment was of recent origin, and designed to have just such an effect, for the rest of the declaration had listed holdings in a variety of small companies in the Midlands, some not even dealt in on the London Stock Exchange. Ivor decided that a few oblique questions must be directed at Bleach before he went in front of the Rota Committee.

At the box, Bleach met Toby, Martin and Wells. It had been Ivor's intention to take Bleach around the Room himself, to introduce him to the other syndicates which the Murchison agency was arranging that the new name might join; but a broker approached with a ticklish problem about a whaling fleet in the Antarctic which demanded his immediate intention, so thankfully – for the new candidate's whining Midlands accent was beginning to grate – he deputed this task to Martin. Then Gasper wandered off to the Members'

Cloakroom, Wells disappeared to his early lunch, and Ivor found himself on his own with Toby.

He was uneasy that he had been over-severe with Blackett. It was not his way to reprimand a member of his staff in front of the others: he himself was at least partly to blame for the goatskin loss, for he had failed to follow his instinct: Toby's intervention in the Petronella deal had been timely, and if his suggestion about offshore reinsurance had been ill-conceived, at least it showed initiative and a proper concern for profit.

'By the way, Toby,' he began – the use of the Christian name signalled that this was a social, not a business, matter – 'by the way, Ursula and I were hoping you might come down to Tickton one weekend soon. There's a local dance at the end of the month: would you be free to stay with us then?'

Toby expressed his pleasure at the invitation; inwardly, he was relieved, for he realised that it meant he was restored to favour and must still be in the line for promotion: the broker Pendragon had done him a good turn.

Soon after, Ivor took Bleach and Gasper Grieve off to the Captain's Room on the second floor, where the head waiter Fred had kept them a table. As lunch progressed, Ivor kept up a discreet questioning on Trevor Bleach's activities. The consultant had no false modesty: as he related how he had taken over and then sold on a company making motor horns in less than a month and how, by a revaluation of fixed assets, he had turned a loss-making manufacturer of washing-machine components into a little goldmine, Sir Woodbine sat back, as pleased with his introduction's prowess as the owner of a labrador is smug when his dog retrieves a difficult pheasant.

'In such cases, do you act on a commission basis?' asked Ivor.

'Commission? No, what would I want with that?' Bleach was scornful. 'Commission is income and income attracts tax. I usually ask for an issue of shares at a discount: it costs the company less and I get my reward from the subsequent capital gain.'

Ivor noticed – and gave credit for it – that while Bleach was quite ready to talk about his company clients, he would say nothing whatever about his dealings for personal clients such as Gasper.

'One thing, Mr Bleach,' he observed casually, 'I was a little surprised to see such a large holding of gilts in your portfolio. Have you held them for long?'

'I know what you're thinking,' replied Bleach, wagging a finger in Ivor's face. 'You're suspecting that they're just window-dressing for my membership here. But there's more to it than that: just as you people at Lloyd's like to boast that you make double use of your capital, well so do I. From time to time, I like to go into the market in quite a big way, and I might not have a hundred thousand to hand; but with a nice fat portfolio of government stock, my bank are quite happy to see me right. Besides,' he went on, 'I stick to the short-dated stock: I'm not interested in the yield but I like the capital gain, which is still tax-free despite this bloody new capital gains tax.'

'I see.' Ivor was satisfied. 'And now, perhaps you'll tell me why you are keen to become a member of Lloyd's. I'm sure Sir Woodbine has told you that in my opinion our profits are going to be well down for a few years to come. Some people here talk of a seven-year cycle, and I don't think they are far wrong.'

'I know. And I'm aware that, in theory at least, I'm risking everything I own when I join. But' – he gave a thin chuckle – 'I don't rate that chance very highly in your good hands, Ivor. Anyway, apart from what you may make me, or even if you lose a bit now and then, there are some useful tax lay-offs. I know what I'm doing, never you fear. And I don't deny it'll be useful to me, to be known as a member of Lloyd's. Besides, I've several other clients in much the same position as Gasper here, and it might be handy for you if I guided 'em your way.'

'There are some agents, I believe, who do pay a commission on introductions; but,' Ivor warned, 'that is not our practice.'

'Never mind,' Bleach returned, 'I expect we could work out something between us. One favour deserves another, that's what I always say.'

54

With luncheon over – potted shrimps, some grey roast lamb and a gooseberry tart – Ivor suggested coffee and a glass of port in the ante-room. 'You'll forgive me for not having port myself,' he said, 'but I must keep a clear head for the brokers on the box this afternoon.'

'I'd like to see a little of the broking side,' Bleach suggested, 'just to complete my picture of Lloyd's.'

By now, Ivor had had enough of Bleach's company: while he was impressed by the man's grasp of business, he did not warm to him personally; so he proposed that, when they returned to the box, he would ask Toby Blackett to undertake this, for Toby had a wide acquaintance among the brokers in the Room.

Meanwhile, at the box, Toby had told Martin of the weekend invitation to Tickton. Martin was cast down by this; a realist, he recognised that the Blacketts were more the Murchisons' own kind than the Coleys would ever be, but he had been beginning to hope that he was in with a chance for promotion to the deputy's seat. This sign in favour of Toby seemed to indicate that his own role was to be subservient, and Toby's own pleasure, not far removed from gloating, made him more depressed. However, this did not last; when Toby went off with Bleach, Murchison restored his spirits.

'By the way, Martin,' he said, 'my wife and I are having a few young people down to Tickton for a weekend: Toby's coming, and we very much hope you will too. You'd better bring a black tie,' he added, 'as there's some kind of local dance on the Saturday night.'

5

At Tickton, Sunday mornings had a regular pattern. Ursula
Murchison liked to go to the early service to leave the morning clear for her tasks in the house, for she cooked Sunday
luncheon herself; and Ivor, who was a churchwarden, always
went to Matins, where he took the collection. Breakfast
was a casual affair and it wasn't until Ivor returned that the
Murchisons saw much of each other. Now, on this bright
day at the end of June, they settled in the sun room, where
Ursula had already put out several bottles of beer for the boys
and a jug of home-made lemonade.

'What are the young up to?' Ivor asked, easing himself into
a creaking wicker chair.

'Mixed doubles.' Ursula nodded through the french window; at the far end of the lawn, behind a thick macrocarpa
hedge, was the hard tennis court.

'Such energy,' Ivor said, smiling, 'and after a late night
too. Did you hear them come in after the dance? I was fast
asleep.'

'It wasn't very late – only just after one, I think.'

'Well, I hope they enjoyed themselves. Was anything said
at breakfast?'

'Just a few grunts over the coffee,' his wife replied. 'You
know what Lucinda is like: she never volunteers anything if
she can avoid it.'

'I wonder if Giles managed to have a good time,' Ivor

mused. 'The rest were a few years older and he may have felt rather out of things.' Giles Murchison, at seventeen and two years younger than his sister Lucinda, had been determined to be of the party. 'Where is Giles, by the way?'

'I've let him sleep in,' Ursula explained. 'Oh, I know he ought to be down by now, but it is his half-term so I thought I wouldn't disturb him.'

Her son Giles was the one chink in Ursula Murchison's armour. She was a thin woman, with large limbs and a broad bosom: her voice was loud, clear and commanding, with the assurance of one who ran her life with efficiency and discipline. Only with Giles, sometimes, she felt her self-control slip. Looking at him sometimes, she felt a strange liquefaction inside her, a welling-up of adoration; and although she seldom indulged him outwardly, she was apt, as on this morning when her son slept on upstairs, to let him have his way. It had never dawned on her that Ivor felt much the same about the boy. Now, in order to divert her husband from Giles' dilatory appearance, she changed the subject.

'How do you think those two young men are shaping up?' she asked. 'Have you come any closer to deciding which one you'll promote?'

'I've reached no conclusion yet,' Ivor answered. 'Toby's very clever, and he's full of ideas; but I think he's inclined to be erratic.'

'He's still only in his twenties,' Ursula pointed out. 'If you ask me, there's no doubt about it, Toby's the man for the job. As you say, he's bright: he's also well-mannered and he does come from the right sort of background.'

'Ten years ago, that might have mattered,' said Ivor. 'Ten years ago, we wouldn't have entertained a newsagent's son for the weekend. But Martin is just as well-mannered as Toby, and he has a real feeling for underwriting, for Lloyd's. I'm beginning to feel that perhaps Toby's talents might be better applied on the broking side.'

'I see.' Ursula trusted her husband's judgment, especially on matters about Lloyd's, and once he made up his mind, she would not dream of questioning his decision. After all, there was nothing actually to be held against Martin Coley; as Ivor had pointed out, times were changing. She gave a loud

57

laugh. 'If that's the case, it's just as well for Toby that Hilary Parsloe has fallen for him.'

'Has she indeed?' Ivor looked over his tankard at his wife, his eyebrows raised in mild surprise.

'Oh yes, hook, line and sinker. I could see as soon as Toby came in on Friday night: Hilary positively lit up.' Hilary Parsloe, the daughter of Hervey Parsloe, joint managing director with Ursula's brother Andrew Draycott of Draycott, Parsloe & Co., was an honorary niece and frequent visitor at Tickton. She had been asked to make up the numbers for the dance – Giles, as a schoolboy, didn't count – but when the invitation was extended, the Murchisons had no idea that she and Toby were already well acquainted in London. Ursula had been a little put out by this at the time, for it might have had the effect of throwing Martin and Lucinda together, and she was relieved that Giles too was to go to the dance, all five of them cramming into Martin's Hillman drop-head coupé. Still, she had made a mental note to have a word with Lucinda at the right time, hinting that whatever Martin's ability at Lloyd's might be, he was hardly to be considered suitable husband material.

Their conversation was interrupted by the entrance of Giles Murchison. Very slim, with his father's aquiline, fair features still blurred by youth, there was a febrile nervousness about his movements and, this morning, a greenish tinge on his fresh cheeks. He mumbled a greeting while heading for the table of drinks, where he opened a beer, then flung himself into a chair. He drank deep and straight from the bottle, an act which caused his father to frown in distaste.

'Would you like some coffee, darling, it's not too late? Did you enjoy the dance? Who else was there? What time did you get back?' Ursula rattled out a salvo of questions.

'For Christ's sake, Mummy.' Giles rose abruptly. 'I can't face a catechism this morning. I think I'll go and find the others.' He disappeared across the lawn without another word, leaving Ivor and Ursula to shrug resignedly at each other across the silence: unspoken was the thought in both their minds, that boys will be boys, that he was just going through a stage of surliness, that he would soon grow out of it.

Ursula hurried off to the kitchen. It was time to put the

Yorkshire pudding in the Aga; whatever the season, there was always roast beef on Sundays, and today it would be followed by strawberries and cream. There was no room in her well-organised life for imagination: in the garden, straight lines, tidiness and order, as exemplified by the platoon of standard Peace roses marching down the drive, as disciplined as a company of troopers: in the house, safe colours, a dim chintz of drab green and dusty pink in the drawing room with the velvet curtains 'picking up' the green; in her dress, in the winter, twinsets in beige or green with a tweed skirt and in the summer, as now, a long-sleeved cotton frock.

When she returned, the tennis party were tumbling in from the garden, hot and clamorous. She called them to order with a reminder that lunch would be on the table in half an hour and they had better hurry up if they were to wash and change in time. The four from the tennis court had called out loud and bantering greetings to Giles, who looked, his mother thought, slightly apprehensive at their sallies, and there was a hint of conspiracy between the young people that puzzled her; but she had no time to probe for its cause before they hurried off to get ready. And even at the dining room table, the conspiracy seemed to be one of silence: despite jocular questioning, she learned little about last night's dance apart from the names of some others present.

The afternoon was spent on the croquet lawn, and early in the evening the boys left to return to London. Toby had offered Hilary a lift in Martin's car, which she happily accepted, so the Murchisons were left on their own. Giles had wandered off on one of his moody, solitary walks, and for some time Ivor and Ursula sat in silence, watching as the setting sun painted the high East Anglian sky red behind the darkened trees.

'The croquet was instructive, I thought,' Ivor observed. 'It's a vindictive game and it often highlights both merits and deficiencies of character.'

'What do you mean?' asked Ursula, who regarded it as any other game, to be won, with due regard to the rules.

'I mean, for instance, that young Toby was quite determined to win. He was ruthless, he never hesitated when

59

making things difficult for his opponents, he even cheated once or twice when he thought no one was looking. And you're quite right about Hilary, my dear' – he nodded acknowledgment to his wife – 'her resolve was that Toby should have just what he wanted – in this case, to be first at the winning post.'

'And what did you deduce about Martin?'

'That he is honest and straightforward. He's also loyal: even when he spotted Toby moving the red ball with his foot, he didn't betray his friend.'

'They're good friends, aren't they, those two?' Ursula observed. 'I wonder why. I shouldn't have thought they have much in common. After all, Martin's background is rather . . . ordinary.'

'I suspect it started off in much the same way that a pretty girl will choose a plainer as her companion: the plainness of the one points up the attractions of the other. But now, they enjoy each other's company: besides, Martin knows he'll learn a lot from Toby's Belgravia friends, and Toby finds Martin's business sense useful.'

'And have you decided which one you'll promote?'

'Not quite. But in the end, Martin won the croquet match,' Ivor answered elliptically.

'I hope he gets the job, too. I think Martin's smashing.' The comment came from Lucinda, who had come in unnoticed to stand above her parents. She was a small, dark-haired girl whose prettiness was marred by her mother's determined chin. 'He plays a terrific game of tennis,' she went on. 'Beat the daylights out of Toby. One would never guess, Martin is so quiet and demure in his City suiting. But in his white shorts, I thought he was really dishy.'

'Lucinda!' Her mother gave a kind of warning bleat.

'Oh, Mummy, don't fuss. I know you think he's n.q.o.c.d.' She grinned down at them both. 'I just said I thought he was dishy, so don't go into a flap.' She perched on the arm of her father's chair, swinging her bare legs. 'Have you ever noticed Martin's eyes, Daddy, when he takes his spectacles off?'

'I can't say I have,' said Ivor drily.

'Well, they're the most amazing, dazzling blue. It's quite

extraordinary. I'm sure there's more to that young man than meets the eye at first glance.'

'I really don't think . . .' Ursula began; but Ivor interrupted her: either Lucinda meant what she said, or, more likely, she was teasing her mother; but, in any case, it would be a mistake to talk further about Martin just now.

'I wanted to ask you about the dance,' he said firmly. 'Your mother and I have the impression that something happened there which you all seem anxious to conceal from us.'

'I see.' Lucinda stood up. 'I suppose you'll have to know sometime, you'd be bound to hear anyway. The fact is that, I'm afraid, Giles made a bit of an ass of himself – an exhibition, you might say.'

'What do you mean?' from Ivor and 'That sounds most unlike him' from Ursula.

'To put it in a nutshell, he got rather tiddly. Goodness knows how, as they weren't exactly lavish with the champers, but he managed it. Then, when he was trying to dance, he twisted much too energetically and fell over a table. We managed to clear up a bit, and Martin was marvellous at getting Giles away, so we thought we'd better leave at once. That's why we were back early.'

Lucinda's account, which she had carefully rehearsed, left out none of the basic facts; but she had skipped the more disagreeable details. The table concerned had collapsed under the impact of Giles' flying body, and he had landed on the floor amid a wreckage of broken glasses and spilling bottles. Giles had smelled strongly of whisky, which their host had thoughtfully provided in the library for his more senior guests and which Giles had obviously broached. And finally, in the silence that followed his crash, he had been spectacularly, expansively, sick.

Martin had been quick to act. Deftly he swept up the broken glass and bottles into a tablecloth and did his best with paper napkins to deal with the vomit. Then, with surprising strength, he heaved the recumbent Giles to his feet, pulled his arm across his shoulders and marched him out of the marquee, leaving Lucinda to make the necessary apologies to their host and hostess. All the while, Lucinda

61

remembered, Toby and Hilary had stood awkwardly apart, trying to look as though they didn't belong to the Murchison party.

In Martin's car and heading back to Tickton, little was said. The two girls were crammed into the bench seat in front alongside Martin; in the back, Toby did his best to keep the lurching Giles upright. Toby's mood was sour: he had been enjoying the dance, enjoying the fact that Hilary was excited to be with him, knowing that he looked his slim, dark best in his mohair suit and the newly fashionable white silk shirt with a polo-neck collar. Now, instead of Hilary's ample warmth in the darkness of the back seat beside him, he had to watch out in case the drunken young sot was sick again over his dinner jacket.

Before they reached Tickton, Lucinda made them all promise not to say a word to her parents about Giles' debacle. It would be a shame to spoil his half-term with a family row. She herself would explain when the time was right, and without making too much of a thing about it all. This she had now done: and it was time to divert their attention from her brother's lapse.

'By the way,' she said casually, 'I rather thought I might spend a week in London soon. Hilary has asked me to stay: and Toby suggested we might all take in a show or two.'

'You won't come to much harm if you're staying with Hervey Parsloe,' Ivor observed. 'You go ahead and enjoy yourself,' he added indulgently.

'Just a minute,' Ursula interposed. 'When just now you said you might all go to the theatre, did that include Martin Coley?'

'Perhaps, Mummy, perhaps.' Lucinda gave a light laugh and left the room.

6

In the flat in Eaton Place, Toby Blackett and his brother Paul were both changing to go out for the evening. It was autumn and almost dark; since the apartment was so high up, they seldom bothered to close the curtains, and looking down for a moment as he knotted his tie, Toby could see the yellow lights from the houses opposite reflected in the wet, seal-sleek pavements.

Since the summer, when he and Hilary Parsloe had spent the weekend at Tickton, a good deal had happened in Toby's life. Through many hot, sultry nights in July and August, he had made the usual rounds of restaurants and nightclubs with Hilary; it had not taken him long to get her into bed. Soon, the evenings ended in the flat; in his untidy bedroom, with a disorderly pile of dirty socks and underpants in one corner, he introduced Hilary to the delights of making love. She was an eager pupil, and although her ample, fleshy body was strange to him after the pleasures of out-of-work actresses and models with their narrow, boyish hips and tiny tilted breasts, the exploration of Hilary's Venusian plentitude pleased him. He was not in the least in love with her – a fact he had no difficulty concealing – but he enjoyed her company, she made him laugh, she got on well with his friends, and, above all, she was a Parsloe of Draycott, Parsloe. Hilary would make him a good wife: and she was more than willing.

Her father, presented with Toby Blackett as a future son-in-law, put up no opposition. When he first met the young man, Hervey Parsloe took care to have a quiet word with Ivor Murchison. The underwriter was glad the topic of Toby's future had been raised, for he wanted to touch on the question of Toby's career anyway. Soon it had been settled between the two: Toby would join Draycott, Parsloe as a marine broker. Toby was delighted when Ivor told him what was being arranged: he relished the thought of the wider horizons that would be open to him on the broking side and since, at the same time, he was told that Ivor would propose him for membership of Lloyd's to start writing on the 1st January, both on Murchison's own syndicate and on the non-marine and aviation boxes with whom the Murchison agency normally placed its names, he felt he was now in a position to marry.

As a working member, Toby would not be required to deposit more than about £8,000, and the entrance fee and other costs would amount to another £1,000. When he approached his mother, Molly Blackett was perfectly amenable, even agreeing that as both her sons were well into their twenties and settled in their careers, there was little point in continuing the discretionary trust: accordingly, this was dissolved, Toby and Paul now having control of their own capital.

Hilary was impatient to announce the engagement; but her father urged caution. It was not that he had reservations about Toby, but rather that it might be wise to have an interval between the time when Toby joined Draycott, Parsloe and the appearance of the announcement in *The Times*. He would not want it to be suggested that Toby's new post owed anything to nepotism.

'Not that I have anything against helping the family, you understand,' Hervey Parsloe explained to Toby one evening over a brandy after dinner, 'and there's still a good deal of it in the City. What my friend Jocelyn Hambro calls enlightened nepotism – and he, of course, runs his own bank very well. But it can make for envy, and we'd be as well to be careful.'

It was therefore decided that the engagement would become public at the end of the year. Meanwhile, the couple spent most of their weekends visiting each other's families, and three or four evenings a week together; which was why Paul was mildly surprised when he learned that Toby was togging himself up other than for a dinner with Hilary.

'Business dinner, eh?' he commented, taking in Toby's dark-blue silk suit. 'You're taking a lot of trouble just for an evening with some dreary clients.'

'Actually, we're having dinner at the Mirabelle,' Toby offered in offhand explanation as he carefully brushed his hair.

'Indeed! Well, I hope you're not picking up the bill. It would make quite a hole even in your lovely new expense account.'

'No, I'm dining with Trevor Bleach, and he can well afford the Mirabelle. I'm hoping for a chance to quote on some of his insurances.'

'H'm.' Paul raised his eyebrows teasingly. 'From all you tell me, your new friend Mr Bleach is a bit of a dark horse. Are you sure it isn't your beautiful body he's after?'

'Oh, rubbish, Paul!' Toby frowned. 'Trevor Bleach is becoming very useful to me, and I think I'm of use to him, too – and I don't mean what you think.'

After their first meeting, when Bleach first came to Lloyd's, he had kept in touch with Toby, at first asking his advice over occasional lunches on Lloyd's matters; later, he had encouraged Toby to take up the offered post at Draycott, Parsloe, which fitted in very well, he said, with some of his own plans. He also stated his approval of Toby's choice of future wife; but most of all, he led Toby to speak his mind, his half-formed ideas, about the as yet unexplored potential that might lie somewhere within the financial chain that bound together broker and underwriter and the re-insurance market.

Although Toby had dismissed Paul's suggestion almost angrily, in the taxi on the way to the Mirabelle he gave it some thought. Trevor Bleach was, after all, without any apparent woman in his life. His style of living, despite the expensive entertaining in restaurants, was curiously modest for a man who was obviously well off: no smart car, not even a modish mews house. When in London, Bleach lived in a serviced apartment in the White House, just beside Regent's Park, where he appeared to blend in with the impersonal furnishings provided by the management; and when business took him to Birmingham, a suite in the Midland Hotel became his base. Nor did he possess any of the apparatus of executive power: no receptionist to protect him from unwelcome visitors, no secretary to sit, obedient to his dictation, no intercom or large desk. He preferred to deal on the telephone or over a restaurant table, making no notes and shuffling no files: all he seemed to require in the way of records was secure behind the combination lock of his black and ever-present briefcase.

At first, Toby had been suspicious of his new friend's detached impersonality; but as he saw more of Bleach, he came to appreciate how effective was this hovering in the shadows; for, if there was a trick to be gained, Bleach never missed it.

As the taxi swung round Hyde Park Corner, Toby found himself wondering if Paul was right, if Trevor Bleach was a suppressed homosexual. He had no experience of that sort of thing, no way of judging: there were, of course, one or two obvious and flamboyant queens at Lloyd's, but they were little more than a running joke among the brokers' queues at the boxes, always willing to be sent up in a jocular, masculine way. And apart from an almost-forgotten memory of adolescent grapplings at school, he had little idea as to what two queers actually did together. How would he react if Bleach actually made some kind of pass at him? Would he even recognise such a pass for what it was? And, worst of all, would his future prosperity depend on his reaction? Damn and blast his little brother for putting the idea in his head, he cursed as he dismounted and paid off the taxi.

Bleach gave Toby a chilly smile as he was led up to the table. While Toby ordered a dry martini and chose from the menu, his host remained silent, sipping at his pale whisky; but when the waiters had moved off, he began at once with what was on his mind: he had no small talk.

'I trust you have settled in well at Draycott, Parsloe,' he asked.

'It seems so. My future father-in-law says he's pleased: and

I've been promised a seat on the board, as an associate director, early next year, leaving what he calls a judicious interval after Hilary and I are married. Also, he's planning to promote Michael Pendragon at the same time, so it won't look too like nepotism.'

'Indeed? That could be very useful,' Bleach observed. Toby didn't see why: Michael Pendragon was a friend of his, but he had no idea that his host even knew of him.

'It so happens,' Bleach explained, 'that Pendragon's mother was born a Draycott. She is a cousin of your chairman Mr Andrew Draycott; but, more to my point, she possesses a considerable holding in the voting shares of Draycott, Parsloe.'

'And so?' queried Toby.

'And so I made the acquaintance of Master Pendragon and we soon came to an agreement. When the time comes, I can count on his mother to vote as I want, because the son will earn a very healthy commission when she does.'

'Why?' Toby paused, leaning back while one waiter placed a plate of smoked salmon and potted shrimps before him, and another hovered attentively with a chilled bottle of Pouilly Fumé for him to taste. His host was, more modestly, served with an avocado vinaigrette and provided with another long, pale whisky.

'Why,' he continued, 'why are you so keen to get control of Draycott, Parsloe? I mean, it's solid enough as far as Lloyd's brokers go and we turn in a reasonable profit; but we don't have all that much by way of assets apart from goodwill. I just can't see why you're bothering.'

'When I joined Lloyd's, Toby, you explained to me very clearly how the big money in insurance revolves in a kind of circle. The premiums come from the clients to the brokers, and the brokers pass them on to the underwriters – after taking their commission. Then, when the underwriters want to unload some of their risk, brokers again place it in the re-insurance market. And when there is a claim, the whole process goes into reverse back up the circle – with the brokers again taking their cut at each stage on the way.'

'I see. Because the broker stands in the middle of the circle, he stands to make most of the money.'

'That's true enough, as far as it goes. But it doesn't go nearly far enough for me.' For the first time, Trevor Bleach's grey eyes were not blank, impassive: instead, there was about them a trace of the faraway look of the dreamer. 'There are two other aspects of the business which, once we secure control of the complete circle, we shall be in a position to exploit to the full. And both these crocks of gold, I am convinced, are to be found in re-insurance.'

Bleach clammed up while the waiters removed their plates; but once his medium steak and green salad was in front of him, he took up his theme.

'We must set up our own offshore re-insurance company. At the moment, I consider the Bahamas the most advantageous, but where it is doesn't matter yet. That will have one use to me . . .' he broke off to give Toby a hard, assessing stare, 'but you needn't concern yourself with that aspect: it's only a somewhat useful device for getting around exchange control. What I want you to consider – and it was your idea, I might add – are the benefits to be had from such a corporation.'

Toby withdrew his attention from his guinea fowl to answer. 'The advantages of an offshore outfit are enormous,' he began. 'Apart from being able to build up a very decent sum of capital away from the attentions of the tax boys, we'd be in a position to dictate exactly where, to our best advantage, the profit should lie. We could manipulate our management fees, and provided we kept our names happy with reasonable cheques each year, the only losers would be the Inland Revenue.'

'Exactly. But to be in a position to do this, we need to control every link in the circle – and that includes the underwriting agency. Then we can be sure of placing our re-insurance business where we want it – in our own hands.'

'I suppose you have your eye on Murchison's,' Toby suggested.

Bleach nodded. 'Why not? Ivor is much respected in the Room, and by the Committee. His presence would give us standing, make us respectable. Do you think he'd play?'

'I don't know.' Toby sounded doubtful. 'The trouble with Ivor is that he's so damned upright. I did air some such wheeze on the box, months ago, and he hit the roof – all that stuff about a conflict of interest, coupled with righteous horror at arrangements for tax avoidance, and ending with a few choice words about all that Lloyd's stands for.'

'Let him have his say. In fact, he'll be all the more useful to us – we can make a virtue of his damned virtue, as it were.'

'I don't follow you.' Toby leaned back to allow a waiter to refill his wine glass.

'I know these upright, honourable men.' Bleach sounded contemptuous. 'They're so fixed on doing the right thing, on not stepping out of line, that if we can only show them that what we propose is the right thing, that it will be good for Lloyd's, good for the insurance market as a whole and indeed good for their names, they'll fall in with us without a murmur of protest. Especially when it dawns on them that they stand to make a great deal of money out of the process.'

'I . . . I think you might have some trouble in talking Ivor Murchison round,' Toby suggested cautiously. 'I mean, I have the impression that old Ivor doesn't altogether trust you.'

'Quite right, Toby, he doesn't.' Bleach smiled thinly. 'I realise I'm not the man to persuade him. Nor are you, for all your public school tie and your well-connected wife-to-be. But I think he'd listen to Gasper Grieve.'

'Of course he would – they're very old friends. That's very neat, Trevor. But even when we have old Ivor's agreement to participate in our new offshore re-insurance fund – which we'd sell to him as our own private catastrophe fund – we still wouldn't have control of the Murchison agency. And I don't think he'd consider selling it: he feels very dynastic and has every intention of passing it on to his son, that little brat Giles.'

'We're in no hurry.' Trevor Bleach shrugged and sipped the last of his whisky. 'In the end, money will talk: it always does. Our first step must be to secure control of Draycott, Parsloe; and in that respect, I want to hear all you've managed to dig up about the controlling shareholders. I didn't get you a comfortable job there just for the sake of your flashing eyes.'

Suddenly, Toby felt cold. Just when he felt relaxed and

assured in the luxurious restaurant, when his dreams of personal wealth, of power, of being in the thick of a successful financial coup, looked like being realised, by one remark he was reminded of his brother's taunt. He reached for his wine glass but it was empty.

His host, observing the movement, suggested a brandy with his coffee. 'Or, I seem to remember, you prefer Armagnac?'

By the time the spirit arrived, in a vast goblet warmed with ceremony over a flame, Toby had recovered his equilibrium. What Trevor Bleach had said, he told himself firmly, was no more than a way of speaking: there was no reason to suspect even a whiff of an innuendo. Nor, glancing at the impassive, grey face of his host, could he detect any anticipatory gleam in the cold eyes.

Relieved, Toby began to explain what he had managed to find out about the share structure of his employers; soon, however, Bleach stayed him, saying that perhaps they had better wait until they were back at the White House, as he himself might need to make some notes. Bleach called for his bill and neatly signed it, which impressed Toby: soon, with luck, he too would enjoy charge accounts and obsequious service at establishments such as the Mirabelle.

At Bleach's impersonal flat, Toby was provided with a large brandy. For a moment, he wondered if he was being made drunk; then he laughed at his suspicions and turned his mind to reporting all he had managed to discover about the shareholdings of Draycott, Parsloe & Co.

The brokers, he began, had gone public in 1960. They had created an issue of three million 'B' shares; of these, their own Pension Fund had taken up half a millon, and the family and their respective trusts a similar amount. The balance had been placed in the market at a price of fourteen shillings, and since 1960 happened to be a record year at Lloyd's, dealings were bullish, soon taking the price well over twenty shillings. Since then the price had been as high as 22/- and as low as 16/-, with the family shedding some of their holdings from time to time when the price rose. At the moment, the shares stood at about a pound, and the family holdings seemed to be less than two hundred thousand.

'This is useful background information,' said Bleach, 'but it doesn't answer my question: who has control?'

'A-ha,' said Toby, enjoying himself. 'That's where Andrew Draycott and Hervey Parsloe have been very clever. Before they went public, they divided the shares into two classes, "A" and "B": it was the "B" shares they sold off and it is to the "B" shares that they themselves look when they want to raise some cash to spend; because the "B" shares have no vote. Only the "A" shares carry a vote, and none of them have ever been sold.'

'It's not an unusual situation,' Trevor Bleach commented. 'Some most respectable companies, like Marks & Spencer and Savoy Hotels, employ that kind of device to give the board absolute control. What I need to know is how, within the families, the "A" shares are divided up.'

'The largest holding, oddly enough, is in the name of the DP Pension Fund.'

'It's not odd at all,' snapped Bleach, irritated at Toby's obtuseness. 'If, as I presume, Andrew Draycott and Hervey Parsloe are the trustees of the Pension Fund, it simply means that they retain in their hands the reins of power. Even if, in the future, some members of the family have to sell their holdings, to meet death duties perhaps, and even if the others fail to take up those voting shares, the Pension Fund holding still gives them enough clout to keep control. Now, tell me how the 'A' shares are divided up.' Bleach opened his brief-case and took out a sheet of paper, then he withdrew his fountain pen from his breast pocket and sat, poised, making notes as Toby explained.

There were only 200,000 voting shares, and of these the Pension Fund held 40 per cent. Andrew Draycott, the chairman, held 20,000 and a discretionary settlement in favour of his two children a further 10 per cent. On Hervey Parsloe's side, he too had 10 per cent, and his daughter Hilary, Toby's intended, had a similar holding. There were only two other shareholders of the 'A' shares: Mrs Ivor Murchison, who was a sister of Draycott, and a Mrs Muriel Stamp; they each held 20,000.

'I haven't been able to find out who Mrs Stamp is,' Toby admitted; 'I suppose she's some kind of aunt.'

'Mrs Stamp is the mother of Michael Pendragon. I think we can say,' Bleach added complacently, 'that we have Mrs Stamp's vote in our pocket, and that's a good start. And I hope we will be able to count on the future Mrs Toby Blackett?'

'Hilary? Oh yes, I think she'll do whatever I want. There's not much love lost between her and her father anyway; and she's so besotted about me' – Toby gave a lubricious grin – 'that she won't ask any questions.'

'You keep her that way.' Bleach glanced at his notes. 'Now, if we ignore the Pension Fund, we've only to gain control of just over 60,000 voting shares to lay our hands on Draycott, Parsloe & Co.'

'How can we just ignore the Fund? I would have thought it crucial.'

'There are ways.' Trevor Bleach laid aside his notes to explain. 'If it came to a full-blooded bid, a takeover offer, we could suggest – and if necessary get a judge to agree with us – that the trustees of the Fund must be seen to act in the best interests of the beneficiaries, who are the pensioners and future pensioners of the company: and that means that they should abstain from influencing the result. Their duty, in the last resort, must be to obtain the best possible price of the Fund's holding. With luck, the mere threat of an application to a judge in chambers should be sufficient to make the Fund's vote impotent.'

'Neat, very neat.' Toby hoped he looked sage as he leaned back to light a cigarette. 'So we concentrate on the family's "A" shares.'

'For the moment, yes. Mind you, if we don't succeed there, I can think of other ways . . . but I won't confuse you with them at this juncture. Now, we have 40,000 shares which we can rely on to vote our way: how do you think our friend Ivor's good lady will react?'

'Ursula Murchison is strong on loyalty. I very much doubt that she'd ever move against her brother. Nor is she particularly interested in money; she has ample for her needs. The same goes for Andrew Draycott; he likes to be thought of as a big cheese in the City. He's a Liveryman and serves on Lloyd's Committee: rumour has it that he may be in line for a

"K" in the next Honours List – "services to Export" and all that rubbish – so the last thing he wants is a takeover battle.'

'Besides,' Bleach observed, 'I don't think Mr Draycott much approves of me. I don't wear the right tie.' His Birmingham twang was suddenly pronounced. 'I think we can take it that the Draycotts will be opposed to us. That leaves us with Hervey Parsloe.'

'I've seen a good deal of Hervey in the last few months. In a way, he's like old Ivor: wants to be thought a man of honour and all that. But underneath, he's very different. For one thing, he's jealous of Draycott's position of power and all the trappings that go with it – the Rolls, the lunches at the Bank of England, the pomp and ceremony of a Wardenship of one of the big Livery companies.'

'If that's his price, he can easily have all that.' Bleach sounded contemptuous.

'He'd want more. For although he must be worth half a million, I'm convinced he's still greedy.'

'Butter *and* jam, eh?' Bleach's thin smile flashed briefly. 'That all seems satisfactory. You start the process of softening Parsloe up, and when you judge the time right, I'll move in. I aim to have Draycott, Parsloe & Co. wrapped up in six months: from that position of strength we can then move out in both directions. I want to have our offshore outfit on the road by the end of next year. And there'll be something in all this for you, by the way.'

'For me?' Toby tried to sound casual, but the eagerness showed in his voice.

'I've been buying up the "B" shares in the market for some time. All in nominee names, of course, so the board haven't any idea who's behind it. And I've earmarked a hundred thousand for you. Without the vote, the "B" shares stand at a substantial discount: I've been paying between 13/- and 14/6d for them, but once we gain control, I'll enfranchise them and they'll go ahead, perhaps to 25/-. You'll make a lot of money.'

'But . . . but I can't possibly pay for a hundred thousand shares,' Toby stuttered.

'Who said anything about paying? They're in a nominee company, just a shell which I have to hand. The day we sew

73

up Draycott, Parsloe & Co., I just sign one transfer and they'll be yours.'

'Gosh, Trevor, that's really handsome of you.' Toby sloughed his carapace of worldly wisdom in his excitement: he sounded like a prefect at school.

'Of course, it's only a start for you.' Bleach made a rare, deprecating gesture with his well-manicured hand. 'But it will give you enough to take part in our new re-insurance corporation and that's where you will clean up. I shall be very surprised if, by the time you are thirty-five, you're not worth at least a million.'

'Good Lord.' Toby shot a quick, assessing glance at his mentor. 'Why, Trevor, why? It's marvellous, needless to say, but I don't understand why you're doing all this for me.'

'My dear Toby, I should have thought that was obvious.' Bleach rose from his armchair and moved to the sideboard, taking Toby's empty glass with him. 'You're useful to me and I'm useful to you. For this operation to be effective, I need your total loyalty – and there's no better way of ensuring loyalty than having a great big dollop of capital attached to it.'

'Yes, I know, but still . . .' Toby was by now slightly drunk and the conversation didn't altogether make sense to him.

'I see.' Trevor Bleach came back with Toby's brandy refreshed and set it down. He remained standing, looking down on Toby's luxuriant head of thick dark hair. 'Perhaps you are wondering if there is by any chance another price tag on your fortune?' His voice was suddenly very quiet.

'I don't know what you mean,' Toby mumbled, taking a large gulp at his drink to hide his confusion. For an instant, he felt almost frightened of the slight, grey man looming above him.

'That's just as well,' said Bleach, moving away. 'And you'll have to wait until you're a millionaire before you find out. Now,' he went on briskly, 'before you go, a few words more about Murchison's. If we are to complete that circle, we need an underwriting agency.'

'I think the best tactic would be to distract old Ivor,' Toby suggested. 'After all, he's been the underwriter on the box since the war; he's probably ripe for a little diversion.'

'My thinking exactly. Gasper must represent to him that it's his duty to Lloyd's to lend his wisdom and, let's not forget, his honour, both to the board of Draycott, Parsloe and to our Bahamian outfit. We must, by the way, dignify the latter with some high-sounding name.'

'M'yes.' Toby was thinking. 'Old Ivor has always been a bit of a stick-in-the-mud. He could easily have done what so many boxes do: set up a small "baby" syndicate on the side. It's just for the working names and a few close chums, but it's easy for the underwriter to cream off for baby's benefit the very best of the risks and the most lucrative premiums.'

'That sounds like good sense.' Bleach liked the way Toby's mind was working. 'But I think we'd have to leave young Martin Coley as the underwriter. How would he react? I hardly know the man.'

'Martin likes to model himself on old Ivor. But I'll have no difficulty in pulling the wool over his eyes if I have to.'

'Oh dear.' Bleach sighed. 'Another man who thinks himself incorruptible?'

'Martin has all the old-fashioned virtues.' Toby laughed and added, 'Even chastity, I should imagine.'

7

As it happened, Toby Blackett was wrong about Martin Coley, but only just. As the Underground train rattled through the deep tunnels under Oxford Street, Martin found himself thinking about Lucinda Murchison, with whom, as so often recently, he had spent the evening before. From the first time they met at her parents' house that summer, Lucinda had made what, with all modesty, Martin had to admit was a dead set at him. It was she who telephoned him first, at the box, early one morning before her father would have arrived, to propose an evening out as a foursome with Hilary and Toby; it was she who suggested which restaurants, clubs and theatres they would visit; and in the end, one evening when they were on their own in Hilary's home (where Lucinda was still staying), it was she who, almost briskly, persuaded him into her bed.

For Martin, the effect was explosive. Now nearly thirty, he was not only inexperienced with women, he was – much to his very private shame – still actually a virgin. There had been, of course, some fumbled gropings with the girls he met in Ealing, at the tennis club or the Young Conservatives; but, despite the fact that he felt the drives of most young men, he had lacked the confidence to 'go all the way'. Nor were the verandah of the tennis club, or the back of the Hillman after a barn dance at the YMCA, places conducive to his breaking his duck. And the girls he met with Toby all seemed to be too knowledgeable, too worldly, too poised for him to approach. Once, very drunk after an evening on the tiles with Toby, he had determined to pick up a whore; but the sight of the raddled figures hovering under the dim street lights of Shepherd's Market combined with natural caution and downright fear to put him off.

His night with Lucinda, therefore, hit his emotions for six (he had caught the habit of cricketing allusions from Ivor Murchison). Quite suddenly, the whole world was aglow, and the centre of the world was Lucinda; she was seldom out of his thoughts, and when he was not with her, he found himself suspended in an abject craving. In short, he was in love, for the first time in his life.

Once she was certain of him, Lucinda's attitude had changed. While still enjoying their congress, she began to keep Martin at a little distance. Now, he was the one in pursuit and Lucinda teased him by cancelling arrangements at the last minute, or if she appeared at all she made sure she was late. For Martin, her new mood was agony; in his mind, from bed to love to marriage was a natural progression; had she not early on extracted his promise of silence, he would long since have spoken to her father.

When she enlisted at the Cordon Bleu School of Cookery, Lucinda continued to stay during the week at the Parsloes'. Meanwhile, she told him, they were in no hurry. She refused to talk of marriage, or even to agree a date by which they would declare their engagement; instead, they must enjoy their secret while they might. Besides, she pointed out, although he knew her parents, as yet she hadn't even met his mother.

This presented Martin with a problem. It was not, he assured himself robustly, that he was in any way ashamed of his suburban origins, about which he was open: it was Muriel Coley herself who was the difficulty.

Even as a schoolboy, Martin remembered his mother's occasional odd moods. He would come home to find her silent and morose, sitting motionless beside the wireless, to whose loud blaring she paid no attention. She would scarcely notice his return, offering only the occasional inconsequential remark which made little sense; and he had become accustomed to finding his supper a charred relic under the gas grill on such evenings. The next night, with her bright hair well done, she would again be her chatty, cheerful self, but Martin realised that she was exerting all her pressure of will to make sure that no mention whatever was made of her condition the day before. At first, Martin had been worried about his mother's moods; but there were no close relations in whom he might confide and it was obviously not a thing to discuss with a school friend, so he just accepted the dark times, putting them down vaguely to some after-effects of the war.

Lucinda was the first person he told; but she had not been very concerned. When she suggested it was merely 'the change', Martin had been puzzled; as she explained about the menopause, she had giggled at his innocence. He was relieved at such a simple explanation, but he still wanted to make sure that Lucinda's first meeting with his mother should go off well, and the only day on which he was sure of Mrs Coley's mood was a Sunday: weekends, of course, Lucinda always spent in Essex, and thus the encounter had never taken place.

Martin had not lost his relish at going to work, and his sense of belonging to the community of Lloyd's was enhanced now that, thanks to generous help from Ivor Murchison and the agency, he himself had been elected a working member. The changes which had taken place on the box, too, augured well for Martin's future. Now that Mr Wells had retired to Penge to devote himself to his begonias, Martin, as deputy underwriter, sat facing Ivor Murchison, whom, rather tentatively, he addressed by his Christian name. With several new names on the syndicate and the consequent increase in their underwriting limits, Ivor had decided they would need two new clerks, and these had both recently started work. One was a pink-and-white public school boy named Philip Hemsley, the son of a neighbour of the Murchisons in Essex, and the other, John Bishop, was the son of a clerk on a nearby box. Remembering the friendly rivalry between himself and Toby on the box, Martin was amused to see the same pattern with the new recruits; for already it was understood on the box that in due course one of the two would have to depart for other pastures to make way for Giles Murchison, when Ivor judged it fit for his son to join.

Despite Ivor Murchison's gloomy predictions of a poor year, the syndicate was not doing at all badly. Word had gone round the market that the bat-buggers were writing more adventurously; with the rush of renewals towards the end of the year, the queue of brokers waiting for the under-writer's attention was busy, and they were beginning to show some new lines to Murchison's. Draycott, Parsloe, in particular, were showing them a good many new, first-class risks, which attention Martin attributed to Toby, both out of affection and to ensure the prosperity of the syndicate he had just joined. Besides, why shouldn't they come to Murchison's?

It was raining hard when Martin emerged from Bank station. Without thinking, he raised his umbrella and set off up Cornhill, the same walk he took every weekday morning. He did not notice the heavy Doric portico of the Royal Exchange, nor the subtle change in the office façades as he neared Lloyd's, where the severe Georgian of the banks gave way to the more ornate baroque of the shipping companies. His thoughts were on his future: married bliss with Lucinda, that went without saying; but in the forefront of his mind as he turned into Lime Street was the proud prospect that in a few years' time he would himself be the underwriter on Murchison's box.

Already, Ivor was showing signs of handing over the reins. The shipbuilding lines were now left entirely to Martin, and Ivor was encouraging him to write as much new business as came their way. Ivor now spent more time in the marketplace; he saw his role as being to nudge the senior brokers in the direction of the box, and in pursuit of this he had embarked on a series of long lunches, not in the Captain's Room or the City Club, but in the more relaxed (and more impressive) surroundings of his club in St James's. Often, after such an engagement, Ivor would not return to Lloyd's at all, instead looking in on the sale rooms of the West End in pursuit of his growing collection of eighteenth-century fire-arms.

Once inside the warmth of Lloyd's, Martin went straight to the members' cloakroom. Here he deposited his overcoat and umbrella (it would be carefully dried and returned to him, neatly rolled, at the end of the day), and took *Lloyd's List* away for his usual ten minutes in the lavatory. He was back on the box by nine. After half an hour with the post, and looking through the possible re-insurance of risks written the day before, he was ready to deal with the brokers.

One of the earliest was Michael Pendragon of Draycott, Parsloe. Martin did not care for the florid, sharp-toothed broker, although he was a friend of Toby's, but he gave him the box's customary, formal greeting.

'Good morning, sir.'

'And the top of the morning to you, too, Martin old lad.' Pendragon had no time for the old-fashioned courtesies. 'I've a couple of beauties for you today, which we've managed to get our hands on from the USA, thanks to our friends at A & A.'

'Indeed?' said Martin, putting up his hand for the slips. American business, if good, was much sought after, and anything that came from New York brokers of the magnitude and reputation of Alexander & Alexander must be worth looking at.

While Martin studied the slips, Pendragon asked casually if Martin saw much of Toby these days.

'As a matter of fact, we're lunching together at Simpson's today,' Martin answered. 'Dot's lamb chops and stewed cheese will make a change from the Captain's Room.'

Ivor Murchison arrived at the box in time to hear this exchange; and as soon as Pendragon had picked up his slips and left, he signalled to Martin that he wanted a private word. Side by side, they walked away from the box.

'So you're seeing Toby today,' he began. 'I wonder if you could find out something for me?'

'Of course . . . Ivor,' Martin answered. 'What is it?'

'All this is fairly confidential, Martin. I had dinner last night with my brother-in-law Andrew Draycott. Between you and me, he's damned worried. Someone – and he doesn't know who – has been buying up shares of Draycott, Parsloe through the market. All the transfers are in nominee names, but he's picked up a whisper that our new name Trevor Bleach may be involved. I never liked the fellow,' he added, 'and I'm regretting that I ever let Gasper Grieve talk me into having him as a name.'

'Do you mean there's a takeover brewing?'

'I don't think there's much likelihood of that,' Ivor laughed easily. 'Between them, the Draycotts and the Parsloes have control pretty well wrapped up. But there must be some reason for this interest in the company, and Draycott badly wants to know what that reason is.'

'I can understand that. How do you think Toby can help?'

'I may be wrong, but I have the impression that he and Trevor Bleach have become quite thick. Bleach may have dropped a hint or two, and if he has, I hope Toby will pass the word.'

At the crowded chop-house, Toby and Martin had to share a greasy wooden table while Dot, the motherly waitress, took their order. Over luncheon, all the talk was of Toby's now imminent marriage. Mrs Hervey Parsloe had determined to do the thing properly, with a full choral service at St Paul's, Knightsbridge, and the reception afterwards across the road at the Hyde Park Hotel. Paul Blackett would be best man, Lucinda a bridesmaid, and Martin himself agreed to act as an usher. To himself, he resolved to buy a morning suit: with any luck, he'd soon need it for his own wedding. The Parsloe present to the couple was the freehold of a small house in Hasker Street, just behind Harrods.

'Hilary's busy furnishing it now,' Toby said, 'and we've already tried out the bed!' He gave his lewd grin, adding, 'And when are you going to make an honest woman of Lucinda?'

'I don't know,' Martin muttered. He found it distasteful to talk of his private life, especially with other ears around the table. 'She says she won't make up her mind yet.'

'Don't worry, she will,' Toby consoled him. 'There's nothing like a good old-fashioned wedding to bring out the bride in every woman. Once Lucinda's seen Hilary trotting down the aisle on my arm, she'll grab you.'

When they emerged from Simpson's cellar into daylight,

they found that the rain had turned to sleet. They dodged through the maze of alleys between Lombard Street and Cornhill as fast as possible, pausing to catch their breath once they reached the shelter of the Leadenhall Street market.

The market was an unlikely thing to find tucked away in the middle of one of the great financial centres of the world. Beneath its intricate roof of wrought iron and grimed glass was gathered a parade of shops such as one might more reasonably expect to find in some prosperous country town: fishmongers, with elaborate displays of lobsters, oysters and whole turbot on their marble slabs, poulterers with rows of still-feathered fowl suspended from a brass rod, butchers with succulent joints of dark red beef, fruiterers with heraldic pineapples crowning pyramids of oranges and lemons, even an old-fashioned grocer's shop, where assistants in brown alpaca coats would weigh out pounds of demerara sugar and grind fresh-roasted coffee to their customer's taste. Above all, the smell was wonderfully refreshing, almost earthy, like a kitchen garden after a shower of rain, overlaid with a faint, salty tang of the sea.

As, outside a small tobacconist's, they lit their cigarettes, Martin remembered Ivor Murchison's request.

'By the way, Toby,' he began carefully, 'do you see much of Trevor Bleach these days?'

'A certain amount. Why do you ask?'

'Ivor's got hold of a rumour that your friend may be trying to buy up Draycott, Parsloe. Do you think there's any truth in it?'

'I know nothing whatever about it,' Toby lied. 'But I would have thought it most unlikely.'

8

The London offices of Ithaki-Hellenic were on the third floor
of a heavy Edwardian building tucked away in an alley
behind Cornhill. Paul Blackett made a habit of being early to
work. His fortunes too had changed since the summer. He
had been surprised to be summoned to lunch with his god-
father, Major Algernon Villiers, whom he seldom saw and
remembered chiefly for a steadfast amnesia in the matter of
Christmas and birthday presents; he had been even more
surprised, over the course of the lunch, to be offered a job
within the London office of Ithaki-Hellenic. He had heard of
Laertes Vathos: indeed at that time, to mention the words
'Greek shipowner' was to conjure up a vision of measureless
wealth. At any rate, Paul hadn't hesitated, for the salary
offered was generous, the duties seemed not arduous and he
could see no real future in the estate agency.

Once he joined Ithaki-Hellenic, he saw little more of
Major Villiers. The major's working day began at eleven, and
by eleven twenty the cocktail cabinet in his room was open; a
succession of cronies would arrive to share its contents, and
then the major departed for a long lunch, from which, often,
he did not return at all. This vacuum Paul filled: he discovered he had a talent for administration, and the hitherto
idle secretaries found themselves busy as Paul made it his
business to deal promptly with the telexes from other Ithaki-
Hellenic offices, to sharpen routines, to install up-to-date

office equipment. Despite all this, and despite learning his way around the Baltic Exchange and, more important, the oil traders, he had plenty of time on his hands; and an idea was forming in his mind that he decided to touch on with his brother.

As he swung into the office one morning in November, his secretary held up a warning hand. 'Mr Vathos is here,' she hissed, 'he's in Major Villiers' office.'

Paul was surprised. He had had no instructions to book hotel suites, no hint of the owner's arrival. Wondering what was up, he went straight in.

The Greek was seated at Major Villiers' desk, its usually empty surface strewn with files and papers. Standing attentively at his shoulder was another Greek, small and dapper with black, smooth hair so shiny it looked as if it had been polished.

Vathos didn't look up from his papers. 'Good morning, Paul,' he muttered. 'Sit down, I want to talk to you. This, by the way, is Masterakis.'

Paul nodded at the other Greek, to whom he had often spoken on the telephone. Hitherto, Paul had only met his employer in the neutral surroundings of hotel suites; this time, as he watched Mr Vathos dealing with his papers, instructing Masterakis and, once, barking some orders in Greek on a long-distance call to Piraeus, he became aware of the shipowner's dominance of his business.

'Now, Paul,' said Vathos, 'when do you think we may expect to see Major Villiers?'

'I . . . I don't know, sir. He often has to make calls on his way into the office.'

'Oh, Paul.' Vathos' tone was reproachful as he leaned back in his chair. 'I see you feel you have to be loyal to my worthless brother-in-law. Loyalty is a great thing, provided it is not misplaced; but you know, as I know, that Algie won't put his nose into this place until well after eleven o'clock and when he does, his nose will go straight into that thing over there.' He gestured at the cocktail cabinet.

'Now you listen to me, young man.' The owner placed his broad, hairy hands on the desk and looked straight at Paul, his black eyes hard under the thick eyebrows. 'It is I who

84

should command your loyalty: do you understand? I, who am your employer and who will reward you well. If you do what I say and follow my orders without question – and some of my instructions may from time to time appear to be . . . unconventional – then you will prosper. Have you anything to say to that?'

Paul hesitated, startled by the Greek's knowledge of the London office, of the habits of Major Villiers. It was too late to try to defend Villiers, even had he wanted to. Already, Vathos was detailing what he wanted Paul to do.

'You have heard about my new ship, the *Katherina Vathos*?'

'Oh yes, sir. How's the building getting along?'

'There's been some delay: she should have been laid down already but I haven't yet completed all the financial arrangements, and that's why I'm in London today. I could easily pay for her myself, out of my own pocket, but this time it suits me better to raise the money in London, and that's why I'm calling on Mauser's this morning. There are a few last details to clear up and then the yard can start work. And, by the way, I want you to come to the bankers with me.'

They set off for Mauser's, threading their way through the network of gloomy alleys that lay between Cornhill and Lombard Street. Vathos had Paul at his side, with Masterakis bringing up the rear, and he set a sharp pace as he fired questions at Paul about the City. When he learned that Paul's brother was a Lloyd's broker, he asked which and repeated the name as if to register it in his mind.

At the bank, in the anonymous conference room which was windowless and featureless save for blanks of blotting paper laid out around the table, Vathos became, it seemed to Paul, very Greek. He paced about the room with extravagant gestures, at times he shouted angrily and at others became wheedling. Mauser's men, three dark-suited, smooth-faced assistant directors, must have been used to such behaviour in some of their foreign customers, but one of them, who by chance was wearing the same Old Stoic tie as Paul, gave him a wry glance of sympathy. From behind Vathos' shoulder, Paul grinned back; later, when he persuaded Vathos to sit down and to add his signature to some papers, he received another complicit look; and after it was all over and a tray of milky coffee was handed round, the banker murmured on one side that they must get together for a natter some time soon and he'd be on the blower to fix a lunch.

On the way back, Vathos put his hand on Paul's shoulder. 'You handled that well, boy,' he said. 'Just keep in with that mob – and others like them – and spread the word that Laertes Vathos is on the level. After all, you're an Englishman and one of them: if you say my standing is OK, then they'll listen to you, and they'll come to believe that I'm not an untrustworthy wog, like some they could mention. That's why I want you to head up Ithaki-Hellenic in London.'

'Me, sir? But what about Major Villiers?'

Vathos did not reply. He quickened his step and, when they reached the office, went straight into the major's room, Paul and Masterakis following.

Villiers was in, and in the act of pouring himself a glass of gin.

'Ah, LV,' he said genially, 'I heard on the grapevine you were in town. I'm sorry I wasn't here to greet you myself, but you didn't let me know. Drink?'

'Thank you, Algie, no.' Vathos settled into the major's chair. 'But help yourself, by all means,' he added, with a proprietorial gesture. 'And when you're ready, I'd like to have a word about our insurance arrangements.'

'Insurance, LV?'

'Insurance, Algie. How, at present, is my fleet covered?'

'Well, as you know, most of the policies are taken out by the Piraeus office; through them, a certain amount of re-insurance comes into the London market, I understand, though we don't handle it here.'

'I consider we should. I think it's time we took our fleet to Lloyd's: I'm advised that we'd probably get better cover and cheaper.'

'You may be right, LV, I wouldn't know anything about it.' The major took a gulp of his gin and tonic and smiled disarmingly at his brother-in-law.

'But Algie, you do know something about it.' Vathos' tone was very gentle.

The major shook his head. 'All quite beyond me,' he mumbled.

'I think not.' The Greek's voice hardened. 'What about my new tanker, the *Katherina Vathos*? Masterakis here tells me that you were insistent that her insurance came to London.'

'The best place, old boy, the best place.'

'I quite agree, Algie. And that's why I'm going to place my whole fleet here, through a Lloyd's broker.'

'Very wise, LV. We'd better use the same people that placed the *Katherina Vathos*. I'm told they're very reliable.' The major spoke as if he was recommending a good gunsmith.

'No, Algie.' Vathos shook his head gently, as if reproving a wayward child. 'We will not use the same people as before. We will use Draycott, Parsloe & Company.'

'Why on earth, LV?'

'Why not? I'm told they're very reliable.' Vathos repeated his brother-in-law's words with a dry relish. 'And what is more' – he leaned across the desk to stare into the major's empurpled face – 'they wouldn't be so foolish as to pass over to you the ten percent of the premiums I pay which at present, I am assured, you receive from these so reliable people.'

Major Villiers looked taken aback and attempted to bluster. 'Here, I say, there's nothing underhand in that. In the City, it's quite normal for a commission to be paid on business introduced.'

'I am not interested in the dubious ethics of the City. I consider such arrangements as disloyal to Ithaki-Hellenic, disloyal to me, Algie. My mind is made up: we will approach Draycott, Parsloe and Paul here will see to it.'

The major looked at Paul. 'I see,' he sneered. 'I get it now. You've a brother at Draycott, Parsloe, haven't you, Paul? I suppose you've tied it up between you.'

'My decision has nothing to do with Paul,' Vathos snapped. 'He will handle the business because he will be acting as the London manager of Ithaki-Hellenic.'

'London manager?' Villiers echoed. 'What the hell . . . ?'

'Yes, Algie,' Vathos silenced him, 'London manager. For some time, I have been considering that you are a somewhat expensive extravagance in my employ, and now that I learn that you have been lining your pockets at my expense, I have no wish to go on indulging you.' As if to dismiss the major from his mind, he turned to Masterakis at his elbow and took from him a sheaf of papers.

'Just a minute, LV.' The major sounded aggrieved. 'What about Catherine, what about Hélène?'

Vathos looked up briefly. 'My decision is of no concern to my wife. And as for Hélène, I have no wish to see my sister-in-law impoverished as a result of her husband's petty greed. I shall make her a suitable allowance, and if she cares to support you out of that, well, that is her business, not mine.' He returned to his papers, and the major, realising that further protest was useless, slunk from the room.

Paul Blackett made as if to leave too, but Vathos stayed him.

'Masterakis is going to Rotterdam tomorrow,' he said, 'and I want you to accompany him. He will introduce you to the spot market.'

'The spot market, sir? I didn't know that Ithaki-Hellenic dealt in oil as well as carrying it.'

'There's a great deal you don't know, young man, and don't you forget it. In fact, I don't play the oil market as yet, but I may well do so at some stage in the future, and I want you to be familiar with its workings. Besides, it will do us no harm to have our faces known there.'

'I see, sir.' Paul paused. 'If I might make the suggestion, sir, and while you are talking of making our face known, would you like to be shown round Lloyd's? The under-writers sometimes like to meet an owner, and I know my brother would be honoured to show you around.'

'A good idea, Paul. By all means arrange it. But it will have to be this afternoon; I leave for Paris in the morning.'

9

In such a close community as the City of London, the word soon spread that something was 'up' at Draycott, Parsloe & Co. Dealings in the 'B' shares were active, some sellers taking a profit and finding ready buyers hopeful that there was substance in the talk of takeover. When the price hit 30/–, Trevor Bleach instructed his brokers to unload: he took a handsome profit, and when the price dipped again to 22/–, because of new rumours that the potential bidder was pulling out, he bought back again. Andrew Draycott had given instructions that he was to have sight of each and every share transfer, but since Bleach's deals were made in the name of nominees, he was none the wiser.

In his head office in Crutched Friars, Sir Andrew (as, since the 1st January, he was styled) began to feel he was under siege. Hitherto, he had always been comfortable in the knowledge that the ramparts of Draycott, Parsloe were unassailable: there might be a scattering of outside shareholders beyond the moat, but the family held the keys to the keep and could always raise the drawbridge and let down the portcullis. Yet he realised this was no traditional siege: no heralds had come forward under the white flag to offer terms of truce, from the walls he saw no sign of the deployment of battering rams, siege-towers or escalades, no soldiery scurrying forward under their shields amid a hail of arrows to raise the grappling ladders.

He glanced down at a letter on the polished walnut of his desk. It opened warmly, in handwriting, 'My Dear Andrew', but the brief typed paragraph was cool.

As you know, Mauser's have been proud to work with Draycott, Parsloe in the past, and I myself remember with pleasure the success we enjoyed a few years ago when we assisted in placing your shares on the market. It grieves me, therefore, to have to tell you that circumstances have arisen which make it impossible for us to act as your advisers at the present time. To be frank, my partners feel that Mauser's might well find itself in a position where a conflict of interest could arise; therefore, we have no alternative but to suggest that you and your board look elsewhere for advice.

The letter concluded, again in handwriting, with warm felicitations on his appearance in the New Year Honours List.

Re-reading the missive added to Sir Andrew's unease. Mauser's had been got at; and they would not play the part of the relief column. It was as if, from far below the foundations, the bedrock on which his fortress was built had trembled: sappers were at work, mining their way under his stout walls. Once breached, there could be no effective defence.

He reached for the intercom and barked at his secretary to present his compliments to Mr Hervey, asking him to come to the chairman's office as soon as possible to discuss a matter of urgency.

It always gave Hervey Parsloe pleasure to come into the room of the chairman. His colleague Sir Andrew was standing by the imitation fireplace with its bolection moulding in pale oak, dressed as usual in a dark-grey suit; across his waistcoat was looped a thin gold chain and, above the blue tie of the Honourable Artillery Company with its discreet red zig-zags, Sir Andrew still maintained an immaculate stiff white collar. He was a big-framed man, with broad shoulders and an expansive belly that told of many Livery dinners; bushy eyebrows almost white against a florid complexion completed a commanding presence. Parsloe's own style was more relaxed: tall and thin, with dark hair turning elegantly grey, he wore an Italian silk suit in just too bright a blue, with soft-collared blue shirt and a floral tie. As they stood, side by side, while Parsloe read the letter from Mauser's, around them on the panelled walls dark portraits of previous chairmen looked down: Mr Jermyn Parsloe, Hervey's father, who had run the firm in the expansion of the Twenties, and the founder, Edwin Draycott, who like another great name, Cuthbert Heath, had done so much to bring the vast new non-marine business to the marketplace at Lloyd's.

'Well, what do you think, Hervey?' Sir Andrew went on without waiting for an answer, 'I tell you, I don't like it, I don't like it at all. I'm convinced this fellow Bleach is behind all this buying, but he won't come out into the open. And I'm sure he's using Mauser's and that's why they say they can't act for us.'

'It looks like it,' Parsloe agreed. 'Damned underhand: we've used Mauser's for years.'

'It's typical of these new boys in the merchant banks,' Draycott declared bitterly. 'In the old days, we all knew – and trusted – each other in the Square Mile; but nowadays, the young men who are coming into positions of power either don't understand or don't know about a decent code of behaviour.'

'Well, it seems as if we'll have to find ourselves another merchant bank,' said Parsloe, replacing the letter on Sir Andrew's desk. 'If there is to be a takeover bid, we'll need someone to advise us. Any ideas?'

'I'd thought of Schleswig-Holstein. I see quite a bit of old Harry Holstein at the Club: I think he's a shrewd bird, and I'm sure he'd be willing to act for us.'

'Fine. You have a word with old Harry Holstein.' Hervey turned to the door. 'Anything else?' He paused.

'Yes, there is,' Draycott snapped. Parsloe raised his eyebrows: was his chairman beginning to lose his nerve?

'Look, Hervey, we can't just sit here and wait for Bleach to gobble us up like a plate of chopped liver on Friday night.'

'I don't think, actually, that Bleach is Jewish,' Parsloe commented.

'What *do* we know about him?'

91

'I've met him once or twice.' Hervey took out his cigarette case and lit up: the next few minutes might be tricky. 'He's a member of Lloyd's, you know, through your brother-in-law's agency.'

'I know that. And it makes our situation more difficult. You see, I can't go off to the chairman of Lloyd's – as in other circumstances I might well do – to complain about Bleach's tactics, to suggest that a bid from an outsider might be undesirable from the point of view of Lloyd's itself. Because, technically, the blighter isn't an outsider: he's a name himself.'

Hervey remained silent while Sir Andrew continued to speculate.

'It would help if we knew just what the bounder's after. I mean, we're a good sound company and, I pride myself, well run; but if you take away our goodwill, we don't have all that much in the way of assets. Not enough to attract an asset-stripper, wouldn't you say?'

'I quite agree,' said Parsloe. This much was obvious.

'Then why the devil is he buying up our "B" shares? They won't give him control, and provided our two families stick together, he can't get his little hands on any of the voting shares.'

'I fancy he can – in fact I think he already has.' Hervey judged the time was ripe to shake his chairman's confidence a little further.

'Has he, by God?' Sir Andrew's face was turning blotched purple. 'Come on, man, tell me, who the devil's ratted on us?'

'I have the impression that Bleach has secured a lien on the holding of Mrs Stamp – of *your* cousin Muriel.' Parsloe placed a slight inflexion on the pronoun.

'That bloody Muriel,' Sir Andrew burst out, 'she always was a shiftless baggage – look at the way she keeps on remarrying! However, she's only got ten percent, and that's not enough to enable Bleach to make trouble.'

'I hope you're right, Chairman,' said Hervey emolliently.

'Still, we can't afford to be complacent.' Sir Andrew began to pace about the room. 'We must demonstrate that we intend to stand firm. I've still got a lot of friends with influence here and there, thank goodness, and I'm going to make sure they're on our side. And as for you, Hervey, it would be useful if we could find out a little more about this Bleach. Perhaps it would be judicious if you were to set up an informal meeting with him, and take some soundings as to his intentions.'

Again, Parsloe said nothing. He wasn't about to tell his chairman that, the night before, he had been Trevor Bleach's guest at dinner at the Caprice and that what he had heard was, for him personally, gratifying; Sir Andrew was too preoccupied to notice that his fellow director looked around the subdued luxury of the chairman's office with a new, almost proprietary air before he left the room.

Draycott now decided to take soundings from some of the younger staff: they might have picked up something in the Room, or from their own set of friends around the City.

'Is young Blackett back from his holiday?' he barked into his intercom.

'Yes, Sir Andrew,' came the disembodied reply from his secretary, 'Mr Blackett returned from his honeymoon last week. He came in this morning to show me his photographs; I thought he looked very fit and tanned.' Toby was something of a favourite with the secretaries at Draycott, Parsloe & Co.

'I am not interested in the young man's health,' was the snapped reply. 'Just send him in to see me as soon as possible.'

When Toby knocked and entered, his chairman was on the telephone. While he was waved to a chair, he had time to look around the room. It was horribly old-fashioned, he thought, with its pickled panelling and second-rate portraits, its beige leather and figured walnut, rather like a saloon on some long since broken-up Cunarder. Now when it was his – for Trevor Bleach had been confident that Hervey Parsloe wouldn't last more than three years in the hot seat – he would really bring it up to date.

'. . . thank you, Governor, see you next Tuesday, then.' Sir Andrew replaced his receiver with smug satisfaction. 'The Bank of England,' he explained. 'I'm determined to rally all necessary support in the City. I'll keep this blighter Bleach out of here if it's the last thing I do.'

It may well be that, thought Toby, while presenting his chairman with a deferential, keen-young-officer smile.

'Now then, Blackett.' Sir Andrew leaned back in his padded revolving chair. 'You've probably heard some rumours about the old firm. Not a word of truth in 'em, of course, we're safe as houses; but I'd like to hear if you've picked up any straws in the wind about what's going on.'

You lying old fool, thought Toby, you pompous lying old bastard, you're shit-scared of being thrown out of your cosy position. You thought you'd inherited that desk for life . . . Just you wait. Aloud, he replied that he had indeed heard rumours, and did the chairman know who was behind them?

'What have you heard?' countered Sir Andrew.

'Well, sir, I've had some strong hints that a chap called Trevor Bleach has been investing quite heavily in our shares.'

'Indeed? And what do you know about this man Bleach?'

'As a matter of fact, I've met him once or twice.' Bleach's advice had been to tell the truth wherever possible: it needn't be the whole truth, of course, but the important thing was to avoid the lie direct. 'Bleach became a name on old Ivor's – I mean Mr Murchison's – syndicate last year, and I was asked to show him the ropes.'

'I see. And did you form any impression of the kind of man this Bleach may be?'

'To be frank, sir, he's self-made.' Toby flashed a quick, deprecating smile across the polished desk, a smile complicit of the gentlemanly, public-school conspiracy. 'I gather he's made quite a fortune for himself in the Midlands and, from the odd remark he's dropped, I think he has ambitions to move in on the City.'

'Has he?' Sir Andrew clasped his hands over his leather blotter. 'Did you come to any conclusions as to why this man should be interested in Draycott, Parsloe & Co. in particular?' The chairman had abandoned his pose of being unconcerned.

'As I said, sir, I think he wants to make his mark in the City. He was very chuffed at being elected a member of Lloyd's; he thinks it's a kind of recognition.'

'Oh, I know that type.' Relaxed for the first time, Sir Andrew gave a brief laugh. 'I suppose he thinks he's the cat's whiskers every time he enters the building. So perhaps I might conclude that his purchase of a minority holding in our stock is no more than an extension of his love affair with himself as a City personage?'

'You might indeed conclude just that,' Toby agreed.

The club to which Sir Woodbine Bulkely-Grieve belonged was a patrician establishment housed in a handsome eighteenth-century building in St James's Street. A feature of the first floor was a projecting bay, whose high Venetian window looked down towards the sentries on duty outside St James's Palace, and here, after a leisurely lunch, Sir Bulkely and his guest Ivor Murchison installed themselves in deep leather armchairs, with a decanter of Taylor '35 between them. After the heavy lunch – pea soup, steak and kidney pie and spotted dick with custard, the school food much relished by the members – both men were relaxed; and Ivor reflected with pleasure that there was no need for him to return to Lloyd's that afternoon: he would look in at Christie's, where an attractive pair of silver-mounted duelling pistols were due to come up for sale.

'I've been meaning to have a word with you,' Ivor began, 'about your friend Bleach. After all, you introduced him, in a way you're responsible for his membership of Lloyd's; and, as you may have heard, he's giving my brother-in-law a lot of worry at Draycott, Parsloe.'

'I'm glad you've raised the subject.' Gasper Grieve took out a cigar case, handed a Havana to his guest and took another himself, carefully biting the end off before applying a match slowly and luxuriously. 'I have the impression that you don't care much for Trevor Bleach?'

'I don't. And I don't think he's the kind of man we want to encourage at Lloyd's.

'I told you when you first met him that he wasn't our kind of chap.' Gasper leaned forward to pick up the decanter and refill their glasses. 'But that doesn't mean he's not someone with whom one can do business, whom one can make use of. He's damned bright, financially.'

95

'That he may be: but I fancy he sails rather close to the wind for my liking. Anyway, what does he want at Draycott, Parsloe?'

'I'll come to that.' Gasper drew on his cigar and exhaled a thin column of smoke that swirled blue above them. 'But first, I'd like to air one or two thoughts I've been brewing up about the City.'

Ivor, too, was lighting up, but he also paid close attention. Gasper Grieve had an instinct about the workings of money that was well worth heeding.

'The trouble with the City is that it's become too damned safe. So many men who are running things now are – like your brother-in-law – the sons or grandsons of the chaps that actually went out to fight for new business, who created new markets and made London what it is today. But the men in the top jobs haven't the interest or the talent to battle for new markets; they're content to sit back, sleek as a farm-reared cock pheasant, to take a good screw and to make sure that as far as possible the status quo is maintained, that things continue to be done as they've always known them to be done. The net result is that your precious City is in danger of becoming moribund.'

'I see your point,' Ivor murmured, 'but I think you're being a little hard. The heavy burden of taxation, for instance, is inclined to suppress initiative . . .'

'Be damned to the tax man,' Gasper broke in. 'You know as well as I do that no tax invented has ever hurt the really rich man. There are always ways and means. Tax is irrelevant to my theme.'

Sir Woodbine sat back in his chair and contemplated his glass of port, held up to the thin winter sunlight. 'What I'm trying to suggest is that Andrew Draycott and his kind sit back complacently and bother with nothing more important than who is next in pecking order for the Prime Wardenship of whichever mumbo-jumbo they adhere to. And meanwhile' – he jabbed his cigar at his guest – 'meanwhile bloody foreigners and especially bloody Yanks are moving in to clean up.'

'You certainly express yourself strongly,' Ivor observed.

'I feel strongly. I feel that unless we do something pretty

96

damn' quick, London's going to become a backwater financially. And that applies especially to international insurance and even more to your beloved Lloyd's. What we need are new men, men of vision and drive who will fight to keep what we have and will make sure that we grab a good fat slice of the global cake.'

'I suppose you mean the likes of Trevor Bleach?'

'I know you don't like him, Ivor, but yes, I do. Bleach has become interested in insurance because he sees a huge unexplored potential; and he feels that if he can knit together the various disparate parts of what he calls the circle of insurance – underwriters, brokers, agents and re-insurance – we would be in a much stronger position.'

'Hence his present interest in Draycott, Parsloe?' Ivor sounded dry, unimpressed.

'Absolutely,' Gasper agreed. 'I wish you'd set aside your personal dislike for Bleach,' he urged. 'As a matter of fact, I don't care much for him myself – I mean, he's not the kind of man I'd want to ask to cast a rod over my salmon – but I do believe he's capable of a real breakthrough. And,' he added, a red glint of greed showing in his narrow eyes, 'we'd all stand to make a great deal of money.'

'We?' Ivor cocked an eyebrow.

'We,' Gasper answered firmly. 'You see, if you would accept that we need Bleach, that he may be some kind of financial genius, then it becomes very important that his associates are men of standing, men of experience and probity, who can make sure that he doesn't go off the rails. I don't just mean window-dressing, Ivor: Bleach's associates must be strong-minded enough, independent enough, to stand up to him should he ever, out of ignorance, propose something even remotely . . . disreputable.'

'I'm sorry, Gasper.' There was a look of icy distaste on Ivor Murchison's face. 'I'd rather not be associated with the likes of Bleach; and I'd prefer it if he kept me and, more important, Lloyd's out of his murky scheming.'

'Don't be so high-hat.' Gasper finished his port before going on. 'Whatever you may wish, you have to face the fact that Bleach is now part of the scene, and he's going to play an ever-growing role, at Lloyd's and elsewhere. Given that, can't you see how important it is for Lloyd's that Bleach has the advice and guidance of a distinguished and honourable man, one respected throughout the market?'

For a moment, Gasper was concerned that he might have laid on the flattery too thick; but an air of preening about his guest as he dusted some cigar ash off his lapel gave reassurance. 'I see what you're driving at,' Ivor conceded, 'but I must think first of my names. My prime responsibility must be to my syndicate.'

'Quite right and proper,' Gasper laughed. 'After all, I'm a name myself. The syndicate won't be affected: rather the other way: they'd have the benefit of preferential access for all their re-insurances direct to Bay Street & Global.'

'And what, pray, is Bay Street & Global?'

'It's an insurance corporation in Nassau already under the control of Trevor Bleach.' Gasper did not add that the corporation had only come into existence three weeks before, and that the grandiloquent name (a suggestion from Toby Blackett) had been decided the night before last.

'So, once he's sewn up Draycott, Parsloe, he'll have his hands on two segments of his circle. And then what? He can't imagine he can just buy up a few syndicates: he must appreciate that they are nothing more than an association of independent men of means underwriting together – that's the fundamental principle of Lloyd's.'

'Of course he knows that. As I see it, you'd become a director of Draycott, Parsloe, and you'd probably have an interest in Bay Street & Global; but, as an underwriter, you would be completely and utterly independent.'

Ivor was hooked.

. . . so you see, it's very serious indeed.' Ursula Murchison sounded distraught, shorn of her usual calm, organised air. Ivor had just returned from the City, and they were in his study in front of a good fire, whose bright flames were reflected back from the locked glass doors around the walls, behind which were displayed some of Ivor's collection of fire-arms.

'Mary Parsloe told me today: she'd only just found out from Hilary. It seems that Lucinda has been seeing a great

98

deal of Martin Coley since they met here in the summer; and from what Mary told me, they've been carrying on ever since.'

'I don't see what's so dreadful about that.' Ivor sipped at his whisky and soda; he had a great deal to think about since his luncheon with Gasper Grieve and, after all the port, he was tired. Besides, Lucinda was his wife's problem, and he didn't think it so very terrible that his daughter had been seeing a bit of young Martin. It probably was nothing important, and he said as much.

'Of course it's important,' Ursula barked. 'And it's all your fault. You've encouraged that young upstart to have ideas above his station, and if you hadn't insisted on inviting him down here for a weekend in the summer, they'd never even have met.'

'I like Martin,' said Ivor defensively. 'I think he's a straight, level-headed young man and if you ask me, Lucinda could do much worse. At least, whatever his background, he's not a Chelsea layabout. He's doing very well on the box; and, I may remind you, he's a member now.'

'He may be a good employee: but I hope you're not suggesting that that would make him an acceptable son-in-law.'

'Has anything been said about marriage?' Ivor's tone was level, reasonable.

'Oh, Ivor, don't be so dense!' Irritably, Ursula finished her gin and tonic and her husband rose, without saying more, to refill it. 'They've been going out together,' she pursued, 'and, knowing the young of today, probably sleeping together. I'll bet you that the wretched boy has already marked down Lucinda as a good catch.'

'Have you asked Lucinda?' Ivor didn't like this mood of his wife's. When she was snapping out orders as if she were leading the St John's Ambulance Brigade into battle, he knew where he stood; but this wailing was not to his taste.

'I rang her as soon as I'd finished speaking to Mary. She didn't deny it; in fact, she was very cool, as if what she got up to in London was none of our business.'

Privately, Ivor rather agreed with his daughter, who was

after all of an age to make her own mistakes – not that he thought marrying Martin Coley would be one.

'She said she'd be down this weekend, unless anything better cropped up,' Ursula continued with a touch of bitterness. 'You'll have to speak to her, Ivor, tell her firmly that young Coley is most unsuitable. Just think what everyone would say if our daughter went up the aisle with a newsagent's son, whose father had been your batman in the war. Honestly!' She shuddered.

'Sergeant, actually,' Ivor corrected. 'Sergeant Coley was never my soldier servant. Anyway,' he went on, anxious to be done with the subject, 'I suggest we leave the question until Lucinda herself brings it up. There's no point in worrying until the time comes.' He smiled appeasingly across the hearth at his wife, amused at her social pretensions. Actually, a match between Coley and Lucinda wouldn't be all that different to his own with Ursula Draycott, a sensible arrangement within Lloyd's; but in Ursula's present mood, there was no point in saying so, and to divert her, he asked if she had been in touch with her brother recently.

'Andrew? It's odd you should ask; he rang me this morning. It was rather a peculiar conversation, come to think of it. He sounded a bit fussed: he wanted to know if anyone had approached me about my shares in the firm. When I told him no one had been near me, he seemed relieved; but he wouldn't ring off until I'd given him my word that if, as he said, it came to the crunch, I'd vote as he instructed me. Naturally, I told him what he wanted to hear – I mean, we Draycotts and Parsloes must stick together – but what's it all about, Ivor? Have you any idea?'

Ivor told her that he had heard rumours of a bid brewing for Draycott, Parsloe, and doubtless her brother was making sure of his defences.

'But I don't understand. I mean, I've always understood that provided we stuck to our voting shares, we were safe. Isn't that true any more?'

'Not altogether. A clever man could find ways.'

'A clever man? A crook, you mean.'

'No, Ursula, I don't mean a crook. The man concerned is called Bleach and he is by way of being a name on my syndicate. At first, my feelings were like yours: I considered him to be an upstart, a jumped-up nobody from the Midlands. But I'm beginning to think I may have misjudged the man. He has both vision and drive, and we must always find a place in the City for talent. We need these new men, my dear, and provided we make sure they don't break the rules, we must make use of them.'

'Not in Draycott, Parsloe, I hope. It's unthinkable.'

'It has to be faced. I've thought it through deeply, my dear, and it cannot be denied that your brother's management of the firm has been cautious, unadventurous. In my opinion, some new blood on the board would revitalise the company.'

Ursula looked up sharply. 'Revitalise' was a strange word to hear from her husband. 'I've no intention of betraying my brother,' she declared, 'so don't attempt to persuade me otherwise.'

'Of course not,' Ivor assured her. 'In any case, whether there is a bid or not, and whether or not it succeeds, it's out of our hands.'

Trevor Bleach arranged his next rendezvous with Toby Blackett at Hasker Street, where he would call in after dinner. When Hilary Blackett heard this, she said she would make herself scarce.

'I'll go round and see Mummy,' she told Toby, 'I've hardly had a word with her since we came back from Barbados. To be honest, I don't like your friend Bleach and I've no wish to have to be nice to him. And you needn't worry: I'm not going to change my mind about my shares: I've promised you that if it comes to a battle, I'll cast my vote whichever way you want, and I won't go back on that.'

'Thank you, darling,' said Toby, squeezing her waist.

'I'll leave you to him, then.' She fished in her handbag for the car keys. 'Just watch your step with your precious Mr Bleach. There's something *louche* about him: I can't put my finger on it, but he gets up my arse.' Hilary Blackett was the kind of girl who likes to use coarse language, and her broad face was flushed with inner pleasure as she slammed the door.

When Bleach arrived, he and Toby were soon deep in

papers relating to the establishment of Bay Street & Global. Toby had taken two days out of his honeymoon to fly up from Barbados to Nassau, taking Hilary with him, to make the acquaintance of the Bahamian lawyer and accountant who were to be the nominal directors of the new corporation. It was to be an 'offshore' company – an euphemism denoting that, although in practice its management might lie in London, it was in name an overseas entity, thereby placing it well out of reach of the depredations of the Inland Revenue.

Bleach looked oddly consonant in the drawing room at Hasker Street. The decoration and furnishings were all new, wedding presents or chosen by Hilary at Harrods and the General Trading Company, and the place was somewhat bare, with none of the bibelots, books and souvenirs that are the wrack of living together. Trevor Bleach, in his grey suit and with his hair the colour of dust, looked as much at home there as he did in his own impersonal suite at the White House. Toby had even bought in the brand of whisky his mentor favoured.

With the paperwork completed and put away in Bleach's briefcase, Toby asked what progress had been made in relation to Draycott, Parsloe.

'As far as the voting shares are concerned, with your wife, Mrs Stamp and Hervey Parsloe on our side, we've reached parity with the existing management: 60,000 shares on each side.'

'But that's not enough,' said Toby. 'They'll just maintain the status quo.'

'It's a question of pressure,' Bleach explained. 'We've been softening up Sir Andrew in the last few weeks and I know he's getting rattled. He was more shaken than he'd admit when we deprived him of Mauser's, and I think he'll break altogether when we reveal to him, at the right moment, that we have his precious managing director Mr Parsloe in our pocket.'

'A-ha,' said Toby, rubbing his hands, 'then we move in for the kill.'

'Oh, no, Toby, nothing as savage as that. We behave in a most gentlemanly fashion. Sir Andrew will be elevated to some high-sounding but impotent position, such as president, and our friend Hervey takes over as chairman and managing director. As a substantial shareholder, I shall be invited to join the board and, if Gasper Grieve has done his job properly, Ivor Murchison will also become a director. All, you see, will be most respectable: nothing to upset the panjandrums of the City.'

'Then there won't really be much change.' Toby sounded disappointed.

'Not that anyone would notice, and not immediately. Remember that we are not planning a full takeover: we just want quietly to take control, and with you and Pendragon also on the board, that we will have. Mind you' – Bleach sipped at his thin whisky – 'I wouldn't give Hervey more than two years as chairman. Within that time, we can contrive some kind of boardroom row and ease him out: that would be the moment, I think, for me to assume the chair.'

'And . . . ?' asked Toby.

'And you, Toby, would be managing director. I flatter myself that it's quite a practical plan of campaign and the time-scale is tolerable – for we mustn't be seen to be in too much of a hurry: the City doesn't like undue haste.'

There was an air of anticipation, of celebration even, in the narrow room when Hilary Blackett burst in. She was back earlier than Toby had expected, and her round face was red with excitement. Bleach rose courteously to his feet with a murmured compliment on her appearance, but she waved him back to the sofa.

'Never mind all that,' she said impatiently, 'have I news for you two! I've just seen Daddy.'

'What's the old fool . . . ?'

'. . . is Mr Parsloe unwell?'

Toby and Bleach spoke together.

'No, no, Daddy's all right: in fact, he says he's come to his senses.'

'Mrs Blackett, do explain yourself.' Bleach's voice was very quiet.

'Well, Mummy was telling me that Uncle Andrew had been working himself up into one hell of a lather – about you, Mr Bleach. Apparently, he's been rushing around the City, lining up as many big guns as possible to come to his support – you know the sort of people, the Governor of the Bank, the Chairman of the Stock Exchange. And, Mummy says, it was old Harry Schleswig who pointed out to Uncle Andrew that his weakest spot was likely to be Daddy himself.'

'If your bloody father has ratted at this late stage . . .' Toby broke in venomously.

'You can't say that about Daddy,' Hilary cried, 'when it was your mob that wanted him to be a traitor in the first place!'

This unexpected defence of Hervey Parsloe from his daughter so surprised Toby that he was silent: and it was Bleach who begged her to continue.

'Daddy came in just now,' she told them. 'He was a little pissed after some grand dinner in Threadneedle Street, but he was also revoltingly pleased with himself. Apparently, all these big shots have been having a go at him, telling him it's his duty to stick by Uncle Andrew and that they'd see him all right if he did. Then, tonight, Uncle Andrew produced his ace of trumps. It will be announced in the *Financial Times* tomorrow.'

'Come on, darling,' Toby pleaded, 'what is this master-stroke?'

'Daddy told me the exact words.' Hilary sat up straight and recited: 'Sir Andrew Draycott today informed the share-holders of Draycott, Parsloe & Company of his intention to retire from the Chairmanship when he reaches the age of sixty in two months' time. While he will remain on the board, he feels that the time has come when he deems it important for the continued health of the company that the active day-to-day management should be in younger hands, in order to ensure the continued robust health of the company and an aggressive plan of expansion; and he is happy to announce that he will be succeeded as Chairman by Mr Hervey Parsloe.'

'The sly old fox,' said Toby softly. 'He's dished us.'

'I wouldn't be so sure,' Bleach answered. He was, oddly, not put out by what he had just heard. 'I still have one or two cards to play.'

10

Madame Vathos was in a sour mood when she arrived in the South of France in September 1964. The summons from her husband had been urgent, peremptory, and it had interrupted the rhythm of her social life in Paris. When she disembarked at Nice airport and stepped down to the tarmac for the short walk to the terminal building, there was a hard, vicious wind blowing straight in from the sea out of a clear blue sky; it whipped flicks of dust into her eyes and threatened havoc to her sleek hair.

She was still discomposed when she reached the car, like a plump black bantam with her feathers ruffled, and she snatched away her gloved hand from the attendant Masterakis as he handed her into the back seat.

'I regret the weather infinitely, Madame,' he said smoothly as he settled beside her. He made it sound as if the wind was the fault of some derelict minion of Ithaki-Hellenic. 'This Mistral is most unfortunate. Indeed it has put M. Vathos himself to some inconvenience. He sends his profound apologies, Madame, but it will be necessary for you to board the *Thermopylae* by way of the tender.'

'*C'est effroyable!*' Mme Vathos shuddered. 'Why?'

'Unhappily, Madame, with the wind blowing thus, it is too strong for the yacht to enter the harbour in safety. She lies at anchor between Les Îles de Lérins.'

They were now on the main road along the shore. The

sea's surface was alive with little scars of white spume and all the flags on the restaurants lining the coast streamed out, flapping wildly in the gale. A few hardy bathers, tempted by the glare of the sun, exercised themselves on the pebbles, but all the bright umbrellas were furled, the deckchairs stacked and the pedaloes hauled well up the beach. Mme Vathos stared out stonily through the tinted glass.

'M. Vathos knows how intensely I dislike travelling in the tender,' she said. 'The motion of the sea discommodes me greatly. Is it not possible that I go straight to the Hotel Majestic and await more clement weather?'

'Alas, Madame,' Masterakis spread his hands apologetically. 'M. Vathos was most insistent. And he asked me to give you this.' He took from his pocket a small pouch in grey wash-leather.

'Ah, the Rose of Alexandria.' Her black eyes shone with pleasure as she took out the diamond clip with its huge central brilliant. Now she understood.

Neither Mme Vathos nor Masterakis had been present when Paul Blackett had first been summoned down to the *Thermopylae*; but as usual, her husband had reported the meeting to her.

The owner had begun with some routine questions about the London office, matters so mundane that Paul began to wonder why he had been so abruptly summoned. Then Vathos reached out for a thick, colour-printed catalogue which he folded open at one page.

'Tell me, do you know anything at all about the London auction rooms?'

'Sotheby's and Christie's, do you mean, sir? Not really, I've never attended any of their sales.'

'Never mind. You're going to, now. I want you to buy this for me.' Vathos handed over the catalogue, his broad thumb on a colour illustration, and Paul found himself looking at the photograph of a diamond clip and matching ear-rings displayed against a purple velvet background. In the centre of the clip was a stone the size of a cherry; the caption informed him it was known as the Rose of Alexandria, formerly in the possession of His Late Majesty King Farouk.

'You want me to buy this for you, sir?' he asked slowly. 'But . . . but it'll cost a fortune!'

'You may bid up to £400,000,' said Vathos carelessly. 'A guy I know in Amsterdam told me I should get it for that.'

'But, sir, why me?' Paul's face was wrinkled in a puzzled frown, like a schoolboy protesting against an unjust imposition. 'I mean, why doesn't your friend from Holland bid for you?'

'I have my reasons.' Vathos paused, staring up at a cloud of cigar smoke still hanging in the sultry air. 'Soon we will be launching my new super-tanker and my wife, of course, will name her. I consider that the Rose of Alexandria would be a suitable gift for Mme Vathos when she launches the *Katherina Vathos*.'

'Of course, sir, most appropriate. But where do I come in?'

'Just think, Paul. Apart from adorning my wife, the Rose of Alexandria' – Vathos uttered the name with relish – 'will have another purpose. Do you know any journalists?'

'Not really, sir, not proper journalists. One of the chaps who writes Paul Tanfield in the *Mail* is a kind of friend, and I have met one of the William Hickeys, but I don't suppose . . .'

'Excellent, Paul, excellent,' Vathos interrupted, 'just what I need. Don't you agree that when it's known that I've spent a large sum – what you call a fortune – on a bauble for my wife, it might have a favourable impression upon your friends at Mauser's?'

'It will do your credit rating no harm, certainly.' Paul was puzzled that the opulent shipowner, relaxing on board his splendid yacht, should be thinking in such terms. He said nothing, but something of his concern became apparent to Vathos, who explained in some detail that once the *Katherina Vathos* was at sea, he planned to build several more such vast tankers; and he would want to depend on the money men of the City of London for much of the finance.

'So that's why I want you to do the bidding at Christie's, and to make it known to your friends of the press that you're buying for me, money no object. Up until now, I've kept pretty quiet – no opera singers for me!' Vathos chuckled.

'But I've decided that a little publicity will do me no harm, so get what mileage you can out of buying that diamond.'

The bid by Laertes Vathos for the renowned stone had been successful, both in the auction room and in the publicity Paul Blackett had secured for the purchase. Its subsequent presentation to Mme Vathos, on the occasion of the launching of the great tanker that carried her name, had attracted a further bout of press attention. All this had benefited Ithaki-Hellenic just as Vathos had intended: he was talked of as being almost in the same league as Livanos or Niarchos, his credit was unquestioned, and now not even the underwriters at Lloyd's raised an eyebrow at his risks.

For Mme Vathos, the effect was less agreeable. Hitherto, she had enjoyed a quiet life, out of the limelight; now she – and her daughters – became objects of attention to journalists as unwelcome as those from *France-Dimanche*, and to those shops and restaurants where until now she had enjoyed privacy and discretion. This she did not like: and even less did she welcome her husband's order that from now on both she and their daughters must endure the presence of (admittedly discreet) guards – a function that presently Masterakis himself was performing.

She took out the clip and fastened it to the lapel of her pale-green Givenchy crêpe-de-chine. After the presentation, Vathos had privately handed her a well-made replica of the brooch, with the instruction that if she wanted to display his gift in Paris or New York, it was this that she must wear. The original would be kept in the safe of the office in Monte Carlo and, it became accepted between them, would only be worn on occasions of significance to Ithaki-Hellenic itself, a private ensign of the new-found respectability of the Vathos fleet. Clearly, she now understood, today's meeting on the *Thermopylae*, however inconvenienced by the Mistral, was to be important. This suited Mme Vathos: she too had some things it was time she said, and she intended to say them with force.

When she entered the saloon of the yacht, she had her opportunity. Her husband was alone, as he rose from his desk to give her a great bear's hug that threatened as much disarray to her *coiffure* as the salty spray that whipped across the tender. Patting back her hair and waving away a steward bearing her usual Turkish coffee, she settled opposite her husband and regarded him steadily.

'Laertes,' she began, 'I am much concerned. I wish now that I had never consented to the building of that ridiculous super-tanker you've given my name.'

'Why, my love? What on earth's happened to give you cold feet?' Vathos frowned across the desk at her, his black brows closed down on his craggy face; but he was not angry, not even affronted; he always heard his wife out, and he trusted her instincts as well as he did his own.

'Nothing has happened – yet. And I concede you may be right when you insist that the future of oil-carrying lies with these vast ships. But do we have to compete? On all sides, I hear that the Japanese and the Dutch, the Koreans and the Norwegians, the Americans and even, late as usual, the English, are all commissioning such vessels, each one more of a monster than the last.'

'So are our compatriots,' Vathos pointed out. 'They are not fools. Ithaki-Hellenic cannot afford to be left behind.'

'But can Ithaki-Hellenic afford it at all? It's plain fact that we don't have their resources. Even to build this ship, we are forced, for the very first time, to borrow from the banks.'

'That's what banks are for,' Vathos shrugged.

'I don't like it.' Mme Vathos spoke flatly. 'In the past, we've paid for our new vessels by selling the old and from our own reserves. But today, the rest of our fleet is worth little more than its value as scrap and every day our liquidity dwindles and we're deeper in debt to the banks. And it's all because of your super-tanker. Do you realise that she is costing ten times more than we've ever before paid for a ship?'

'And she'll cost more by the time she's ready to sail. A lot more.'

'More than ten million dollars?' Mme Vathos' voice rose, as did her arching eyebrows.

'Oh, yes. Every month I have to raise the insurance on the hull. I'm determined that the *Katherina Vathos* shall possess every up-to-date aid to navigation and efficiency. These things cost money.'

'How do you do that? I mean, by what system do you increase the insured value?'

Vathos gave his wife a curious glance. It was unlike her to be so concerned with routine administration. 'Every month,' he explained, 'Apallson's send in a statement certifying what we have spent so far. Our office in Monàco attaches to that any other relevant invoices and sends it all off to London, where Paul Blackett presents them to his brother at the Draycott Group. Acting as our brokers, they effect the increased cover with the underwriters at Lloyd's. Why do you ask?'

Mme Vathos shrugged. 'It could be useful to know . . . if anything should go badly wrong.'

'What could go wrong, my love? Even if we were to suffer the catastrophe of a total loss, we would be fully covered at Lloyd's. And that brings me to another matter. You may be wondering why I have indicated that today is an occasion for the Rose.'

He pointed to the brooch. He was anxious to distract his wife from further discussion of the liquidity of Ithaki-Hellenic: in fact, her feeling that they were running low in funds was well founded. It was not just that the super-tanker was costing much more than they had anticipated; acting on a tip from one of their charterers, Vathos had indulged in some speculation on the spot market in crude oil in Rotterdam. This had gone badly wrong, and although the Vathos wealth was considerable, a loss of six million dollars hurt. It was just as well that his credit remained good and that Mauser's continued to be an obliging merchant bank.

'I've invited Trevor Bleach to pay us a visit,' he announced. 'I've also asked your sister Hélène to make up the party. She is to accompany him from London. They will arrive on the afternoon flight and we will have dinner here on board tonight.'

'Oh, no, Laertes, no!' Mme Vathos wailed. 'Let us rather have dinner in my suite at the Majestic. There at least we will be comfortable, but here, with this terrible Mistral, it will be most disagreeable. Please let us have dinner ashore,' she pleaded, looking out of the window with a delicate shudder. Beyond the shade of the promenade deck, the sunlight was

110

hard, strong and glaring, but the short, sharp, spume-flecked waves flung spray onto the glass and the unsteady motion of the yacht was most disturbing.

'It is arranged. We will have dinner here.' Vathos' tone was firm, final: he was not about to have his plans disrupted by a mere wind. 'I want to meet Mr Bleach on my territory, for him to see me – and you, my dear – against the background of this our splendid yacht, and not in the anonymous surroundings of a suite at the Majestic.'

'Why is this Mr Bleach so important that you should wish to impress him?'

'On all sides, I hear that he is a clever man. He understands money, his acquisition of the Draycott Group was masterly, in the City of London even they are beginning to talk of him with respect. He could be useful to us. Also, I suspect he's brewing up some new scheme and I'd like to find out what it is.'

'So I wear the Rose, Hélène's at hand to charm the pants off him if that's what he wants, and you overwhelm him with a gourmet dinner and a fat cigar to follow. I see. Or, rather, I don't quite see. Why should this Mr Bleach rate such four-star treatment? Unless . . .' she gave her husband a shrewd glance, 'unless it has something to do with Paul Blackett?'

Vathos gave his great laugh. 'You're right, my dear! That too. I am curious to know why Bleach is so interested in that young man and his brother and how best I can make use of it.'

That night, the dinner party on board the yacht *Thermopylae* was uneasy. Although the Mistral had abated with the coming of darkness, the sea was still restless, and Mme Vathos felt far from comfortable: she waved away a platter of crawfish, demanding instead a bowl of consommé, and although with the aid of some pills she managed to avoid the onset of *mal de mer*, she felt distant, somehow apart from the round table about which they sat, and quite unable to contribute much to the conversation. Her sister Hélène Villiers was dressed *en fête*, in a low-cut dress of gold lamé and with her tawny hair elaborately coiled (by the hastily summoned Majestic hairdresser) on top of her head. Hélène knew

111

perfectly well why she was present: she never forgot that after her husband's dismissal she was dependent upon Laertes Vathos for her comfortable life in London and she had set out determined to sing for her supper. But, even on the flight out from London and the drive into Cannes, she had drawn a blank with Bleach: her best drollery received no more than a thin smile from him and any question was answered in a brief, curt monosyllable. At the table, she gave up on him and instead concentrated on her brother-in-law. He, expansive in his dark blazer and white silk roll-neck, responded and soon they were both laughing, bringing something of the party spirit to the dining saloon.

Trevor Bleach had refused champagne. He sat at the table, occasionally sipping at his whisky as he wondered what Vathos wanted out of this meeting. No doubt he would find out in due course. He knew why he himself engineered and accepted the invitation: partly curiosity, the opportunity to meet, on his home ground, the rich tycoon, partly because such a meeting might well prove advantageous, both to the Draycott Group who now handled Vathos' insurances and, possibly, to Bleach's further plans.

It had crossed Bleach's mind that he might propose to the Greek an investment in Bay Street & Global, and it was with this in view that he had recently begun to cultivate Toby's good-looking young brother. The connection would be useful and although the Nassau corporation was growing rapidly, a further injection of capital could be applied to even more rapid expansion. On the other hand, he reminded himself, he had heard rumours that Vathos had burnt his fingers in the spot market; in which case, how Vathos reacted to such an offer might be a gauge of his losses.

Meanwhile, Bleach saw no reason why he should put himself out, and especially not for the flashy woman with bulging bosoms and jangling ear-rings who had been his companion on the journey from London. Mme Vathos, on the other hand, might be worth talking to: her few remarks had been shrewd and to the point, but now she seemed to have withdrawn from the party. Glancing across at her, his eye caught a bright flash from the brooch above her heart: he recognised the famous Rose of Alexandria. He would not,

112

he decided, vouchsafe any remark about the stone: better to wait until it was pointed out to him.

The glacial atmosphere was broken by an accident. As the steward was serving the béarnaise sauce, the yacht, tugging at her anchor, gave a lurch and a spoonful of hot butter ran down Bleach's grey lapel. Hélène Villiers leaped to her feet, napkin at the ready, but Vathos remained seated, ordering the steward to take Mr Bleach to the owner's state room at once and to tell his valet to make good the soiled jacket.

When Bleach returned in his shirt-sleeves, he accepted Mr Vathos' voluble apologies with a shrug. But, deprived of his coat, he appeared less armoured against conviviality; for the first time he unbent, even, against his earlier resolve, complimenting Mme Vathos on her diamonds. By the time the dinner was over, he had taken several whiskies and seemed ready to talk.

Mme Vathos chose this moment to withdraw, sweeping Hélène away with the excuse that they hadn't had a moment for a good sisterly chat. Installed with their coffee in the aft saloon, Catherine Vathos began at once.

'So what is M. Bleach like?' she asked. 'He seems a cold fish to me. Does he fancy ladies much?'

'Not at all.' Hélène was definite.

'You would know.' Mme Vathos lit one of her fat Egyptian cigarettes. 'Pederast?' The question came sharply through a cloud of blue smoke.

'Possibly. Probably.' Hélène shrugged her magnificent bare shoulders. 'Who cares? All I know is my warpaint has been wasted.'

'But don't you see?' Catherine pressed on. 'If Bleach fancies young men, that might explain rumours about his interest in Paul Blackett.'

'Maybe. And I did notice Bleach's cold eye linger on your steward once or twice. But what does it matter?'

'Laertes wants to find out the extent of Bleach's influence over Paul. And to put a stop to it. Do you think Paul is that way inclined?' Mme Vathos knew she could rely upon her sister's judgment in sensual matters.

'I wouldn't have thought so, not as a general rule. But Paul

113

is quite pretty, I suppose, and he is English public school, so perhaps . . . He is, after all, very fond of money.'

'How disgusting.' Mme Vathos shivered with distaste. 'These English are quite bestial.'

'Just very commercial, my dear – especially Mr Bleach. I think he likes money for the power it brings, rather than what he can buy with it. And if he buys their bodies as well as their minds, he thinks that extends his power over them even further.'

Back in the dining saloon, conversation touched only briefly and ambiguously on the Blackett brothers and then turned to Bleach's success in the City of London. Vathos was adept at acute questioning, disguised under layers of gruff flattery and, while the steward was attentive to Bleach's whisky glass, Bleach dilated on his triumphs and his machinations, explaining in some detail how, through Bay Street & Global, he was able to manipulate the underwriting profits to his own maximum profit and, he conceded with a thin smile, at the probable expense of the Inland Revenue.

'It's not only at the expense of the tax man, surely?' Vathos observed through the smoke from a fat Havana. 'If I understand you aright, although what you do may just be legitimate in the eyes of the tax authorities, it is at the expense of the people at Lloyd's, the – what do you call 'em? – members of the original syndicates that first underwrite the risks?'

'The names?' Bleach was offhand. 'I don't weep tears over them. They don't understand the business and they never will. As long as we manage matters so each name makes enough every year to keep them quiet, they'll never kick up a fuss – in fact, they couldn't.'

Vathos sat up. 'So what would happen,' he asked bluntly, 'if my beautiful new super-tanker the *Katherina Vathos* should go to the bottom? Would there be enough left in the syndicates, after you've all helped yourselves in Nassau, to pay my claim?'

'Mr Vathos, I assure you you have nothing to worry about.' Bleach was beginning to regret his boasting, but he continued smoothly. 'The loss of one tanker is not likely to cause problems.'

'I'm glad to hear it. But if the loss coincided with another disaster, or some vast natural catastrophe?'

'Then it is possible that we might have some small amount of difficulty,' Bleach conceded, 'but even then you would have no cause for concern.'

'Why not?'

'Because, my dear Mr Vathos, your risks are written under Lloyd's policy, and Lloyd's would never countenance that one of their policy holders with a legitimate claim should suffer from a default. Whatever might happen your claim would be met in full.'

The next day, the Mistral had departed and the sea was again flat calm, dazzling blue under the Mediterranean sun. As the *Thermopylae* inched her way through the crowded yacht harbour to tie up, Mme Vathos was waiting at the quay. She looked out of place in her blue silk suit and white gloves; under the broad-rimmed hat, her plump face looked peevish and her high-heeled shoe tapped impatiently as the passerelle was rolled ashore for her to come on board.

She went straight to the aft saloon, where her husband was at his desk.

'I must say,' she began at once, 'last night's little party was a waste of time and effort. Did you achieve anything with that cold English fish?'

'Not much,' he admitted.

'Hardly worth dragging me down from Paris, and Hélène all the way from London.'

'I dare say Hélène was glad of the trip.' Vathos paused. 'I did sound him out about taking a small share in the *Katherina Vathos*.'

'Did you indeed? Why?' she snapped.

'I thought it would be no bad thing. Bleach is no fool and he might be useful to us later. Anyway, he turned me down. In fact, he hinted that he would only do so if I in turn invested in his Bahamas operation. Then it was my turn to decline.' Vathos chuckled, as if dismissing the episode, but his wife stood up, straightening her skirt as she went over to the desk.

'I'm relieved that nothing came of that,' she said flatly, 'but I believe there's more than you've told me. What's the real reason that you've been so anxious to cut in outsiders on our super-tanker?'

115

'I've already explained . . .' he began in a conciliatory tone.

'Oh, I know what you've told me,' she interrupted, 'but this time I want the truth.'

Vathos frowned, his dark brows heavy, his jowl sunk. For a moment, he considered losing his temper, but then realised that his wife would have to know at some stage, so instead he gave a rich laugh.

'You must admit it's quite funny,' he said, 'when you realise that a bunch of outside investors – including the canny Captain Dougall – paid for your precious Rose of Alexandria.'

'I don't understand.'

'It's simple: I used the money they invested in the ship to pay for the stone.'

'But why, Laertes, why? Surely we still have plenty of *liquide*?'

'Not any more, my dear: not since six million dollars went down the scuppers.' Succinctly, he told her about his unfortunate speculation on the spot market; as she listened, Mme Vathos sank back onto the sofa, her gloved hands to her face.

'Laertes, how could you?' she said quietly when he had finished. The reproach uttered, she fell silent as her mind raced, assessing the implications of what she had just heard.

'The most immediate problem,' she began, 'is how we are to pay for the completion of your monstrous ship.'

'No problem at all. The banks are all tied up and they'll meet the payments as they fall due. The *Katherina Vathos* will sail on her maiden voyage on time.'

'But the banks will want to see their money back. When do we have to start making repayments?'

'Not until six months after her first voyage. And we can easily manage the interest until then.'

'But if the banks should have even a suspicion that we might be . . . experiencing problems, what then?'

'In theory, they could foreclose. But in practice, as long as our credit remains good, we've nothing to worry about.'

'I do not like it, not at all. We are in the hands of the banks, and they could pounce at any time.' Mme Vathos reached for her handbag and took out the chamois pouch. 'Take the Rose,' she said, 'take it and sell it. It has not been bought

116

with your money, Laertes, and I do not want it. Let us use it to repair the damage to our *liquide*.'

'In no way, my dear. We're not on the rocks yet. And it's important to remember that the Rose is the symbol of our credit.'

Mme Vathos shrugged. 'I would still have the replica.'

'It's not the same. People would find out. And besides . . .'

'Besides what, Laertes?'

'Well . . .' he looked away from her, down at the papers on his desk. 'If things should go wrong – not that I'm suggesting that they will, mind you, but if – then, at the very worst, the Rose would be a handy and very portable asset. We must keep it.'

'I see. I see too that you have been giving thought to the risks of our present position. *Enfin*,' she continued firmly, lapsing into French to emphasise what she had to say, '*enfin, il faut que nous parions à l'imprévu* – we must, as your banker friends would say, make contingency plans.'

'You're right, of course,' he admitted. 'But have you any ideas?'

'Certainly.' Her answer was crisp. As she explained what she had in mind, Vathos listened intently, his beetling eyebrows raised in growing incredulity. He was shaken, more shaken than he had ever been, by the stark practicality of his wife's thinking. But he was, first and foremost, a mariner, a man of the sea, and what she was saying was deeply abhorrent to his instincts. Sputtering with shock, he began to say as much, but Mme Vathos stayed him by raising her hand.

'Hear me out, Laertes. You are a seaman yourself and you know the seas as well as any man: surely it would not be beyond your skills to conceive of a circumstance such as I have suggested?'

'It is possible, yes,' Vathos conceded, 'but what a betrayal of the world of the sea.'

'Then would you rather betray me?' she cried, her voice shrill.

Vathos sighed deeply and sat down again, his broad, strong hand to his brow. 'Very well, my dear,' he said slowly, 'let us consider your suggestion, at least in theory. For a start, it is obvious that I could not be on board myself – that

117

would arouse immediate suspicion. Therefore, we would have to involve some of the crew.'

'How many?'

'Probably one or two officers would be enough.'

'Then there is no problem,' she declared. 'We know we can trust Captain Dougall. We know that money – enough money – will quieten his sailor's conscience.'

'And Ulysses Stavros,' he suggested. 'He too will do what he is told, if the price is right. But' – he sighed again – 'there's really no point to this, my dear. At the end of the day, we'd be little better off. We'd have risked everything for just a few hundred thousand dollars. It's just not worth it. Unless . . .' he broke off, suddenly deep in thought.

Mme Vathos was silent. On her husband's face she could see what she had been hoping to see: his cupidity was allying with his taste for plotting, to swamp his instinctive sailor's repugnance for her proposal.

'I think I have it,' he growled, his eyes straight at her. 'Look, do you remember how I explained, only yesterday, the way in which I up the insurance on the *Katherina Vathos*?'

'Of course. You pass the certificates and invoices to Paul Blackett and he hands them on to the brokers, who increase the cover accordingly.'

'Exactly. It's just occurred to me that I might, without difficulty, be able to inflate the insured value well beyond what the tanker will actually cost us. It would only be a matter of slipping in a few extra invoices here and there.'

'That's brilliant, Laertes.' Mme Vathos breathed out with relief: at last her husband was following her train of thought. 'We are fortunate that the vessel already has the reputation of being one of the most expensive tankers ever built. No one is likely to notice the extra charges.'

'Especially since they'll be handled by Paul: and he won't spot anything – he couldn't tell a capstan from a corkscrew.'

Vathos was hooked, and husband and wife were once more of one accord. With the air of one settling to an enjoyable task, Mme Vathos peeled off her gloves and tucked them into the handle of her bag.

'And now, Laertes,' she said happily, 'let us settle to the creation of our contingency plan.'

11

For Martin Coley, the spring of 1965 should have been set
fine. In the two years since becoming a member of Lloyd's,
he had also achieved his other ambitions: he had been formally confirmed as the underwriter for I. P. Murchison &
Ors. Although Ivor Murchison still looked in at the box
almost every day and was on hand should his advice be
needed, Martin was in charge and, he noticed with gratification, the clerks had begun to answer the telephone as 'Mr
Coley's box'. In his private life, his hopes had been fulfilled
when Lucinda Murchison agreed to marry him.

Lucinda had made the suggestion, quite suddenly, one
night over dinner. It was not long after Toby and Hilary
Blackett had returned from their honeymoon almost a year
ago, and they had just left after having drinks with the
newly-weds in their bright little house in Hasker Street.
Perhaps Toby had been right when he suggested that there
was nothing like a wedding to make a girl realise there was
something missing from the third finger of her left hand. At
any rate, Martin's whole universe had lit up with happiness
as he looked into the future: visits to both families, the
announcement in *The Times*, the jocular banter of his friends
at Lloyd's, a white wedding in Essex to be followed by con-
nubial bliss in a small, smart home like that of the Blacketts.

It hadn't worked out that way. He did indeed spend a
weekend at Tickton; Ivor Murchison had been urbane and

hospitable, but Lucinda's mother had been icy in her welcome of her future son-in-law. And when, the evening before the engagement was due to appear, Lucinda was at last taken to Ealing to meet Martin's mother, the occasion was disastrous. Mrs Coley had been in one of her worst moods, mumbling over her words, repeating herself endlessly and, which made Martin rigid with distaste, attempting a saloon-bar merriment. When Lucinda was out of the room, Mrs Coley lurched over to her son, jabbing him in the ribs as she hissed, the words for once clear, 'So you think you've made good, marrying the boss's daughter. Just watch your step, that's all I have to say: and never forget where you came from.'

As she spoke, a dribble of saliva came from the garishly painted mouth and Martin watched with disgust as it trickled down his mother's chin. He made some excuse to take Lucinda away and ever since she had not returned to Oaklands Drive, Ealing. Martin paid a duty visit about once a month, generally on a Sunday morning, when he found by experience that his mother was in a better state; even so, he found these calls difficult to bear: his mother was apt to refer to herself as 'old Mother Coley' and come out with arch references to grandchildren yet to appear.

Faced with Ursula Murchison's implacable opposition, Lucinda had agreed to forswear a traditional wedding.

'Anyway,' she declared, 'lots of people nowadays think that orange blossom, and pages in kilts and all that is dreadfully passé in the middle of the Sixties.'

Ivor, who was giving them both dinner at his club, gave her a nod of approval. 'Mind you,' he went on, 'you'll be disadvantaged in the matter of wedding presents, but since I'm to be relieved of the cost of a slap-up reception, I'll see you don't suffer.'

Under Ivor's detached but approving gaze and across the polished table of the club's dining room in the Ladies' Annex, they had agreed to a quiet ceremony in a registrar's office in London.

'I think you're being wise,' he told them. 'Your mother will come round in the end, Lucinda, but I don't think she'll come to the wedding.'

120

'In that case,' Martin had contributed, 'there'll be no need for my mother to be there either.'

'Are you sure about that?' Ivor made the point for form's sake: inwardly, he was relieved that he wouldn't have to endure a waggish, all-parents-together afternoon with his sergeant's widow, who he recalled, was rather too brassy for his taste.

Ivor was conscious of a glow of satisfaction as the dinner progressed. He felt he was behaving in a commendably open-minded, modern manner, with no hint of the 'stuffiness' with which Lucinda sometimes charged him. So, when Martin opened the subject of where they were to live, he made another gesture of benevolence.

Martin had been saying that he had worked out what they could afford, and he could see no way that a house like the Blacketts would be within their means.

'I'm afraid we'll have to start off in a flat,' he told Lucinda, whose dark eyes clouded with disappointment: she had been looking forward to starting off their life together, if not actually in Hasker Street then in one of thirty similar pretty streets, with their terraces of sometime artisans' cottages done over to make them fit for those who wished to live within walking distance of Harrods.

'I admire your caution, Martin, and you're right to be careful,' said Ivor, 'but I think we might be able to arrange things a little better between us. As you know, Lucinda is the beneficiary of a small trust fund – nothing substantial, you understand, but a handy little sum of capital. If you work out how much you can afford to raise by way of a mortgage – and you're a good risk, in good health, with a good job and a working member of Lloyd's – then I think I can persuade the trustees to match the figure.'

Although, as he said, Ivor's offer was generous, it gave Martin a twinge of unease. He was already substantially in debt to Alfred Murchison & Son Ltd, the underwriting agency that had advanced him the capital he needed to become a name: a mortgage on top would make his borrowing seem enormous. But he could not bear to let Lucinda down – she was now more determined than ever on a house, and spent her days clutching a sheaf of estate agents' particulars – and when

121

Ivor assured him that, so far from being imprudent, it was wise for him to borrow to the hilt at his age and in his position, he went ahead with the plan. Even so, there was not quite enough capital for the likes of Hasker Street, for London prices had started to move up sharply: in the end, they had to settle for a modern, three-bedroomed house in Bayswater, in a close of neo-Georgian terraces just north of Kensington Gardens. Adelaide Place might be, as Lucinda was apt to complain, north of the Park, but it was hard by the Central Line and most convenient for Martin's journey to the City.

On this March morning, Martin was for some reason less of an automaton as he boarded the train. There had been a heavy shower and the carriage was filled with the clammy smell of damp umbrellas and dripping mackintoshes, mingling, he noticed, with a sweet, musky scent that must come from the miniskirted girl strap-hanging above him. A drip of water fell from her elbow onto his *Times*, folded to the crossword, and as he looked up, he could see her thighs, apparently naked beneath the brief hem; they were good legs, taut and plump with the promise of delights just hidden under the pelmet of her dress. The brief stab of lust that he experienced put him in mind of his wife.

Lucinda, in bed, was everything he desired, loving, lascivious and surprisingly inventive. But, he had to admit, in other respects she did not fit in with his dream. He had expected to fall into a regular rhythm of living, returning home each evening to a quiet drink before a good but simple dinner. This was not Lucinda's way: although she liked to show off her Cordon Bleu skills when friends came in to dinner, on their own she was careless, unproviding. Too, she was a messy cook, using up a multitude of pans and dishes which she abandoned all over the kitchen; and, if the erratic Irish daily failed to appear, the wrack of her culinary enterprise was often still scattered around the draining-board, congealed and dirty, when Martin returned. She might not even be there to greet him, but would burst in later, laden with parcels from Fortnums and the General Trading Company, to demand that he take her out for dinner to one or other of the cramped Chelsea restaurants where there was a chance they might run into some of her friends.

The trouble was that they couldn't really afford to dine out so often, a fact that Lucinda failed to comprehend. To her, it was simple: where Daddy had picked up the bills before, now it was Martin's job. Martin himself would have liked to be able to afford a few decent pieces of furniture for their home, for he was developing a good eye for antiques and there were still bargains to be found, even in the Portobello Market which they often explored on Saturdays; but, by the end of the month, there was never any money left: even now, in his pocket, there lurked the bill from Peter Jones, well overdue for settlement.

Martin would have been easier in his mind if Lloyd's had been prospering: but it was not. Each name's account was closed three years in arrears, to ensure that all claims due in that year were met from the appropriate premium income: thus, the year ended on 31 December 1961 had only been settled after the end of 1964. A month or so ago, each name had received his annual cheque for his net underwriting profits, plus such capital profit as had been engendered from the investment of the premiums received. On the Murchison syndicate, these cheques had been on average for almost £3,000, the amount varying according to the individual's share. This was only a little less than the names had received the previous year, and they would be happy; but the years still open looked much less healthy. 1962, now nearing closure, would, Martin estimated, bring them in something like £1,000 less, and for 1963, the year Martin had been appointed underwriter and at the end of which he himself was elected a member, the signs were gloomy.

Ivor Murchison assured him he need not be too concerned about this: it was worrying, of course, but the insurance market had a habit of running in seven-year cycles, and it just so happened that Martin had taken over when it began to enter the trough of declining profits. Nonetheless, the competition from overseas and a hard squeeze on the rates of premium were, as Ivor had foreseen, beginning to bite hard.

At least there was one bright star in this darkening and stormy sky. Bay Street & Global, the Bahamian re-insurance corporation, had from the day they began to trade a beneficial effect on Martin's underwriting tactics. With Toby

123

Blackett, he had been able to negotiate some very favourable blanket cover for several of the more risky lines he wrote; moreover, in return for giving Bay Street & Global a favoured position, the box benefited considerably from the commissions that Bay Street remitted back, and these might prove a useful buttress to the syndicate's perhaps vulnerable profits. At one time, Toby had half-hinted that these commissions might be payable to Martin himself, suggesting tentatively that he believed this was the practice on several boxes and that, moreover, some of these men made arrangements to retain their commissions overseas. It was a neat way, he said airily, of building up a useful sum of capital out of the taxman's grasp. But Martin would not hear of it: as he replied that in his view and as a matter of good faith, all such commissions must adhere to the syndicate as a whole, he was gratified to hear an echo of Ivor Murchison's honourable tones.

Thinking of Toby, it occurred to him that he hadn't seen his friend for some time; they must lunch together soon. He was pleased that the other man was doing so well: ever since Toby left the box for the lush pastures of broking, the two had remained close; and the Blacketts and the Coleys often went out in the evenings as a foursome. Lucinda and Hilary Blackett were close, too, and it was often with Hilary that Lucinda went to the hairdresser, browsed through the newly sprouted boutiques down the Kings Road, explored the department stores. Martin was glad of this: at least he knew he could trust Hilary, who was no fool and who could restrain Lucinda from the worst extravagances.

In the managing director's office at Draycott House, Toby Blackett was already at work. He had been in the post for a year now and had long realised that, if he was to accomplish all he needed to do, he must be in his office early and prepared to stay late. He had been reassured to find in himself a gift for management and an ability to take a quick decision; just as important, his leadership, derived from a secure power-base on the board and the steady support of Trevor Bleach, was now unquestioned. At first, some of the older men had resented his youth and his casual style: accustomed to the gentlemanly formality of Sir Andrew Draycott and Hervey Parsloe, they regarded Toby's long black hair, his soft silk shirts and his informal mohair suits, and, most of all, his universal use of Christian names, as symbols of a loose grip.

One of Toby's first changes had aroused all their opposition. Toby did not need Trevor Bleach to remind him that his task was to build up the broking firm from a secure but sleepy position in the middle ground of the market to one of dominance. He soon decided that the traditional means of rewarding most of the brokers in his employ, by way of part of the commission on the business they introduced, operated against the interests of his company in the longer term and, though incidentally, against the interests of their clients. A broker whose prime concern was the scale of his commission would target the easy sell for a quick turnover: he would have no interest in exploring his clients' needs in greater depth, to devise, perhaps, special policies to meet their own especial circumstances. His men, he told them, would in future be salaried: and they were not to regard themselves as salesmen, but more as consultants. Only by identifying with their clients, through a thorough knowledge of their business operations, would they be able to identify each one's insurance requirements and then to devise, in conjunction with underwriters in the Room at Lloyd's or within the insurance companies, the appropriate cover. This expertise could then be shown to other concerns in a similar line of business and although it would take more time than the traditional deal, the benefit to Draycott would be much greater.

The older men had all gone now, their place taken by a team of sleek, smooth recruits who modelled themselves on the smart informality of their managing director. Another thing they had in common: avarice. The new policy was beginning to pay off: seated at his desk, Toby glanced through a typed run-through of each man's monthly achievements and knew that Trevor Bleach would be pleased. And pleasing Trevor Bleach was an activity out of which Toby was doing very well.

When Hervey Parsloe had gone back on his pledge to support Bleach within Draycott, Parsloe, Toby had been apprehensive lest his part in the planned takeover should

125

jeopardise his future. He need not have worried: a second scheme was well prepared and, in the face of what he called Parsloe's treachery, Bleach moved into action. There was a stalemate on the voting shares; but within the three million non-voting shares, he became very active. The Pension Fund's holding of half a million was, as he had demonstrated already, on ice, and therefore if he had one and a quarter million 'B' shares proxied in his favour, and if he then secured their enfranchisement, he would be home and dry.

Trevor Bleach might be regarded as a jumped-up outsider by the mandarins of the City, but he had his own old-boy network, as effective in its way as the City's men of power. One of his friends, Harry Jones, also originally from Birmingham, was now the Investment Manager for Probity Life Assurance. Probity, like the Pearl and the Pru', handled colossal sums for investment, and Jones had invested modestly in Draycott, Parsloe "B" shares when they first came to the market. Under Bleach's prompting, Probity had quietly built up this holding to around 400,000. At the same time, working through the merchant bankers, Mauser's, the shares under Bleach's control now totalled half a million. Mauser's had also bought in smaller holdings for some of the men of substance for whom Bleach acted as financial consultant: Gasper Grieve, for instance, was in for 50,000. By the spring of 1964, Bleach and his associates had secured control of more than half the non-voting equity of Draycott, Parsloe.

Both Harry Jones, from the sheer size of the funds at his disposal, and Mauser's, an old-established and much respected bank, would command attention from the City in a way that was, as yet, beyond Bleach. Working together but from different angles, they began a well-orchestrated campaign for the remainder of the equity to be enfranchised. Their message was simple: it was undesirable, in these days of enlightened capitalism, for control of a publicly quoted company to be exclusively in the hands of a small (and family) group of shareholders: it didn't look good, they would have to watch their step in the City if a Labour Government should come to power in the autumn, and above all it was undemocratic.

These arguments told where it mattered: with the

126

Governor of the Bank of England, the Chairman of the Stock Exchange, the Chairman of Lloyd's and (as Mr Jones made sure) with the other great assurance companies and the pension funds who between them had so much muscle on the stock market. A strong board could have resisted these pressures (as other, similarly arranged companies like Savoy Hotels did); but Toby Blackett and Michael Pendragon worked hard on the other directors while Hervey Parsloe vacillated; then, quite suddenly, he gave in, and Trevor Bleach was elected a director of Draycott, Parsloe.

Once within the walls of the citadel, Bleach had no mercy on the besieged. Although he retained Sir Andrew Draycott in the honorific post of president – that would seem like fair play to the City and the old man might still be useful – Hervey Parsloe's resignation was demanded at once, and Trevor Bleach was duly elected chairman.

Bleach's revenge did not stop there. As soon as he embarked on the reorganisation he wanted, he changed the company's name: the hated word 'Parsloe' disappeared and it became the Draycott Insurance Group Ltd, an umbrella for a number of subsidiary companies each covering a separate activity, such as Draycott Insurance (Home) Ltd, of which Toby became managing director, Draycott Properties, and a web of overseas companies such as DIG (Australasia) Pty Ltd, DIG Inc. in New Jersey, and others in Hong Kong and Toronto. All these names were displayed on a carved granite display in the foyer of Draycott House; but neither here nor anywhere in the published accounts of the group was there any mention of Bay Street & Global Insurance Corporation of Nassau, Bahamas, for it was not in any sense a subsidiary. Officially, the directors were a Nassau accountant and a lawyer; in fact, it was closely controlled by Bleach and owned, apart from himself, by a small group of his allies, including Toby and Sir Woodbine Bulkely-Grieve.

The stock market in general, and the shareholders in particular, were delighted by Bleach's emergence in the chair, and his various changes were enthusiastically endorsed, both at General Meetings and, more importantly, by the financial press. From being a dull market, shares in Draycott became bullish and, as Bleach had predicted, they moved ahead sharply. Every morning, the first thing Toby looked at on his desk was the closing price of the previous day, and he was gratified to see that Draycott had closed at 36/9d.

He still owned about 15,000 shares, bought openly and registered in his own name, taking advantage of a useful share option scheme which Bleach had introduced for the benefit of his executives. The original holding, which Bleach had bought for him through a 'shell' company in Bermuda, had long since been sold, realising for Toby a net profit of close on £90,000. This profit remained overseas, safe from the greedy paws of the tax man, and he had resisted the temptation to pick up some of the change, to blow a little of his new wealth. As Trevor Bleach had suggested, it would have been foolish thus to draw attention to his good fortune, and in any case Hilary Blackett had done very well too from her shareholding: he put the whole of his profit into Bay Street & Global.

Toby checked his desk diary and then began his morning work, ploughing through the incoming mail and a variety of reports from the departments under his control. He was about to summon his secretary when the door opened, quietly, and Trevor Bleach came in; he liked to arrive unannounced. He went straight to the corner of the sofa where he established himself, the contents of his ever-present briefcase spread on a low table in front of him.

It was one of Bleach's idiosyncrasies that he preferred to work thus. He refused to make use of the chairman's office, with its panelled walls and portraits: that was left for Sir Andrew and seldom used for anything more than drinks after a board meeting. Bleach just settled wherever he found table space and a telephone; and since, in a dry way, he seemed to like Toby's company and enjoyed watching his protégé at work, it was usually Toby's office that he chose.

Bleach's private life was still, to Toby, an enigma. Despite his now considerable wealth, he remained in his impersonal service flat in the White House; he enjoyed few of the perquisites of his position, not even a company car – although Sir Andrew retained the use of the big Daimler, and Toby's Jaguar was parked in the garage under Lloyd's. Even the lavish dinners that he gave in London's most expensive restaurants seemed to provide him with little pleasure, for he seldom ventured beyond a steak and a thin whisky. Sometimes he would call in at Hasker Street after dinner, and on these occasions Hilary would absent herself while the two men talked their business, generally Bay Street & Global, which Bleach was reluctant to discuss in the office. No files relating to the Bahamian company were kept at Draycott House and, on Bleach's instructions, the few papers that Toby retained were tucked away in a locked briefcase at the back of the spare-room wardrobe in his mother's house.

This morning, however, Bleach was breaking his own rule. Bay Street & Global papers were scattered all over the coffee table when he called Toby over.

'I've just received the latest figures from Nassau,' he said, 'and I thought you'd like to cast your eye over them. I'm sure you'll agree they are quite satisfactory.'

Toby glanced down the column of figures and whistled. 'My God,' he said, 'these reserves are pretty impressive. How have we managed to build up so large a sum in so short a time?'

'Several factors have helped.' Bleach leaned back on the sofa; he enjoyed expounding to Toby. 'First, we don't pay anything much in the way of tax. Second, we aren't subject to the strict rules that Lloyd's imposes on the investment of premiums received: we can and do pursue a more advantageous programme of investment, taking advantage of opportunities all over the world – and we can move quickly. Third, because when we pay on the premiums on the risks we ourselves re-insure, we don't go through Lloyd's Central Accounting System: we can and do take our time over payment, making use of the money meanwhile. On the other hand, what the London market owes us in premiums does come through Central Accounting; so we get our money quickly, and pay out slowly. It's surprising how quickly it mounts up.'

'You can say that again. We appear to be solid enough even if a major catastrophe occurs.'

'H'm. It's not a question of if, Toby, but *when*. We've been fortunate so far that we haven't suffered any major claims, and let us just hope we don't suffer one within the next year. After that, we might just consider ourselves home and dry.'

Toby picked up another sheet of paper. 'Management funds,' he quoted; 'what exactly are they?'

'Yours, Toby, yours and mine and those of the other shareholders. You must appreciate that, operating as we do offshore, we can tailor what we call our management fees to match the underwriting profits. These are then divided up, and allocated in proportion to each of us who stand behind Bay Street & Global.'

Trevor Bleach reached into his briefcase and took out a small note, covered with figures in handwriting. 'I worked out how your fund stands at the moment,' he said. 'You might just like to see how you're doing.'

'My God,' said Toby, glancing at the total, 'that's incredible. I put in £85,000 and already it's doubled.'

Bleach gave a satisfied smirk. 'I said you might be a millionaire by the time you're thirty-five. You've a few years to go yet, but you're on your way.'

For a moment, Toby's face was expressionless as he contemplated his new-found spending power. An extravagant holiday in the South of France, a good power boat, a spot of rather too high gaming at Asper's, even (for he owed his wife something for her loyalty and her initial support) a move to a larger house with a better address – Eaton Terrace, maybe, or Cadogan Lane.

'Mind you' – Bleach's unattractive voice broke into his thoughts – 'you mustn't consider withdrawing any of your capital yet. For one thing, a sudden splash of spending might just attract the attention of the Inland Revenue, whose curiosity seems to increase daily; and for another, left where it is, and under my management, it will continue to grow rapidly.'

'But where is it?' asked Toby.

'Where mine is, mostly. And Gasper's, and the rest of us. All tied up in neat little parcels and distributed discreetly all over the world, in places where it will arouse no one's curiosity: Panama, Singapore, Bermuda, and just for safety, quite a bit with some good friends in Berne. I dislike the Swiss and their negative interest, but I consider it judicious to keep a tidy sum in their hands.'

'I see.' There was a touch of nervousness in Toby's voice. 'We're all very lucky to benefit from your expertise, but . . .'

130

'But what, Toby? Go on.'

'What I'm trying to ask is, if anything ghastly should happen to you, then where will we all stand?'

Trevor Bleach smiled thinly. 'You are right to ask such a question. After all, men die but money lives on. It would have been imprudent of me not to make some arrangements should I fall victim to a plane crash. Now, listen.' Toby returned to his desk and sat attentively, pen in hand. 'No, Toby, no notes please. It's very simple. You remember Mr Plender?'

'The Bahamian lawyer? Yes, of course, I met him on my honeymoon. And he's on the board of Bay Street & Global.'

'Just so.' Bleach nodded. 'In the event of my demise, you should go straight to the Bahamas. Mr Plender has instructions to hand you the key to my safe deposit at the Royal Bank of Canada in Nassau, and there you will find all the details you will need, together with the appropriate certificates and bearer bonds.'

Bleach began to stow his papers away in his briefcase. 'One last thing, Toby: we don't seem to be making much progress in the matter of Ivor Murchison's agency. Whenever I bring up the subject, he evades the issue, and I'm beginning to lose patience. We need an underwriting agency if we're to complete control of the circle of insurance.'

'I know. And it would be a shame if we had to look elsewhere, because Murchison's would suit us ideally. We can't put down his reluctance simply to some idea that his independence is beneficial to Lloyd's: several other agencies have already been acquired by brokers, and the Committee has raised no objection.'

'It can't be the money – goodness knows, I've offered him more than enough. No, there's something else, some other reason, and I'd like you to find out what it is.'

'I owe Martin Coley lunch,' said Toby. 'I'll sound him out and see if he can give me some clues.'

The next morning started badly at Martin's box when John Bishop arrived to report that a smaller freighter, the *Guadalcanal Star*, had been posted missing.

'She's overdue on passage from Valparaiso to Hong Kong.

I know we've written a line on her.' Bishop was thumbing through a ledger.

'I remember that risk,' said Martin. 'We wrote a line on a policy for a shipbreaker's in Hong Kong, and not long ago we had advice from the broker to include the *Guadalcanal Star*. Does the missing bulletin say anything about the cargo?'

'It's believed to be scrap metal.'

'Scrap? Now wait a minute. I can't believe we'd be so silly as to write a vessel on her last voyage packed full of cargo like scrap that's liable to go through her sides like a knitting needle into butter.'

'You're quite right.' Bishop had found the entry in the Risks Book. 'The slip we were shown specifically excluded scrap. And the brokers were Kitto & Co.'

'Ah-ha. I think we'd better have a word with Kitto's. Would you cut along to the Caller and ask for Mr Benson of Kitto's to come and see us as soon as possible?'

'No need, Martin.' Bishop could see down the aisle. 'Freddy Benson's on his way here now.'

'Good morning, sir.' Martin's greeting to the broker was his most formal.

'I know, I know, you want to haul me over the coals about the *Guadalcanal Star*.' Benson was very young and breezy. 'I thought I ought to put your minds at rest about that bloody scrap metal.'

'It sounds to me like non-disclosure,' said Martin grimly.

'It's a balls-up,' answered the broker. 'We were advised by our clients and we simply failed to tell you chaps, so I've come to put it right. We've already taken out Total Loss cover on our own account, so you're in the clear, but Mr Kitto was very insistent I came and told you right away – and to express our apologies.'

Benson's insouciant air contained no hint of regret and Martin decided to emphasise the point at issue.

'I'm glad to hear that Kitto's have made themselves responsible.' Martin's tone was remarkably that of Ivor Murchison. 'If we underwriters can't trust what we're shown by the brokers, the whole system at Lloyd's would break down. All sides – including the clients for whom you are responsible – must show the utmost good faith.'

'I know – *uberrima fides* and all that.'

'Indeed, *uberrima fides*,' Martin agreed gravely.

By now there was a small queue of brokers waiting to see Martin, but Benson stood his ground. 'By the way, sir,' his tone was uncertain and, for the first time, respectful, 'I wonder if you've had time to think about that proposal I showed you from the Galveston Shipping Construction Corporation. As it's bat-buggery business, we were hoping you'd lead the slip.'

Martin reached into his belly drawer and took out a sheet of paper. 'As I told you, I needed time to think about this one, and I wanted to have a word with one or two other underwriters. These oil rigs for the Gulf of Mexico are a new kind of animal to us.'

What Martin did not add was that he had already been shown the risk by another broker. It was clear that the Galveston Corporation were putting their risk out to tender, and that wouldn't be just in the Lloyd's market. It was obviously beneficial to Lloyd's that they put in an attractive quote, and they would have to trim their price to the bone if they were to have any hope of beating the American competition.

'I wouldn't like to sign for more than two percent,' Martin pronounced.

'Oh, I was hoping we could put you down for five,' said the broker. 'After all, you're the leader, and if you take a bigger slice it'll encourage the others.'

'That's all very well, but I'll have to effect some re-insurance. And you ought to try the companies.' Martin nodded his head towards the first floor, where the big insurance companies had their offices, contributing their weight to the underwriting resources of the Room. 'I'm sure some of them will take a view to help you.'

Benson went on his way and Martin began to work through the line of brokers. It was all routine stuff; as he initialled a slip, Martin noticed that the broker was remarkably young, then laughed at himself: it must be a sign of advancing years if brokers, like policemen, suddenly seem like callow youths.

Martin began to think about his morning coffee and then

133

Ivor Murchison appeared at the box. Although Ivor was scrupulous in leaving the day-to-day underwriting to Martin, he came to the box regularly and always liked to glance through the Risks Book.

'H'm,' he commented, 'that's quite a line you've written on Galveston.'

Martin explained his reasons.

'I'm sure you're right: these oil rigs are going to be big business and we must be on them.' Ivor leaned his backside against the table and folded his arms, a sign that he was about to expound a philosophy of insurance. 'The trouble is that some of these new risks are such colossal lines, it makes it difficult to set an appropriate rate. To some extent, we're groping in the dark until such time as there is a disaster.'

'You sound, sir, as if you're hoping for a huge claim,' John Bishop spoke up from his seat, doubt in his voice.

'In a way, that's just what we need,' Ivor answered. 'It's like these blasted super-tankers, trundling their way around the oceans of the world and each of 'em worth five or six million pounds. Every underwriter in the Room and every insurance company in the world wants to be in on them and the result is that the premiums are cut to the bone. But just think what will happen when one of those monsters crashes into another, rounding the Cape or jostling for position in the Gulf of Oman.'

'The loss would be enormous.' Bishop sounded awed.

'It would indeed. In the short term. The point is that Lloyd's could stand the loss and would pay the claim promptly, gaining reputation in the process. Thus, many owners would decide to switch their underwriting back here, to the Lloyd's market. And meanwhile, in the face of such a loss, we'd be able to push up the premiums and make a bit of profit for a change. In the long run, a spectacular loss does Lloyd's a lot of good. Even so, Martin' – Ivor stood up – 'I'd re-insure quite a slice of that Galveston risk if I were you.'

Ivor then proposed that he and Martin should take their morning coffee together and side by side they moved off. In the lift up to the Captain's Room, Ivor enquired after Lucinda. 'And when are you two going to start a family?

It's not that I much relish the role of grandparent, but I think my wife . . .'

The lift doors hissed open and the subject dropped; but Martin knew what Ivor meant. It would need the arrival of grandchildren for Ursula Murchison to accept him as a son-in-law. He himself was keen enough, but Lucinda remained reluctant: there was plenty of time, she said, and she intended to enjoy herself while she was still young.

The Captain's Room at Lloyd's was what, in a company of similar size, would have been regarded as the executive restaurant. Its name came down from the days when the captains of vessels just arrived in port and those about to hoist the Blue Peter would assemble, to exchange news of the high seas, also being a valuable source of information about marine risks for the underwriters themselves. These days, it was no more than a functional, characterless dining room, and the ante-room, where Ivor and Martin now found themselves a table, was equally impersonal: a great many leather chairs, a blue carpet, a few portraits of past dignitaries on the cream walls and, hanging over all, a blue cloud of tobacco smoke – the only similarity with the old Captain's Room of Mr Lloyd's Coffee House.

Ivor ordered coffee while Martin lit his first cigarette of the day. Unable to smoke in the Room, it gave added pleasure to his morning break.

'I've been meaning to have a word with you about the box,' Ivor began.

'I know the figures don't look good,' said Martin. 'We'll have to look for gains on our investments if we're going to pay our names anything worth while, and I am rather concerned about the effect on the gilts market if Mr Wilson should win the autumn election.'

'I shouldn't worry about the Labour Party too much if I were you. Wilson may mouth a few shibboleths to placate the gods of socialism but I believe in his heart he understands the City very well, and won't want to tamper with it. After all, the unions themselves – and their pension funds – are all huge investors in the stock market. Whatever the result of the election, I don't think we've much to fret about.'

Ivor set down his coffee cup. 'What I really wanted to air

135

with you was the question of the staff on the box. Have you come to any conclusions about the appointment as deputy?'

'John Bishop,' Martin answered at once.

'I thought you might say that.' Ivor was not surprised; after all, young Bishop was much in Martin's own mould. 'What have you against Hemsley?'

'Oh, nothing. Hemsley is bright and keen, and he's already told me he's anxious to become a working name — apparently, his father is prepared to put up the money.'

'But . . . ?' Ivor prompted.

'But, I think he's inclined to be erratic. Whereas, in my opinion, John Bishop is developing a real instinct for underwriting. I feel I can rely on him.'

'Well, it's your decision, and I'll abide by what you say,' Ivor conceded. 'If you promote Bishop, you'll be needing another clerk?'

'I suppose so. Hemsley will be sure to move on somewhere else.'

'In that case, I'd like you to consider Giles. He's quick-witted, and I believe he's learned a lot in New York. I've had good reports of him from Draycott's office there, but I think it's time he came back to the Room and started to learn about underwriting.' There was pride in Murchison's voice as he advocated his son.

'Yes, of course,' said Martin cautiously. He too had had reports of Giles Murchison's presence in Manhattan, from broker acquaintances on their return from the United States: unlike the carefully edited opinions presented to the father, Martin's impression was that young Giles had plunged deep into the hectic life of New York City, and had made more of the sybaritic opportunities open to him than of the chance to apply himself to learning about insurance. 'I've always known that you wanted Giles to join the box,' he continued; 'I just wonder if he's quite ready for it yet. In some ways, he's still very young.'

Giles Murchison had been round to Adelaide Place once since his return to London. At dinner, Martin had not been favourably impressed: Giles had sounded forth his opinions of America, with all the arrogance of a callow Etonian. Lucinda had agreed that her brother seemed too fond of the brandy bottle, that he seemed a mass of nerves and that, with his pale face still acned and his hands apt to shake, New York didn't appear to have done him much good. At the moment, he was sharing a flat in Knightsbridge with three other friends from school; and Lucinda had already suggested what her father was now urging, that Martin should find a place for Giles on the box.

Ivor misinterpreted Martin's hesitation. 'Come now,' he said, 'I know the boy's my son and your brother-in-law, and I'm aware that the very concept of handing one's business on to one's son is regarded as old-hat. But in Giles' case, if the boy himself is keen, and if you find him suitable, I don't think it is fair that his parentage should tell against him.'

'I agree.' Martin was very aware that he owed Ivor Murchison not only his present job, but his whole career at Lloyd's and indeed his membership itself. Moreover, Ivor had been a quiet support over his marriage to Lucinda, without ever showing disloyalty to Ursula Murchison. Ivor himself was far too gentlemanly to press such points, but his very restraint increased Martin's sense of obligation. 'Very well,' he said at last, 'I'll give Giles a ring and ask him to come and see me at the box. I'm sure we'll be able to work something out.'

Back in his place at the box, Martin applied himself to the rest of the morning's work. While there were few brokers around, he ploughed through the stack of notices, advices and alterations to risks already written that fell, thick as autumnal leaves, on to the table from the hands of circulating waiters.

He broke off when a broker approached the box, with the slightly hang-dog expression of one seeking a favour.

'Good morning, sir,' he began, 'I was wondering if you had been able to reach any decision on the *St Elmo* claim?'

'Ah, yes. Dig out the file for me, would you, John?' Martin was playing for time; in fact, he remembered the facts of the claim very well. The *St Elmo* was a small freighter, on passage between Macau and Tai-Pei when she had disappeared. Apparently she foundered with all hands, and the only wreckage that had been picked up by a passing junk (the

Lloyd's agent in Hong Kong had reported) was a drifting life-raft and a few bales of cargo. There was nothing untoward in that, for the South China Sea was notoriously uncertain; nor were the owners suspect. On the contrary, they were a solid, wealthy Chinese company, who had been placing their insurance at Lloyd's for many years. Murchison's had first written the risk in the Thirties and since then they had become the leaders on the slip, which was why the broker now addressed himself to Martin.

Glancing through the file, Martin confirmed that there were two elements of doubt over the claim. The first was that, whereas the port of destination had been named as Manila when the risk was written, the Lloyd's agent had confirmed that the *St Elmo* had been bound for Taiwan, in quite another direction. The second doubt concerned the cargo: the manifest declared this to be electrical components, but the few items recovered had proved to be part of a consignment of cotton.

'I don't think this claim stands up,' said Martin, looking at the broker.

'I quite agree, legally,' the broker answered. 'But we're satisfied it was a genuine mistake. You've seen the owners' affidavit: they say that when another of their vessels had engine trouble, they switched cargoes and destinations at the last minute. They just failed to advise us.'

'Are you satisfied it was just carelessness on their part?'

'Our people in Hong Kong have been into it very carefully, and they're satisfied. Moreover, they are most concerned about the adverse effect a rejection of the claim might have. They're facing some hot competition, especially from the Japanese companies, and a refusal to pay up, however justified according to the letter of the policy, might jeopardise a number of good risks. You know how clannish these Chinese are,' the broker added wheedlingly.

'I realise it might be good for the Lloyd's market to settle, but it would be at the expense of our names,' Martin pointed out.

'It's not a big claim. And we'd pay all our commission over to you to soften the blow.'

'That's the least you can do.' Martin closed the file. 'Well,

I've had a word with the other leaders. We have decided that although we are under no legal compulsion to settle the claim, we will none the less honour the spirit of the risk. Just give the owners a good spanking and make sure you come along with some first-class slips in the near future.'

Gratefully, the broker, after tentatively offering Martin lunch, gathered up his papers and left.

'Giving my money away, I see, Martin.' Toby Blackett had appeared at the box and was grinning down at his friend.

'Toby. Good Lord, I'd quite forgotten; we're lunching together, aren't we?'

'We are. I've booked a table at the Wessex. It'll do you good to get away from the school food in the Captain's Room just for once.'

The Wessex was an establishment comparatively new to the City. Its thick carpeting, velvet banquettes, obsequious waiters and vast bills seemed alien to the older hands accustomed to the traditional chop houses; but Toby seemed very much at home in there and was ushered to a place with a deal of fuss. He ordered a Buck's Fizz while Martin had a sherry and they studied the vast menu. After they had ordered, Toby leaned back and looked at his friend.

'You're looking rather troubled, Martin,' he observed. 'Is it that claim you had to settle this morning?'

'Oh, no, that was run-of-the-mill. Although I ought to warn you, as one of our names, that the syndicate profits won't amount to much this year.'

'Then what's troubling you?'

At the back of his mind, Martin had been brooding since morning coffee about the impending arrival of Giles Murchison on the box; he had just, he considered, got things as he liked them, and he feared that Ivor's son might be disruptive.

'Ivor's asked me to take Giles into the box,' he explained. 'I'm in no position to refuse him, but I must admit I don't relish the idea.'

'So the heir-apparent is to assume his inheritance? And you, I suppose, are inclined to feel that for all your hard work, your job has really been to keep his seat warm for him? I do see you must resent that a little.'

This, Toby realised, was the clue to Ivor Murchison's obduracy over the sale of the agency; Ivor wanted to hand that, and the box, over to his son intact.

'To be honest, I do feel that, a bit,' Martin admitted. 'But I've always known that Ivor would want something of the kind. It's just rather sooner than I expected. And . . .' He hesitated, toying with his glass.

'And what?'

Martin made up his mind. 'Look, Toby, I wouldn't say this to anyone else. But the fact is, I don't like Giles and I don't trust him. I know he's Ivor's son, and he's my own brother-in-law, for God's sake, but he's got too much charm and very little else. And there's something else. Do you remember that dance at Tickton, the first time I met Lucinda?'

'As far as I recall, young Giles got plastered, didn't he? And you did some kind of rescuing act.'

'Exactly. I'd forgotten about the incident, considering it no more than a schoolboy's lapse. But recently, one or two brokers who've been in New York have come back with tales of Giles' life there; they all suggest that Giles has been hitting the bottle in a big way, and other things as well, if half what I'm told is true.'

'That's odd,' said Toby. 'I've seen the reports coming back from Draycott's office in New York, and they've all spoken well of young Giles.'

'Maybe. They probably judged it wise not to offend Ivor, now he's a director of Draycott's.'

'You may be right. But why don't you square up to old Ivor and spill the beans yourself.'

'I can't, don't you see? He'd only think I was using it as a way to prevent Giles joining the box.'

'What about Lucinda, then? Couldn't she have a word with her father?'

'Lucinda's useless. She just shrugs her shoulders and says that Giles' wild oats are nothing to do with her.'

'You do have a problem.' Toby broke off to taste the chilled Sancerre proffered by the wine waiter. 'I think what you deserve is a long, leisurely and slightly pissy lunch. And as for young Giles, you'd better leave him to me.'

12

The Toby Blacketts did not entertain much at home. For one thing, Hilary loathed cooking; for another, while they could dine their friends on Toby's expense account there was little point in not making use of that comforting facility; and, in any case, Hasker Street was much too small. Nor was Hilary the kind of wife to put herself out for her husband. The first fierce lust which he had aroused soon burnt out, at much the same time as Toby realised that her usefulness to him in regard to her family's business was ended. They now lived together in an atmosphere of cool friendliness – what Toby thought of as an open marriage – and although he had a suspicion that Hilary was not faithful, this did not concern him provided he didn't know about it. He had no sexual jealousy and, he admitted to himself, it would be foolish for him to be possessive about his wife's body when he had only married her in the cause of his own advancement.

Nor was Toby himself promiscuous. It was not for lack of opportunity, for he retained his good looks and there was, besides, an air of success about him – a thrusting, fighting-cock aggression that attracted the casual girls with whom his brother Paul still consorted. But all Toby's energies were directed to the Draycott interests, to listening to Bleach's ideas and putting them into practice and to developing others of his own. It was curious, he reflected as he lay in the bath at Hasker Street on the evening of his party and looked down at his smooth, lean body stretched out under the soapy water, how un-sexed his life had become. Perhaps he'd better do something about it, he told himself with a laugh, before he turned into a eunuch, emasculated by the pursuit of wealth.

Toby had suggested to Hilary that they threw a drinks party. Their drawing room had room for no more than fourteen, but that was enough for his purpose. He told his wife that the occasion was to bring together some of his business friends on a social basis. Also, he explained, a cousin of his, a publisher named Charles Harris, had expressed a mild interest in putting up for Lloyd's, and the party would give Charles an opportunity to meet Ivor and Martin informally.

Apart from the Coleys and the Murchisons – for Ivor had told Ursula that it was a three-line whip, they must both show their faces and she couldn't lie low in the country – the guests were all youngish brokers, among them Michael Pendragon, lately returned from the Far East. Also of the party were a sprinkling of assorted wives and girlfriends. After reciting the list to Hilary, Toby added, 'And we ought to ask young Giles Murchison too. We wouldn't want him to feel left out: you might give him a ring.'

It suited Toby's plans that he had secured the attendance of Humphry Chase. Chase, the managing director of one of the largest and most reputable brokers, was a personage at Lloyd's. In his early forties, he had already served a term on the Committee and was spoken of as a potential future chairman. Once or twice, Chase had gone out of his way to be civil to Toby, giving the impression that he rather approved the new buccaneering style of Draycott's by saying that Blackett should not be discouraged by the murmurings of doubtful older members, for what the market needed was fresh thinking, provided always that it did not bring Lloyd's into disrepute. Chase's presence at the party, however, was due less to his quiet patronage of Toby than to a family connection with the Parsloes – showing that Hilary still had her uses.

Gasper Grieve was a last-minute addition. Toby had encountered Sir Bulkely in the lift at Draycott's and the baronet, at a loose end in London in July, was pleased to accept. He was one of the first to arrive and barked with happiness at the drink Toby offered – a White Bear, a concoction of chilled vodka and champagne. Soon the room was full, with the baying of the upper middle classes spilling out through the open windows into the narrow, dainty street.

Michael Pendragon, smooth and fish-like as ever, elected to swim close to Giles Murchison. Flashing his sharp teeth at intervals, he seemed content to listen to Giles' loudly expressed, dogmatic views of America, of Lloyd's and insurance in general, even of politics; but he was assiduous in making sure that Giles' glass was never empty. Toby glanced across the room approvingly as he watched Pendragon adding a larger slug of vodka than was usual to each of the young man's refills.

The climax came just before eight. The party was all amity and euphoria: the drink had not yet worked to bring bile and bitterness to the surface. Ursula Murchison had brought herself to be civil to Martin, Ivor and Humphry Chase were comfortable in their common seniority, exchanging views about the need to recapture lost markets in Australia, Lucinda and Hilary were in a huddle by the fireplace. Looking over his mother-in-law's shoulder, Martin caught sight of Giles and frowned. Aware of a double responsibility for the boy, as probable employer and as brother-in-law, he didn't like what he saw. Giles's face was very white, a few late spots flaring red against the pallor. His loud speech was slurred, his hands trembled and he lurched as he turned yet again to the drinks table.

Martin wondered if he should intervene. To give himself time, he took off his spectacles and polished them. Ursula, watching, suddenly remembered Lucinda's remark, in the garden at Tickton two summers ago, about his eyes: they were indeed a deep, astonishing blue. They also looked anxious and she turned to see what had engaged his concern. Then she moved, brushing past Martin as she sped over to her son.

'Giles dear . . .' she began. It was not within Ursula's capabilities to murmur, but she made an effort to lower her tone. 'Giles dear, don't you think you've had enough? Your father and I are just leaving and . . .'

'For God's sake, Mummy, don't nag!' Giles swayed a little. 'I'm not ready to leave yet, and anyway, Micky Pendragon and I are going out on the town, aren't we, Micky?' He peered around, but Pendragon had edged away and was now on the far side of the room. Meanwhile, Ivor had detached himself from Chase and came over to flank his son on the other side.

'Just be quiet, Giles,' he said quietly, his lips tight with self-control. 'You'd best come along with us before you make an exhibition of yourself. You're just starting at Lloyd's and we wouldn't want you to begin there with a reputation for drunkenness.'

'We wouldn't, would we, Daddy dear?' Giles sneered. 'Well, all I can say is fuck Lloyd's and fuck you Daddy and fuck Mummy too for all I care.'

As Giles spoke, the room was by chance silent, the kind of silence that makes people utter banalities about passing angels. Ivor was embarrassedly aware that the whole room was listening, including a member of the Lloyd's Committee. His back rigid with distaste, he made a last attempt to exert his authority.

'Pull yourself together, Giles! You'll come along with me this minute.'

'Oh, piss off, Daddy, don't come the guardee gentleman with me.' Giles turned back to the drinks table. 'All I want is to be left alone,' he mumbled. Then he downed half a tumbler of vodka and staggered back.

Toby, moving forward as anxious host to intervene, caught him by the shoulders. 'I think you've had more than enough, Giles,' he said quietly. 'We'd better stow you away in your father's car, if you'd give me a hand, Ivor?'

'Yes, of course.' Ivor looked around for Hilary. 'Thank you so much, my dear,' he said. 'We were enjoying ourselves so much and I'm deeply sorry . . .'

'Think nothing of it,' replied Hilary, who was not sure what had happened.

Ursula Murchison had already left the house, unable to bear the public disgrace of her son. She was waiting by the

144

car when Ivor and Toby emerged, half-carrying the slumped Giles between them. After they had eased him into the back seat, Ivor turned to Toby.

'I can't apologise enough,' he began. 'We'll take him straight back to Tickton tonight, for he's in no state to be left alone in London.'

'I'm sure that's the best thing,' Toby agreed. 'I'm afraid the poor boy probably needs specialist help.'

'What do you mean?' asked Ursula loudly. 'After all, most young men get drunk from time to time, more's the pity. It's just most upsetting that Giles had to do it here, tonight, in front of all those people.'

'I wish I could agree with you, Mrs Murchison, but I honestly don't think that Giles's is just a case of occasional over-indulgence.'

'What are you trying to tell us, Toby?' Ivor's tone was sharp; his stance was stiff, the car keys dangling motionless from his hand.

'I've heard things – unofficially, of course – from our office in New York. I'm sorry to have to tell you this now, but it would appear that Giles had been hitting the bottle pretty steadily for at least the last year.'

Ivor shook his head. 'I can't believe that. You must have seen the reports on Giles from your people in New York: there wasn't even a hint that Giles was in any kind of trouble.'

'I agree. In fact, those conduct sheets were too damned good. I took the chance of asking a bit more about him when Jack Matthews, our Number Two in New York, was over here last week. I'm afraid he spilled the beans: Giles was into everything Manhattan has to offer – drugs, orgies, but most of all, and increasingly, drink. In fact, it seems that Jack had to bail him out on more than one occasion.'

While Toby recited this catalogue of misdeeds, Ursula's long jaw had dropped, her face drained by shock. 'How dreadful,' she cried, 'New York must be a positive sink . . .'

'Never mind about that,' Ivor snapped. 'What I want to know is, why wasn't I told the truth?'

'That's just what I wanted to know, too,' answered Toby smoothly. 'It seems that old Tom Hudd, who's in charge of our New York outfit, was worried that, because you had become a director of Draycott's, young Giles' misdoings might be blamed on him. He regarded them as a spree, from which Giles would recover once he was home.'

'It's obviously worse than that,' said Ivor grimly. 'Blast the man for his deceit.'

'I'm of your mind: that's why I've removed Hudd, and given the job to Jack Matthews.' In fact, just such a switch had been in Toby's mind for some time: Hudd was an older man, who had been with Draycott, Parsloe all his working life: his loyalties had lain with Hervey Parsloe, and he had been outspoken in his criticism of the new regime. And, because some of the dealings with Bay Street & Global had had to pass through the New York office, Hudd had been suspicious and critical of that too. Toby had been glad of grounds to retire Hudd (with a pension big enough to secure his silence) and to place in charge of New York a man whose loyalty to the Bleach regime was solid.

As Ivor drove off, Gasper Grieve came to the front door.

'You handled that very well, Toby,' he said approvingly.

Toby couldn't decide whether Gasper was referring to his conversation with the Murchisons, or to the way in which Giles had been shown up; but he had no time to explore the matter, for by now several other guests had taken their cue to leave and the narrow hall was crowded with thanks and farewells. The Coleys, who had been asked to join the Blacketts for dinner after the party, hung back, talking to Toby's cousin Charles, who showed no signs of leaving.

Since Sir Woodbine had helped himself to another drink and seemed likely to become a fixture, Toby extended the invitation for dinner; so it was as a party of six that they set off for the Mirabelle. Here, Mr Blackett's table was a good one, under the open roof and with a full view of the floodlit garden. Toby placed Lucinda on his right, with Gasper next to her, while Martin sat next to Hilary. He kept Charles Harris on his other side, for he wanted to see if he could nail his cousin's entry into Lloyd's. He had already recruited several new members from among his friends, mainly through Murchison's agency: he felt it strengthened the connection with Draycott's. But Harris was proving reluctant.

'You're very persuasive, Toby,' he said, his moon face with large round spectacles shining, 'and I'm taken by the concept of using my capital twice over. But publishing is a high-risk business anyway, and I think I'd be unwise to add to my liabilities at this juncture.'

Martin found himself isolated at the table. While Toby was applying himself to his cousin, Gasper Grieve made himself agreeable to Lucinda, who was, after all, the daughter of his old friend Ivor. The baronet had, without consulting Toby, called for more champagne as soon as he sat down and this he quaffed in bumpers as his loud voice boomed out a succession of slightly salacious tales from his past. To judge by Lucinda's face, alive with laughter, she was enjoying his attention, but then, thought Martin, she probably hadn't met anyone quite like Gasper before, so utterly confident of himself and so skilled at deploying a roguish charm. This left Martin with Hilary Blackett, with whom he had little in common, and who cut off his main source of conversation at the start by begging him for no more talk of Lloyd's that night.

'I've had a bellyful of insurance already tonight,' she told him. 'Most of Toby's friends can talk of little else. Tell me, what theatres have you been to recently?'

This ploy didn't help Martin much, for he and Lucinda didn't go often to the theatre; still, he did his best with references to Brecht's *Mother Courage* at the Old Vic, of which he had read the reviews. From this they passed to the abolition of the Death Penalty and the novelty of Mr Heath's election as leader of the Conservative Party, but it was hard going and when a waiter came round with the smoked salmon, he was glad to sit back and look around.

The restaurant was busy. Martin's glance went casually around the other tables, then focused on an alcove placed discreetly at the side. There were two men sitting there, side by side on a banquette looking out onto the restaurant, and at the sight of them he sat up.

'I say, Toby,' he said quietly across Charles Harris, 'I think you ought to know that Trevor Bleach is also here tonight.' He nodded towards the alcove; his concern was for his friend, for he was worried that Toby's boss might take a dim

147

view of such a dinner party on the expense account of Draycott's.

Toby twisted in his chair to peer across the surrounding tables.

'Good Lord, so he is.'

'So that's your famous Mr Bleach,' said Charles Harris. 'But who's the pretty boy with him?'

'That's my brother,' answered Toby, sounding very disconcerted, 'my brother Paul. And I'd very much like to know exactly what it is that they are celebrating.'

There was indeed something festive about the demeanour of the two men. By a trick of lighting, the alcove seemed to those watching like a stage, and it was almost as if Trevor Bleach and Paul Blackett were aware that out in the main body of the restaurant they commanded an audience. On cue, a sommelier arrived, followed by a commis waiter carrying an ice bucket; with theatrical ceremony, a squat green bottle with a gold label was tendered and then, with a discreet pop, opened and poured for Bleach to sample.

'Dom Pérignon, by God,' said Toby quietly. Since he'd first met Bleach, he'd never known him drink anything but whisky.

They continued to stare as the sommelier withdrew. Bleach and Paul took up their brimming glasses and clinked them together in some unheard toast; then they turned and grinned into each other's eyes.

13

The sudden death of Ivor Murchison took place a few days after the Blacketts' small – and, from Giles' point of view, disastrous – party. Ivor suffered a severe heart attack on the 5.35 from Liverpool Street, but his fellow commuters thought he was just sleeping off the effects of a heavy lunch, a relief enjoyed by most of them from time to time, and the body was not discovered until the train reached Cambridge.

Ursula Murchison, whatever her inner feelings, remained icily in control. The funeral was efficiently arranged at Tickton, announcements appeared in *The Times*, the *Telegraph* and, with a short obituary, in *Lloyd's List*: the obsequies were timed to chime with a convenient train from London, and there was a good turnout around the grave, the coffin heaped with cut flowers (as instructed by Ursula, so that they could be sent to the local hospital afterwards). The only exception was a huge wreath of lilies and carnations, sent 'with deepest sympathy from Trevor Bleach', and this was left to one side, propped up against an adjacent gravestone.

Afterwards, the mourners assembled at Tickton House, where there would be sherry and an appropriately cold collation. Ursula received them briskly, flanked by Lucinda and Giles, with Gasper Grieve hovering near to hand. Gasper had been staying at Tickton for the past few days and Lucinda, who had also hurried to her mother's side, had been glad of his cheerful presence and his robust, no-nonsense attitude to

149

death. Looking across the room, Martin, who had only arrived from London this morning, was surprised by his wife's good spirits: she looked animated, excited even, as she made conversation with the guests. Giles, by contrast, looked in a bad way, his thin face ashen and his hands trembling so much that his sherry spilled onto the carpet.

For Martin, Ivor's death had been a shock. There had been much to do at the box, of course, and he had written personally to all the names as well as acknowledging calls and notes of condolence. With the departure of Ivor, who had been his mentor and had remained as a guiding hand for the syndicate, Martin felt a deep sense of loss, and he grieved. At the same time, he felt isolated, vulnerable: not only was there no one to turn to, but the whole future of the agency must now be uncertain.

When, as soon as was decent, the mourners began to take their leave, Ursula asked Toby Blackett to remain behind. 'We think of you as an old family friend,' she said, 'and I may need your advice later. I'm sorry,' she added, 'that Hilary is not with you.'

Hilary Blackett had declined to attend, on the grounds that she couldn't stand funerals, although adding that she'd be interested to hear what that old stick Ivor had cut up for.

'I'm just going to have a little conference with Sir Woodbine first,' Ursula was saying. 'As you may know, he's one of Ivor's executors. Meanwhile, we'll leave you young people to look after yourselves.'

She withdrew Gasper Grieve into her late husband's study, installing herself at his desk. While she shuffled some papers, Gasper, who had already provided himself a balloon glass of brandy, settled to lighting a cigar.

'I've had the stockbrokers give me a valuation of Ivor's portfolio,' she began, 'and I'm very worried.'

'Let's have a look,' said Gasper, with his usual interest in the financial affairs of others. 'H'm, not bad, not bad at all. Over a quarter of a million, mostly in sound blue chips. I don't see what you have to worry yourself about there.'

'It's the death duties,' said Ursula crisply. 'Ivor's only other major asset was the agency: have you any idea what it might be worth?'

'Oddly enough, I discussed that with Ivor not long ago. He was of the opinion that, given the right circumstances, he might whistle up something around seventy thousand.' Sir Woodbine knew, but did not add, that this was the figure which Trevor Bleach had had in mind to offer.

'In that case, the duty will be enormous,' said Ursula, her fears confirmed. 'Well, I shall just have to face it: Tickton will have to go. Without Ivor's income, I could never afford to keep it up; and anyway, with Lucinda off my hands I don't need such a large place just for myself.'

'Now Ursula,' Gasper held up his hand, cigar firmly between the fingers, 'there's no need for a hasty decision. I've seen enough widows rush in and flog their homes, only to regret it later. You take your time, my dear.'

Sir Woodbine was a little puzzled at Ursula's urgency. Tickton House, he knew, was already in her name and besides that, she was well off in her own right, even apart from the holding she still retained in Draycott's. It was out of character for old Ursula to panic financially; she must have something else on her mind and doubtless it would come out in the wash. First, they must clear their heads about the liability for Estate Duty. 'The tax man will probably want more than fifty per cent of the estate,' he guessed. 'I don't know the exact rate, but I expect young Blackett will. It's the sort of thing he carries in his head.'

'We'd better have him in, then,' Ursula agreed. 'And while we're about it, we'd better talk to the children too. They've a right to know the terms of their father's will.'

She went to the door and called out. 'Lucinda, Giles, darlings, would you come in please? And Toby too: I'd like the benefit of your advice. Oh, Martin,' she added, 'you may as well join us.'

They trooped in and arranged themselves around the desk. 'Christ, Mummy,' said Giles, 'is there to be a formal reading of the will? I didn't think people went in for that much nowadays.'

'Not formal, dear,' said Ursula, giving her son a brief smile, 'but Sir Woodbine and I think you two ought to know what your father's will says.'

'It's very simple,' Gasper told them. 'You're each left five thousand quid: that's all, because of course you've already enjoyed the benefit of some modest settlements. The bulk of the estate, after payment of Estate Duty, goes into trust for your mother for her life, after which time it will be divided between you. There'll be no further duty to pay then, by the way, as the law stands now.'

'A fine help that is to me now,' said Ursula bitterly. 'The tax looks like being huge. Toby, can you advise me about the rate of tax?'

'The incidence of the duty depends on the size of the estate,' Toby answered. 'Can you give me some idea of the figure involved?'

'Say about three hundred thousand,' suggested Gasper.

'I'm afraid you'll have to be a little more precise,' Toby pressed. 'You see, £300,000 is a threshold above which the rate of duty rises: below, it would be levied at sixty per cent; above, it cops sixty-five per cent.'

'You'd better explain more exactly,' Ursula suggested to Gasper, 'and about the Agency too.' Lucinda and Giles were silent: it was the first time they had been privy to this kind of money talk, and both were slightly overwhelmed by the large sums being bandied about. Martin too was very quiet: the fate of the Agency concerned him very directly.

'Our problem, Toby,' Gasper explained, 'is that to be exact, we need to set a value upon the Agency. Could you perhaps suggest a possible figure?'

'I could. But it would depend upon Ursula: does she actually want to sell it?'

'It's not a question of whether I want to: I have to, if I'm to pay these bloody duties.'

Toby felt a spin of excitement. Since he had first heard of Ivor's death, he had realised that his complex plan for the disgrace of Giles Murchison had probably been superfluous: here was the Agency, about to drop into his – and Trevor's – lap. He answered gravely and, now, formally. Mrs Murchison must be aware, he suggested, that for some time the Draycott Group had been anxious to acquire a suitable underwriting agency to round off their insurance activities, and sporadic negotiations to that effect had taken place with the late Mr Murchison, who had been himself a director of Draycott's. While no conclusion had been reached, a general agreement had been reached that when the time was right, a deal would have been clinched. 'I know it was Ivor's wish and intention,' Toby concluded.

'Had any price been agreed?' asked Ursula.

'Not precisely. But something between sixty-five and seventy-five was in the air.' While speaking, Toby managed to avoid Gasper's eye.

'Sir Woodbine suggested seventy thousand. I'd be prepared to settle for that, if I can have a quick deal.'

Ursula snapped a file shut and looked up. Suddenly, she was aware of the impropriety of discussing such business matters in front of Lucinda and Giles, not to mention Martin, and in some haste she began to tell them of her plans to place Tickton on the market.

'But Mummy, you can't,' Lucinda protested. 'I mean, it's home, your home, and we all love it so much. It's the *family* home.' She spoke as if the Murchisons had been in Essex since the dissolution of the monasteries, instead of the twenty years since the war.

'Rubbish, my dear. It may be useful to you for the occasional weekend, but it costs a fortune to run and it's far too big for me and Giles on our own. It isn't as if you've provided me with any grandchildren to fill it,' she gibed at her daughter. 'No, my mind is made up. I shall sell Tickton and buy a small house in London, in Campden Hill perhaps, which would be nice and handy for you, Lucinda, and where there'll be room for a little flat for Giles in the basement. That way, I'll be able to keep an eye on him too.'

Giles' jaw dropped as his mother sketched out her plans. He had been trying to calculate whether his £5,000 legacy would stretch to a small flat on his own and a decent car: the thought of being cooped up with his mother, her considerable energies restricted to keeping an eye on him, was horrendous.

'Mummy, I was rather thinking that I would find a place on my own,' he protested but she swept over him.

'Out of the question, darling, you couldn't possibly afford it and I'm in no position to give you any help. No, you and I will set up house together, and then we must set about

153

finding you a job.' She looked from Martin to Toby: no fool, she realised that once the Agency was sold, she would have little clout to wield on her son's behalf. 'Between Toby and Martin, I'm sure we'll be able to give you a good start to your career. And now, if you'd leave me with Sir Woodbine, there are some other things to settle.'

While the others filed out, Toby contrived to remain behind. He had taken out his chequebook and was jotting down some figures on the back.

'Look here, Ursula,' he began, reverting to informality, 'I've got an idea that might help you with the tax men, but I need to know the precise figures. What is the current valuation of Ivor's equities?'

'£255,000,' said Gasper succinctly.

'I see. If we add to that seventy thousand for the Agency, the total estate is worth £325,000. That lands us with a duty of sixty-five per cent, leaving a net residue of £113,750.'

'Good God Almighty, is that all?' Ursula burst out. 'How the hell do those vultures expect me to live on that?'

Ursula's voice was shrill, and Toby recognised the symptoms. She was suffering from the affliction of apparent financial disaster that affects most people of means from time to time, especially in old age, when penury and destitution seem to loom. In fact, as he knew well, Ursula Murchison would be comfortable, wealthy even by most standards; but it suited his book at the moment to spin the wheels of her panic.

'The tax is savage,' he agreed, 'and it is our duty to see what we can do to mitigate it. If, for example, the estate could be brought in at under three hundred thou', then the duty levied would be at only sixty per cent.'

'Only?' Ursula interjected bitterly.

'Well, it's a start,' Sir Woodbine observed, realising that Toby had something up his sleeve. 'How would you propose to effect such a reduction?'

'There's nothing we can do about the stocks and shares,' he told them, 'because they will be valued on the day old Ivor handed in his dinner pail. But let us suppose, for the sake of the exercise, that the Agency was sold for, say, £35,000.'

'Daylight robbery!' Ursula snorted. 'I'd never agree to that. I've no call to put money in the pockets of your ghastly Mr Bleach.'

'If you'll bear with me,' Toby urged, 'I think you may find what I suggest will be very much to your advantage. To begin with, with the lower rate of duty, the net residue would be slightly larger.' He glanced at his scribbled figures. 'I make it £116,000. But that's not all. As you rightly point out, the Agency is worth a great deal more than £35,000. I think I might be able to persuade Trevor Bleach to an unofficial deal, as it were, on the side.'

'I hope you're not suggesting anything illegal, Toby.' Ursula was at her most chilly.

'Of course not,' he replied easily. 'It's very simple. We buy the Agency for thirty-five grand. But in addition, we'll arrange to make available for you a kind of *douceur*, and quite a good one – say another twenty – which would be payable to you wherever you wanted outside the Sterling Area.'

'Twenty thousand? In cash? Where?' She was hooked.

'The Bahamas, probably. We have a company there called Bay Street & Global, and they would make the payment, through nominees, of course, so it would be quite untraceable – and all yours, it goes without saying.'

Sir Woodbine coughed heavily through his cigar and gave Toby a hard look.

'I'm not sure I should be listening to this,' he muttered. 'After all, as an executor of Ivor's will, I also have a duty to the ultimate beneficiaries, Ursula's children, and unfortunately they have been privy to our previous talk on the subject of the price. Your ingenious scheme might be said to be against their long-term interests.'

'Balls, Gasper,' said Toby. 'All we have to do, the three of us, is to agree to keep our mouths shut, and no one will find out. Besides, it's to everyone's benefit: Ursula, because she saves on the duty and pockets a tidy little sum of capital, the children because in the end they'll fare better at her death, the Draycott Group because we buy the Agency a little cheaper than otherwise. The only losers are the Exchequer, and we don't need to waste any tears on them.'

'Very well.' Ursula had made up her mind. 'I'll go along

155

with your plan. But on one condition: I want nothing whatever to do with your Mr Bleach. It must be understood,
Toby, that I'll only deal through you.'

'Done!' he cried, elated, and solemnly the three of them
shook hands. Then Gasper, aware that his glass was now
empty, hurried off to the dining room where there was, he
knew, a refreshing decanter of brandy. Toby, with the same
intent, followed him.

'You did well with Ursula,' Gasper remarked, affable once
more with a full glass in his hand, 'but I wonder if you were
altogether wise to tell her about Bay Street & Global? I mean,
old Trevor doesn't like the thought of outsiders knowing too
much.'

'Old Trevor will be damn' pleased with the deal I've pulled
off,' Toby returned, 'and anyway, Ursula isn't likely to blab.
She's involved now.'

'I know. And I appreciate that it's the money that'll hold
her. But my worry is that, at some point in the future, she
might get a bad attack of moral rectitude. If she blew the
gaff, we'd all be very unpopular – and not just with the
Revenue boys. Trevor wouldn't want the Committee of
Lloyd's to poke their noses into his dainty arrangements,
would he?'

'On the other hand, Ursula wouldn't want to blot the
noble name of the late Ivor: and he, let me remind you, was a
director of Draycott's. I think she'll keep her trap shut.'

While Sir Woodbine and Toby conferred in the dining
room, Martin was making plans to return to London. 'We
ought to leave soon, little one,' he said to Lucinda, 'if we're
to miss the rush-hour traffic in Seven Sisters Road. Are you
all packed up and ready to go?'

'I wish you wouldn't call me little one,' she said petulantly,
'it's so patronising. And I'm not coming back to London.
Not yet. I can't just walk out and leave Mummy on the day
of Daddy's funeral, and Giles isn't going to be much use.'

She looked at her brother, who had been making the most
of the convention that alcohol should flow after a funeral. His
thin hands grasped a tumbler of dark whisky as he attempted
to anaesthetise the thought of living under the same roof as
his mother in London.

156

'But, Lucinda,' Martin protested, 'you did promise you'd come back with me today. After all, Sir Woodbine will be staying on for a day or so, so your mother won't be on her own.'

'I'm staying,' she answered flatly. 'And I may need the car, so you'd better hitch a lift with Toby.'

Martin was dismayed. He wasn't accustomed to living on his own, and although he liked their little house, it seemed cold and unwelcoming without his wife's presence. Nor was he the kind of man to relish the prospect of a 'pink ticket', as his acquaintances at Lloyd's called the licence to indulgence and masculine bad behaviour conferred by a spouse's absence. Such suited neither his inclination nor his pocket.

'I don't see why you feel you have to hang around here,' he muttered.

'You wouldn't, would you?' This came from Giles: it could have been a light remark, but there was a sneer in his tone that Martin put down to the effects of the whisky.

'You keep your mouth shut,' Lucinda snapped at her brother, with some effect, for he slumped into an armchair with a shrug. 'Look, Martin,' she returned to her husband, 'if Mummy really plans to flog Tickton, there's a hell of a lot to be decided. I've simply got to stick around for the next few days.' She was trying to keep patient reason in her voice, but Martin was puzzled, for he detected in her a bubbling high spirits, an excitement that he could not relate to the loss of her father. He took off his spectacles to polish them, his bright blue eyes staring into Lucinda's face, her chin raised in determination.

Reluctantly, Martin gave way and went off to take his leave of his mother-in-law and of Gasper Grieve. The latter, expansive in florid affability, seemed to have assumed the role of host, even suggesting that Coley might roll down to Tickton again for the weekend, if he had nothing better to do.

In the car heading back for London, Toby glanced sideways at his friend. It's always the husband who's the last to know, he thought to himself. Certainly Lucinda had made little secret of her real reason for staying behind and, equally certainly, Giles had guessed what she was up to. Lucinda's

157

bedroom, the one she had had as a girl, was only one door away from the spare room where the baronet was installed, and Toby was sure that there was a good deal of creaking in the corridor at night. What he hadn't yet decided was Lucinda's motive: she had been throwing herself at Gasper since the Blacketts' party, and Toby knew that they had met often enough in London since then. It would be trite to suggest that she found in the baronet a substitute father-figure; maybe it was just plain old lust, or perhaps Lucinda had an ambition to become the second Lady Bulkely-Grieve.

What did worry him was the effect on Martin when, as was inevitable, he found out about his wife's infidelity. Martin Coley did not regard his marriage vows casually, and it was obvious that he was still very much in love with Lucinda. He would be hit badly.

They were now passing through Epping Forest, the narrow main road clogged with lorries. Martin was still slumped in gloom. Poor trusting chump that he was, even he might soon work out what was going on, so Toby decided to distract him, to misinterpret his silence.

'You've nothing to worry about, you know, Martin,' he began. 'About the syndicate, I mean. The change in the ownership of the Agency won't affect your position as underwriter: all that'll happen is I'll join the board of the Agency, and one of my first acts will be to invite you to join me there.'

'You can promise me that neither you nor Trevor Bleach will try to interfere with my underwriting?'

'Of course not. Mind you, there are areas where the Draycott Group could probably help you. But the decision would be entirely yours.'

'Meaning?'

'Meaning re-insurance, for the most part. I know you already have a quota share with Bay Street & Global, but you're still spreading your re-insurance all around the market.'

'Of course. It's one of the basic principles of underwriting, to spread the risk.'

'Naturally, Martin; you don't have to teach your grand-mother to suck eggs. All I'm suggesting is that it might be to the syndicate's advantage to negotiate a larger quota share with Bay Street & Global. After all, you're for ever moaning that your underwriting margins are cut to the bone, and the commission you'd receive back will make a hefty addition to your profits.'

'M . . . yes, there is that. I'll have to think about it.'

'Good man. I'll send a broker round soon to discuss it with you.'

Toby concentrated on a roundabout and began to think about a route that would take them across London so he could drop Martin at Adelaide Place. Then he had an idea.

'I say, I'm going to take a drink off Paul this evening. He's just come back from one of his sudden summonses to attend upon his lord and master in the South of France. Why don't you come along with me – I know he'd be glad to see you.'

'It's kind of you, Toby, but I don't think so. I'm not feeling very convivial, and I've a lot to do at home. The house is a bit of a mess and I'd like to get it straight before Lucinda comes back.'

Poor fool, thought Toby. But, he decided, he couldn't leave Martin on his own; he again urged him to tag along and in the end, too indifferent to put up much resistance, Martin agreed.

When Toby and Martin entered Paul Blackett's flat, they were surprised to find the little drawing room full. There were several other young men and a sprinkling of Paul's casuals draped about the sofas and window seats: the room was full of high-pitched chatter and of several different and expensive scents. Paul provided them both with drinks and then took his brother's elbow.

'I'm glad you've looked in, Toby,' he said. 'There's something I want to ask you. You won't mind, will you, Martin?' and without waiting for an answer, he took Toby off to his bedroom.

'Have you noticed anything odd about your boss Trevor Bleach?' Paul flung himself down on his bed, heaving aside a pile of coats and furs.

'No. Not especially.' Toby was noncommittal: he in turn

159

had questions for his brother, but first he would hear what was in Paul's mind. 'Give me a clue.'

'Well, for a start, you know that a while back Trevor took off to the South of France to see Vathos?'

'Yes, he told me. The meeting seems to have been very inconclusive, although since then the Draycott Group have tied up all Ithaki-Hellenic insurances, as you well know.'

'But you and I could have done that on our own. It didn't need a personal encounter between the great men. And there's another peculiar thing. When I got to Cannes last weekend, there was no sign whatever of Vathos. Masterakis wouldn't – or couldn't – tell me where he was, and I was left kicking my heels in the Carlton for three days until the *Thermopylae* sailed in.'

'I don't see anything odd about that. You can't expect your mighty shipowner to be concerned about wasting your time. I think you're just jolly lucky to be given a few days' hookey in the South of France.'

'Yes, but even when I did see Vathos, it was only about something very trivial. It could perfectly well have been dealt with on the phone.'

'Oh, forget it, Paul. There's no future in trying to read the mind of a Greek shipowner.'

'I wonder. You see, it did cross my mind that Trevor Bleach might have been trying to interest Vathos in that Bay Street racket of yours.'

'No way.' Toby was certain. 'And it's not a racket, by the way. Even if Trevor did think of it, I can tell you for sure that nothing of the kind has happened. Mind you, isn't it possible that it's the other way round? That Vathos tried to persuade Bleach into an investment in this new super-tanker?'

'The *Katherina Vathos*?' Paul sat up. 'Why should Vathos do that?'

'There are rumours that your wily Greek caught a considerable cold in the spot market. And the new tanker is costing a bloody fortune. I tied up her final cover while you were away last week, and the *Katherina Vathos* is standing him in for well over fifteen million dollars now she's on the high seas. She must be the most expensive tanker afloat.'

'Fifteen million?' Paul echoed. He was shaken. Then,

noticing that both their glasses were empty, he suggested it was time they rejoined his guests in the next room.

'Just a moment, Paul. I've a question for you. Just what was it that you and Trevor were celebrating the night we saw you at the Mirabelle?'

'Nothing much. It was just his way of thanking me for setting up the meeting with Vathos.'

'It looked like more than that to me,' Toby pressed. 'I've never seen Trevor drink champagne before.'

'Perhaps you haven't appealed to him in the right way.'

'I don't know what you mean,' said Toby stiffly.

'No? Anyway, old Trevor was so full of good will I thought the time was right to touch on a little scheme I've been brewing up – a property venture on which I could clean up in a big way, only I don't happen to have the starting capital.'

'How much did you touch him for?' Toby was becoming angry.

'Half a million was what I needed.'

'Bloody hell, Paul, that's a fortune.'

'Well, it was my chance to make a decent pile, which I'll never get out of Vathos. And I thought I knew how I could clinch it there and then.'

'Clinch it? How?'

Paul spreadeagled himself on the bed among the heaped-up furs, his legs wide apart. 'Just lay back,' he said with a giggle, 'and thought of the Bank of England.'

'Paul, you didn't! You mean . . .' Toby spluttered.

'Oh come off it, Toby,' Paul sat up again. 'You must have guessed that Trevor, dry old stick though he is, must be a suppressed queen. Haven't you had the friendly arm on the shoulder, the pat on the bottom in the lift?'

Toby didn't know what to say: he was startled to find himself shocked; yet, at the same time, he reminded himself, he too had received some such hint. Perhaps he had better find out more. It would be as well to be prepared.

'I had no idea what might be expected of me,' Paul went on, 'but after all that Dom Pérignon, I didn't much care. So when Trevor suggested that we came back to my flat for a night cap, I thought, well, this is it.'

'What was what?'

'The time for me to earn my half million, of course, you idiot. The trouble was that Trevor squatted down on my sofa with a stiff whisky and began talking business. I couldn't concentrate on that, and I decided that perhaps he was shy and didn't know how to open the next stage of the proceedings. With girls, I'm quite good at turning them on – you know the technique, hang up your jacket, slip off your shoes, fling away your tie and undo a few buttons of your shirt. Then you perch on the arm of the sofa and leave it to them to make the next move. They always do.'

'My God, Paul, you're talking like a tart. A nasty little male tart.'

'Oh, don't be such a prig. I'm only telling you this so that you're forewarned. Anyway, I didn't seem to have much effect on Trevor: he just sat there like a squeezed lemon, babbling away about bank rate. I thought we'd never get anywhere if I didn't make a further move so after muttering something about being a little hot, I undid a few more buttons of my shirt. That at least had some effect on him: he stood up and said, in that precise little voice of his, that perhaps before anything else he'd better go and have a wash.'

'That was your cue, I suppose?' Toby observed.

'I took it as such. The bathroom is through there' – Paul pointed to the wall behind his bed – 'so while he was splashing about, I threw off my shirt, slipped out of my trousers and lay down, all pink and pretty in my Y-fronts, waiting for him to make some move.

'And did he?'

'It was most odd.' Paul's voice was puzzled. 'He came back and just stood there, looking down at me for what seemed like ages. Then he just gave a dry little cough and turned away.'

'That left you with egg on your face. Didn't he say anything?'

'When he reached the door, he paused. Without looking at me, he said he assumed I must have taken too much champagne and that he would leave me to sleep it off. Then, after adding that he didn't suppose our paths would cross again in the future, he left.'

162

Toby burst out laughing. 'That must be the most expensive strip-tease in history,' he exclaimed.

'It was a bit of an anticlimax,' Paul agreed, 'but at least I'd done my best to keep what I thought was my side of the bargain. And you do see now that the old stick is a great deal more peculiar than we thought.' He picked up his empty glass. 'We'd better go back to the others,' he said. 'And I don't mind admitting that telling you all this has made me terribly randy: I must go and cut out one of the swingers before they're all booked for the night.'

Martin Coley, left to his own devices in Paul's drawing room, made no effort to join in the party. He was thoroughly depressed by Lucinda's determination to stay on at her mother's house: he wasn't feeling in the least sociable and yet he remained sitting there, reluctant to return to his empty home. All around him elegant young women, sleek in their carapace of sophistication and glamour, were talking brightly with Paul's assortment of friends – stockbrokers, estate agents, advertising account executives as well as Lloyd's men. At one time, Martin would have made an effort to join in, to be one of them: but this evening it seemed futile. He had no part in their confident, aggressive and greedy world; he had to face it that to them he was, and always would be, an outsider, what they would describe among themselves as a jumped-up nobody. Lost in gloom, Martin stared down at the carpet, an island of silence in the sparkling sea of the party.

Above and behind him, Michael Pendragon was gossiping with two girls. All three had piercing voices, made the sharper by Paul's drink, and Martin couldn't help listening.

'Have you heard the latest about Gasper Grieve?' Pendragon was saying. 'Apparently he's serious this time.'

'The bad baronet?' cried Kerry (or it might have been Kim). 'I've never been out with him myself, more's the pity, for I ache for those middle-aged, craggy men.'

'Really, darling,' said Kim (or Kerry), 'he's old enough to be your father.'

'I know, darling,' answered the first, 'that's just why I fancy him. It must be so deliciously dirty to sleep with your father.'

'Well, I'm sorry to disappoint you,' Pendragon put in, 'but from all I hear, Gasper is no longer up for grabs.'

'Oh well,' sighed Kerry, 'I expect he'll be back on the market sooner or later. By the way, who's the lucky girl? Is she here? Is she one of us?' She looked eagerly round the room.

'Of course not.' Pendragon gave a harsh laugh. 'Gasper's much too fly to shack up permanently with one of you lot.'

'Well, come on,' urged Kim, 'do tell.'

'I don't see why not.' Pendragon was enjoying the attention of both girls, and he lowered his voice before continuing. 'Actually, she's the wife of a Lloyd's underwriter. I don't suppose you know her.'

'Don't be mean,' chorused both girls, 'you've simply got to tell us who she is.'

'She's called Lucinda Coley.'

Martin dropped his glass. Blindly he rose and pushed his way through the crowd to the door.

'Good gracious!' said Kerry, startled into gentility. 'Who on earth was that?'

'I'm afraid,' said Pendragon, 'it was Martin Coley, Lucinda's husband. Surely he must have known?' he added, excusing himself. 'Silly sod.'

14

In the Underwriting Room at Lloyd's, John Bishop was a little anxious as he approached the box. For the second morning running there was no sign of Martin Coley, and since Martin had always been punctilious in his timing and about telephoning on the rare occasions he had been absent, Bishop's anxiety grew. He had hoped that there might have been a note among the pile of broker's advices that made up the mail, but a quick glance revealed no letter. There was nothing for it, he decided: it was beyond him to cover up for Martin any further. Luckily, Toby Blackett was both a director of the agency and a personal friend of Martin's: Toby would know what to do.

Toby's response was to appear at the box almost at once.

'It's most unlike Martin,' Bishop began. 'I've rung his home several times but there's been no reply. Is Mrs Coley away?'

'Yes, she's staying with her mother.' Toby didn't explain that he had just spoken to Lucinda: she had no idea where her husband might be and she made it plain she didn't care much. 'Actually,' Toby went on, 'I was with Martin the night before last. He left a party very suddenly, after receiving some bad news. I think you can say that he has been called away on urgent private business. Meanwhile, you're the deputy: it's up to you to keep the box ticking over as best you can. Any problems?'

Bishop hesitated. He knew that Martin had expressed a

concern that some of the syndicate's lines on one or two risks, especially a new super-tanker, were rather larger than might be prudent: he had been planning to go through them with a view to laying them off through re-insurance but, to the best of Bishop's knowledge, he hadn't yet done so. Should he mention this? For, on the other hand, here was his opportunity, his chance to show that he could act on his own initiative, to take decisions on behalf of their names: it wouldn't look good to run whimpering to Toby with just a routine matter.

'Nothing to worry about,' he said finally, 'nothing I can't handle.'

'Good man,' said Toby, looking at his watch. 'I've got to get back to Draycott House, but I'll try and look in later this afternoon to see how you're getting on.'

As he dodged through the Leadenhall Market on his way back to his own office, Toby wondered where on earth Martin had holed up. He had heard from Michael Pendragon of the unfortunately overheard conversation, and of Martin's abrupt departure; but he hadn't expected Martin to go to ground so completely. Or to go to pieces. He remembered vaguely that Martin's mother lived somewhere in West London: it might be worth glancing at a directory to see if he could give the old bag a ring: she might know her son's whereabouts.

Back in his own office, Toby found Trevor Bleach installed at a table with his open briefcase. He put Martin out of his mind – there was no need yet to tell the chairman of the underwriter's disappearance nor of the reasons – and for some minutes they discussed the prospering affairs of the Draycott Group.

'Now we've secured the Murchison agency,' Bleach was saying, 'we've completed our hold on the circle of insurance. We can control the profit at every stage.'

'Not quite,' Toby cavilled. 'We can't claim to control the individual names.' He was, after all, a name himself.

'I'm not concerned about the names.' Bleach dismissed the members of the syndicate with a shrug of his thin shoulders. 'They'll be quite content with whatever we throw them, while we maximise the profits elsewhere.'

'Which means, in practice, Bay Street & Global.'

'Just so. The management funds are building very satisfactorily. You're going to be a rich young man, Toby, as I promised.'

'Surely there's still an element of risk? I mean, we haven't been in the re-insurance market long enough to avert catastrophe in the face of a few disastrous claims at the same time.'

'Our reserves within Bay Street are not inconsiderable,' said Bleach primly. 'And in any event, your own personal funds are tucked well away, far out of reach of any possible claim.'

'Well, that's good to hear.' Toby paused. Now, perhaps, was an opportune moment to clear up the question-mark which had stood over him since his association with Bleach began. 'Look, Trevor, I wish you'd tell me just why you've been so generous. I mean, I've got a good job, which I flatter myself I'm doing rather well, but ever since we started together, you've gone out of your way to cut me in on your plans. It's not that I don't appreciate all you've done for me: but I wish you'd tell me your reasons.'

'Ah.' Bleach stared over at Toby: his eyes behind the thin-rimmed spectacles were cold slate-grey. 'I think you have been talking to your brother. As far as he is concerned, let me just say that Paul was under a misapprehension and made himself look very foolish.'

Inwardly, Toby heaved a sigh of relief: thank God he was off that hook.

'As to my motives,' Bleach continued slowly, as if he had not often spoken of what moved him, 'I am interested in money: what I might describe as absolute money, for I am not concerned, as you will have observed, with the trappings of wealth. My interest lies in the ways that money can be made to work, like yeast in a loaf of bread, to grow and grow. I have no wish to eat the loaf; but I do like to watch it rising.'

'There's no point in baking bread if you're not going to eat it.'

'I don't agree. The baker, after all, doesn't eat every bun that comes out of his oven: he sells them, to make more money, to make more buns, and I do the same.'

167

Toby was listening intently; he had never before heard Trevor Bleach so eloquent, but he was still no nearer an answer. 'That dooesn't really explain where I come in,' he observed.

'Money yields more than dividends and profit,' said Bleach. 'It may be a cliché, but it's a fact that money equals power: thus, it will be true that the absolute money at which I aim will bring an absolute power. Along the road, I need able lieutenants, such as yourself, Toby, young men of ability, certainly, but also fired by both ambition and greed. If I am to exploit the former, it makes sense to slake your appetite for the latter, provided always that I remain in control, that I have power over you. After all, you may have accumulated a handsome sum of capital, but you can't get access to a penny of it without my say-so.'

Toby had learned a good deal from this exchange, and it was clear that Bleach was not going to say more: he had, however, one more question, which he posed while Bleach was engaged in shuffling his papers back into the briefcase.

'By the way, why did you go and see Vathos in the South of France? Oh, I know we've secured the Ithaki-Hellenic account, but I think we'd have managed that anyway, and a trip on a yacht in the South of France doesn't sound like your style.'

'No, indeed.' Bleach's narrow-lipped smile flashed briefly. 'I was curious to meet him: there was of course an element of each exploring what the other might, at some stage, do for the other, but in the same way you've just asked me about my motives, I wanted to see what drives a Greek shipowner.'

'And what does?'

'He's a spender.' Bleach's tone was censorious, puritan. 'He's interested in making money all right, but he only wants it to spend and to gamble with. He likes to show off, too: that yacht, for one thing, and flashy objects like his wife's jewellery, they're extensions of his own ego. So, too, is his much-vaunted merchant fleet. He'll go on building more and more ships to fly his flag, like that elephantine super-tanker he's just launched . . .'

'The *Katherina Vathos*,' Toby broke in. 'We've just completed her insurance cover. She's cost him a fortune.'

'Just so. And she may not even pay her way. The freight scene is changing fast, and in a few years ships like her will be lying idle all over the world. But that doesn't matter to Vathos: it's enough that he's built the biggest, the best, the most expensive.' Bleach shook his head. 'Vathos will never be serious, as far as money is concerned.'

For Bleach, as Toby knew, to be less than serious about money was a scarlet sin.

Martin Coley awoke slowly, his mouth sour, his head like flannel. As he came to, he realised he was in his old bedroom at 31, Oaklands Drive, lying in the narrow bed he had slept in as a boy. As, blearily, he focused on the wan light filtering through the thin curtains, recollection came flooding back: a patchwork of scenes, shadowy, unconnected. He could recall Pendragon's voice, high and sharp as he pronounced Lucinda's name; then, as if he were an extra standing in the wings, he saw himself in Paul's room, surrounded by a circle of Paul's friends, all with shining faces and idiotic grins as they looked down, jeering at the cuckold in their midst. In another flash of memory, he heard the sudden silence that fell over the party as he elbowed his way to the door, he felt their stares in his back, and as he closed the door behind him, he heard the chatter rising again in a new crescendo of laughter.

The next scene was in the street – any street. He was stumbling aimlessly along the pavement when a bus drew up beside him. He saw that its destination was Ealing Broadway: without thinking, he swung on board and when finally it stopped, his feet took him automatically along the quiet, tree-lined streets to his mother's house. Here the lights were on, the door unlocked.

His mother had been slumped in an armchair. Her hair was unkempt, its blotchy gold streaked with grey, her face bare of make-up save for a garish smear of red lipstick from which a trail of saliva dribbled down her chin. Her jaw hung slackly as she stared into the flickering television screen intently, as if she was searching for some message; but whatever it might be, she would not learn it, for the sound was turned off.

She had looked up briefly when he came in. 'Hullo, Martin,' she slurred, 'where's that pretty wife of yours then?' She did not wait for an answer, but turned to the table at her side, where there stood a bottle of Gordon's gin. She refilled her glass to the brim with neat, clear spirit, knocked half of it back, and repeated her question.

As Martin watched, everything fell into place: his mother was a drunk. The answer, which he was amazed had never occurred to him before, was both starkly simple and at the same time far too complicated to think about at that moment: his mind was too full of the bile of his own bitter misery. Instead he fetched himself a glass and sat down beside her, helping himself to a large gin.

'That's right, dear,' she said with an attempt at cheerfulness, 'you help yourself. There's nothing like a drop of gin to perk up the spirits. Where's that pretty wife of yours then?' she asked for the third time.

Martin began to explain. In his mother's state, there was no point in saying more than that he and Lucinda had had a row and perhaps he could stay at Oaklands Drive for a few days. His mother looked up sharply: despite the mists of alcohol, her son's white face and shaking hands and his air of hopeless despondency registered.

'It's more than a row you've had, isn't it? She's left you, hasn't she? Well,' she sighed, 'I always said it couldn't last. She's too lah-di-dah for the likes of us, that's the long and short of it.' Then her tone changed; it became derisive, venomous. 'You were a bloody fool to think you could hold on to a girl like that. She was bound to go off with one of her own kind in the end. And you were even more of a fool to think that by marrying her, you would become one of them. You're not, and they know it, and the sooner you accept that you're just a nobody from Ealing, the better.'

This delivered, Mrs Coley had fallen silent, such attention as she had returning to the television, and to her glass. Martin felt no wish to say any more, no urge to utter any defence; in any case, his mother would have forgotten all that was said by the morning and would have to be told again. So they sat there, side by side, without speaking, their only communion the gin bottle that stood between them.

Lying in bed, Martin was reluctant to rise, to start the day at all. Apart from further explanations to his mother, in the sober light of the morning there were practical matters to be faced. He accepted without question that the conversation he had overheard contained the truth: looking back, he could now see clearly all the signposts of Lucinda's infidelity to which before he had been blinded by love. That passion was now dead, killed by betrayal and by his wife's now obvious indifference to him; but he must at least make some effort to communicate with Lucinda, to tell her that he realised their marriage was over.

Of Lloyd's, of his job, he refused to think at all. The acrid, bitter misery that still lay in his stomach like a layer of grease on a stew suffused his mind. What he needed most was simple kindness, and he did not think he would find that in the Underwriting Room: even if Toby's friends did not actually jeer at him, there would be knowing glances, hushed voices, sudden silences at his approach. Better by far to lie low, at least for a day or two.

Throwing back the eiderdown, he swung his legs out of bed. Earlier, he had heard the creaking of the stairs that told him his mother was on her way down to the kitchen: perhaps she would have coffee ready and perhaps in the morning quiet she would extend to him a hand of comfort.

Martin padded downstairs barefoot and went into the kitchen. His mother was lying on the floor, her head at an odd angle against the oven door. Her shabby pink quilted dressing gown had fallen open, revealing her flabby breasts; she was unconscious, though her eyelids fluttered and her breathing came in short, shallow gasps.

He looked down at her for a moment: then, almost automatically, he went through to the telephone in the hall. The ambulance drew up amazingly quickly, and soon the men had shifted Mrs Coley's shapeless bulk on to a stretcher. One of them took her particulars, and the name of her doctor: then he told Martin which hospital would receive his mother, adding that there was no point in his coming along.

'She'll go straight into Intensive Care as soon as we get her there,' he said. 'Give them a ring in an hour or so and they'll tell you the form.'

Left alone, Martin wandered into the front room. The curtains were still closed, the air heavy with the smell of stale cigarettes: the coffee table was ring-stained from the sticky glasses and the ashtrays overflowed. He'd better clean up, he decided: it would give him something to do until the time came to speak to the hospital, and work, just physical house-work, might damp down both the despair he still felt at Lucinda's desertion and the guilt which grew, minute by minute, as he began to take in the nadir his mother had reached in the face of his neglect.

From the cupboard under the stairs, he fetched the Hoover and dusters, stumbling over a stack of empty green gin bottles which he took out to the bin. The kitchen too, he saw, was filthy, with a fat-streaked sink: grimly he settled to his task, obscurely gratified that there was so much to do; and so absorbed was he that he did not notice the whine from the telephone receiver, which he had left off the hook after dialling '999'.

15

Up on the bridge of the *Katherina Vathos*, Captain Dougall felt rather than heard the explosion. From the bowels of the ship there came a muffled clang and, as his hands rested on the rail, he felt a quick tremor, as if the huge vessel had been struck by a rogue wave. Then, in the next instant, all the lights went out and suddenly the tanker seemed to be ghosting along in the dank darkness: within the bridge house, a klaxon began to blare and a red light to flash. In a few seconds, the emergency lights came on, dull and yellow, and as the captain opened the door to the bridge house, he was greeted by a bank of thick, acrid smoke that filled the interior.

Inside the bridge house, all was chaos. Officers and men stumbled about, coughing and shouting through the black fumes, while the klaxon's wailing filled their ears: then, with the draught of fresh air from the door, the smoke began to clear. Nykiadopolou burst out from the radio room, his face blackened and his right arm limp.

'My radio!' he cried, 'he blew up, whoomp, just like that, in my face!'

'Pull yourself together, man,' said the captain. 'Take hold of yon fire extinguisher and see what you can do before the fire crew arrives.'

Below decks, the off-duty watches, roused by the alarms, were scurrying to their emergency stations; fire hoses were

173

unreeled, hydrants made ready following a well-practised drill. Mr Manises, the first officer, who had been at dinner when disaster struck, ran up the companion way to the bridge. He still clutched a white napkin in his hand and as he reported to the captain, Dougall had time for the wry thought that he looked more like a wop wine waiter than ever.

'Mr Manises,' he said, 'you'd best take charge of fire-fighting below decks. It looks like some kind of electrical fire, and the intercom's out of action, so please give my compliments to the chief engineer and tell him to report to me here as soon as he's assessed the damage.'

Manises hesitated. 'What about the engines, sir? Shall I tell the chief we're going to heave to?'

'Certainly not,' said the captain. 'Tell him to maintain half speed ahead if there's no damage to the engines.' Manises still stood his ground and Captain Dougall glared at him: then he decided to explain his decision to his first officer. 'When in doubt, stand out to sea: that's what I'm always telling young Pissou here. A vessel is much safer with plenty of sea room about her and with a bit of way to keep her navigable. Besides, over there' – he nodded over his shoulder – 'away to port we have a lee shore and a very hostile coast the north of Scotland is too. We wouldn't want to wallow about out of control and find ourselves on the rocks; we'll go steady as we are, heading out to sea. Mind you, with the radar out of action, we're fortunate that there's no other shipping about.'

Manises sketched a salute and disappeared below, and the captain began to survey the damage to his bridge. The radio officer emerged to report that he had managed to extinguish the fire in the radio room, but radio communication was out of the question for at least several hours. The radar screen was blank and the automatic pilot clearly out of action, its once smooth grey plates buckled and blistered. But there were few other signs of damage except for scorch marks where banks of cabling ran across the bulkheads; the flames were now extinguished and with the last of the smoke billowing out through the door and into the inky night, he ordered the klaxon to be turned off. The sudden silence fell on a bridge where some order had been restored; and, from

174

the throbbing under the decks beneath his feet, the engines sounded undamaged. The captain now needed to clear the bridge house of the remaining officers before he could embark on the next phase of the operation.

'Mr Enikos,' he summoned the second officer, 'will you take a party and make the rounds of the weather deck to check for damage. And you'd better inspect the forward tanks too, in case there's any danger of a flash fire from fumes. I know we're in ballast but you'll have to make sure. And Nicky' – this to the radio officer – 'you ought to take that arm of yours to the Sick Bay.' Then he turned to the cadet, hovering at his side. 'Mr Pissou, we don't want to be sailing blind, with all those contraptions knocked out.' He kicked at the silent radar. 'We'll have to navigate by dead reckoning. Hop along aft and stream the log, and then set a hand to report to me every half hour how many sea miles we cover.'

With Pissou gone, the bridge house was empty of officers. Able Seaman Privas stood by the helm, and, by the door to the wrecked radio room, two hands were standing by, extinguishers at the ready in case the conflagration should flare up again. Now another officer came in, dressed in oil-stained overalls, his face smeared and his cap at a jaunty angle. This was the second engineer.

'Mr Stavros' compliments, sir,' he began, stumbling over the courtesies that Captain Dougall demanded on his bridge. 'He say for me to tell you the engines is OK. Also the hydraulics for the rudder though he's not happy about all the pumps yet.'

'Very well.' The captain nodded gravely. Stavros seemed to have contrived matters very neatly, he noted to himself with relief.

Dismissing the young officer, he went over to Privas. The able seaman's English was very limited, but he was an experienced hand and he knew his drill; applying himself to two hefty crank handles, he disconnected the controls of the automatic pilot. Beside him was the wheel; with its turned spokes and gleaming varnish, with its unashamed wood, it had seemed an anachronism amid the electronic efficiency of the bridge house; now, with the old-fashioned binnacle that stood beside it, it would come into its own. Able Seaman Privas took up his station at the wheel, hands on the spokes, to await his captain's orders.

Captain Dougall cleared his throat and straightened his cap. 'Steer one-seven-two degrees,' he commanded.

'One-seven-two,' the able seaman chanted, bending his shoulders as he spun the wheel to bring the ship on to the captain's declared course.

Dougall turned away. The moment of decision had passed and with his seaman's sense he could feel the first change of motion as the great ship began to answer the helm. Privas might feel it too; but, good sailor though he was, he would be unlikely to question his captain's orders and would probably put down the change to the ship's loss of direction during the minutes of the fire and the consequent need to restore her to course. Fortunately, outside it was still very dark. Then he remembered the cadet Pissou, streaming the log on the afterdeck: despite the black night, it was just possible that the young man might spot a tell-tale arc in the ship's wake, perhaps shown up by phosphorescence in the trail of turbulent water: the cadet might have some awkward questions. He despatched a rating to retrieve the cadet from the stern and when he reported back, he was set to prepare a report on the damage to the radio room which, perforce conducted by torchlight, might keep him occupied for a crucial hour or two.

He turned from the cadet to find the first officer back in the bridge house and, what was worse, heading for the binnacle.

'Mr Manises,' he called out sharply, 'over here if you please. And what,' he went on more quietly but with all his authority, 'what are you doing on the bridge? My orders were that you should assist the chief engineer in preparing a full damage report.'

'Stavros has no need for me, sir, so I thought . . .'

'You *thought*?' the captain bellowed. 'Are you questioning my orders?'

'No, sir.' Manises was respectful, but standing his ground. 'I felt my place was here on the bridge. If the ship is in danger . . .'

'Danger?' Again the captain interrupted. 'The ship would

only be in danger if we'd followed your hare-brained suggestion that we hove to.'

'I must disagree, sir.' Manises squared his shoulders. 'We have no radar, no radio communication, we are sailing blind. Once we have assessed the damage, then we must head for the nearest port where we can obtain assistance and effect repairs.'

'Just so, Mr Manises. And those are my decisions, which I will take only when I am fully informed of the condition of my vessel. You will assist me best by returning to the engine room and speeding the preparation of the damage report.'

'Very good, sir.' Manises gave in and made to leave. On his way out, he paused behind Able Seaman Privas. 'By the way, sir,' he asked casually, 'what course are we on?'

'The same as before the explosion,' said the captain. 'Just about due west,' he added, carefully avoiding the use of numbers which the able seaman might understand, 'and a safe course to take us out to sea.'

With the departure of Manises, Captain Dougall was alone on the bridge with the helmsman. To his ears, accustomed to the steady clicking of the automatic pilot, the ping of the radar, the chatter of tape machines from the radio room and the murmured words of officers of the watch going about their duty, it was strangely quiet. He glanced at his watch: not yet nine o'clock. Less than half an hour had passed since the explosion, and several hours to go before the plans so carefully laid in Cannes were fulfilled. During these hours, he must endeavour to impose an air of normalcy upon his crew, to dismiss the fire as a minor hazard which Stavros would soon have repaired, and at the same time, with the aid of his hidden Radio Direction Finder, he must navigate his ship towards her secret destination.

If Manises were kept away from the bridge, the other officers should prove easy to distract. Fortunately, he thought grimly, they trusted their captain and his seamanship without question and in the aftermath of the explosion there was plenty to occupy them. It was perfectly natural that during the emergency the master of the vessel should remain on his bridge, in active command. Dougall was aware that he

177

was keyed up, his nerves on edge in anticipation of the most difficult feat of navigation he had ever faced. There was also, at bottom, a residual, sinking horror at the implications of the secret orders he had accepted from Vathos: no seaman would relish, at any time, deliberately placing his ship in peril; one error of navigation would mean disaster and very real danger for his crew, for the fierce and barren northern coast of Scotland was no place for mistakes. The landfall for which the *Katherina Vathos* now headed was a tricky one, complicated by the tidal stream now making from the west; although, from the point of view of the necessary secrecy, it was lucky that the night was dark and misty, he would have no visual bearings from any lighthouse to aid his navigation; apart from the RDF, the super-tanker was sailing blind into dangerous waters.

To distract himself from these dark thoughts, Ben Dougall turned his mind to the comforting subject of his private fortune. He was not a spendthrift, a gambler, or in any way extravagant, and his wife never failed to receive enough for her needs. But whenever he had had a bonus from Mr Vathos – and these had not been infrequent – the whole sum had been salted away, and there now lay, in a variety of bank accounts and portfolios in Geneva, Hong Kong and the Bahamas, enough capital to provide the captain with a deep pocket for the rest of his life. He knew, to the last dollar, franc or yen, exactly how much he was worth, and the total, stored not on paper but in his memory, was a constant source of gratification. For Ben Dougall loved money: not for power, not for display, but merely for the possession thereof. All in all, he was worth a tidy sum, and the thought of the bonus that would accrue from this particular voyage of the *Katherina Vathos* gave him a glow of satisfaction. Whatever happened now, soon he would be, by his own terms, a rich man.

While engaged in his mental arithmetic, the captain had been staring out from the windows of the bridge house over the weather deck far below. Without the arc lamps on the stumpy masts, the nine-hundred-feet length of the great ship disappeared into the solid blackness of the night: only the flicker of flashlights showed where Second Officer Enikos

178

and his party were going through the laborious task of checking each tank. There were fourteen wing tanks and thirteen more amidships; it would take some time.

He came to to find a sailor at his elbow, waiting patiently for his captain's attention. It was one of the hands from the afterdeck, come to make the half-hourly report of the sea miles covered; on his chart and making much of protractor, dividers and rule, he added these miles to the ship's putative course, almost due west; then, when the seaman had gone, he swiftly placed a small dot on the chart to show the vessel's real position as she ploughed steadily south at seven knots.

Still on edge, the captain waited impatiently for the appearance of the chief engineer. It was some minutes before the stocky, overalled frame of Ulysses Stavros shouldered through the door and came up to him with a formal salute.

'I regret to have to report, Captain, a most unfortunate accident.'

'Well, what is it, man, what is it?'

'First Officer Manises, sir, he has suffered a severe concussion. I have had him removed to the sick bay, sir, but I fear he may remain unconscious for some time yet.'

'Manises?' The captain arched his thin eyebrows. 'As if I hadn't enough on my plate. What the devil happened?'

Slowly, in his thick accent, Stavros explained. His voice was loud and he used frequent gestures, as if he were anxious that his report should be understood, not only by the captain, but by the three or four hands still on the bridge and by Cadet Pissou, who had come to the door of the Radio Room to listen.

It seemed that the chief engineer had suggested to Manises that one of the hydraulic systems was malfunctioning. Perhaps the first officer would inspect it himself? Unhappily, since they were relying on the stand-by generator, and because the gangway to the pump concerned was ill lit, the first officer had tripped up: he had gashed his head against a stanchion.

'I see,' said the captain, staring down at Stavros as he wondered how his chief had contrived the accident. It was not his side of the affair, however, and he knew better than to

179

enquire. Instead he asked, 'Is he badly injured? Will he need medical assistance?'

The chief shook his head. 'He'll come to in six or seven hours with a bad headache.'

'Good. And what is the state of my ship?'

Formally the chief engineer made his report. There was no damage to the engines or to the steering gear; the fire had been confined to the main generator, and was now under control. No other outbreaks had been reported, and the captain could be assured that he had full control of the vessel.

'Apart, that is, from the pumps,' he concluded. 'They seem to have suffered some damage, and we're still working to find out the extent.'

'So it seems,' the captain summed up, 'that we've lost the radar, the pumps and the automatic pilot, and the Radio Room's a shambles. What on earth happened?'

'The main generator seems to have malfunctioned, sir. It appears that there was a sudden, massive surge of power, and that's what caused the damage.'

'I see. Well the worst thing is to be without radio communication. Pissou!' he called out, 'how are you getting on in the Radio Room?'

'We've cleaned up, sir, and Vassilou – he's good with electronics – thinks he can get the stand-by radio working, if Mr Stavros can give us a power line.'

'Aye, lad, but how long will Vassilou take?'

'He says, maybe four, five hours. By dawn anyway.'

'Good. Well, keep him at it. And make the round of all officers, will you? I want all officers to report to the bridge at 24.00 hours. I shall then give my further orders.'

Cadet Pissou disappeared with his message and the captain turned to Stavros. 'I don't know about you, chief, but I think we've earned a drink.'

The two men retired to the captain's cabin. As soon as the door was shut, Dougall said quickly, 'You'd better make sure that power line to the radio room is defective. We want to keep radio silence as long as possible.'

The chief nodded and settled into a chair as he took the offered brandy. 'Well, Ben,' he said comfortably, 'I think we can say so far so good.'

Captain Dougall frowned at Stavros. The familar use of his first name, even in the privacy of his own cabin, jarred. Captain Dougall had always maintained a distance between himself and all members of his crew. Admittedly, Ulysses Stavros was more than just his chief engineer, more than just an old shipmate, for he had just as crucial a part to play in the present drama as Dougall himself. Still, it was just as well that when all was over, they would have to take care that their paths never crossed again.

'Your fire was most accurate,' the captain said, 'and just what was required. How did you contrive it?'

'You need not concern yourself with that,' Stavros answered easily. 'I had an idea, and it worked. And by morning, all trace of what caused the surge of power will be gone. As will the little black thread over which First Officer Manises so unfortunately tripped.' He chuckled and lit a black cheroot.

'There is still a great deal to be done,' said the captain severely, sitting down at his RDF. Listening intently, he tuned in on each beacon in turn and then noted down on his crumpled chart the ship's exact position. Stavros looked over his shoulder. 'Where are we thought to be?' he asked.

Dougall pointed with his pencil to a spot about ten miles north of the mouth of Loch Eriboll.

'But in fact we're heading for the coast, and right on course. That's fine navigation, Ben.' The chief's tone was jovial.

'Not too bad,' the captain admitted. 'But I shall have to make a slight adjustment to the course shortly. It's a narrow entrance we're making for, and we don't want to end up on the rocks.'

'How will you explain a change of course?'

'Oh, I'll just remark that I want to test the steering, to feel how the ship answers. Privas will swallow that.'

'And when do we . . . arrive?'

Captain Dougall glanced up at the chronometer high on the bulkhead.

'High water in the Kyle of Pogue is at 0.44 hours. I'm aiming to get there a few minutes before. I've called the officers together at midnight, and I want you to be a few

181

minutes late. When you do join us, make an issue as Manises would have done – urge that we turn and run for the shelter of Loch Eriboll. I'll argue with you, and that should distract the others. I don't want them to notice that we'll have run into calmer waters as we come under the lee of Whiten Head. My intention is that we . . . arrive while we're all on the bridge. By that time, it'll be too late to do anything.'

'It's almost too late now,' Stavros observed, looking at the chart. 'We're steaming at seven knots. It would take us three or four hours to lose way, even if we had room to turn and manoeuvre.'

'Yes,' said the captain, 'nothing can stop her now.'

After Stavros finished his brandy and left, leaving a cloud of thick blue smoke and a smell of cheap tobacco, the captain returned to the bridge. All was quiet, so he went out on to the wing.

The weather had closed in. Way ahead in the far distance, a faint glow was all that could be seen of the forepeak light; the air was clammy and the captain felt a fine mist settling on his face as he peered about. Suddenly, his eye caught the flash of lights. His heart leaped: surely he had made sure, before the radar blew up, that the seas were free of other shipping? Staring into the distance, he decided it must be some inshore fisherman, feeling his way along the coast: it was away to the east, much too far to concern him.

The trawler *Andy*, homeward-bound with a good catch of cod and halibut, was almost awash to the gunwales as she ploughed steadily east, helped by the flooding tide. She was so low in the water that she wallowed in the valleys of the seas and when she climbed, engines thrumming, to the peak of a wave, the whole ship vibrated as the screw was lifted momentarily clear. She was keeping inshore, where they would make the most of the tidal stream, and with any luck they would be unloading their catch at Wick by noon.

That night, of the crew of seven, two men were on watch. The wheelhouse was little more than a wooden shed, but by contrast with the black and misty night it seemed snug under the yellow lamplight and the two men, bulky in their thick sweaters, woollen caps and rubber boots, made it appear

182

crowded. The older man, Mory Fraser, was at the helm, one of his reddened hands on the wheel and the other nursing a mug of strong sweet tea: the other, Hamish McKay, was much younger and still fresh-faced; he too held a mug between his hands. The cramped cabin stank overwhelmingly of fish, as indeed did both men and the whole ship, but many days at sea had inured them to the smell.

As the trawler rose on the back of a long roller, Hamish happened to be looking aft. With an exclamation he scrambled to his feet, grabbing for the binoculars, but by the time he had them to his eyes, they were once more pitching down the scend into the trough of the sea.

'What's up with you, Hamish?' asked Mory.

'I thought I saw some lights, away to the stern of us.'

'What's that to do with us?' Mory shrugged. 'D'ye no ken the high seas are open to all, as we should know with all them pesky foreigners fishing out our best waters?'

It was an old grievance, but Hamish was not listening. Bracing himself at the aft window, he waited, binoculars at the ready, until the trawler heaved itself to the top of the next wave.

'There it is again,' he cried. His voice changed. 'And Mory, she was showing a red light.'

Mory was not particularly interested, but the sighting of another ship would make a break in the routine of the night watch, so he turned to join Hamish, staring out through the salt-caked window as the trawler's stern was lifted over the next summit. By some freak of the weather, there was a momentary break in the clouds away to the west and both men saw it now, a long black shadow on the horizon, silhouetted against the sky.

'Did you see that!' Hamish exclaimed, shaking Mory's arm. 'Yon's a fucking great ship all right.'

Mory returned to the wheel. 'Aye,' he said over his shoulder, 'one o' they super-tankers, like as not.' Fraser's interest had flickered out: his concern was to stand his watch and, he knew, the skipper was anxious to make port as soon as possible and to get the catch landed.

'Don't you understand, man?' Hamish was urgent, excited. 'She's showing us her port light and she's crossing

183

our stern. That means she must be heading almost due south, straight for the cliffs.'

'Nay, lad, don't take on so. I've seen them super-tankers before. She'll be that packed out with electronic gadgets, maybe they won't even bother to set a proper watch. I've seen that before. Call themselves seamen!' Mory's dismissal was contemptuous.

'That's just the point, Mory. I'm thinking they haven't an idea that they're standing into danger.'

The ancient phrase, the warning that every sailor learned when first he went to sea, stirred the helmsman's interest. 'Oh, aye?' He stared at Hamish. 'You could be right at that.' He thought for a moment. 'Maybe you'd best rouse the skipper – though he won't be pleased to be routed from his warm bunk.'

Grumbling and rubbing the sleep from his eyes, the trawler skipper came into the wheelhouse. The men explained what they had seen and when next the little ship peaked, the skipper took the binoculars. 'Well, mebbe,' he conceded, 'but my sight's not what it used to be and I'm no altogether sure.'

'I am,' declared Hamish. 'We have to do something to warn them, surely?'

'I'm no turning back,' said the skipper at once. 'We'd miss the tide through Pentland any road and there's nothing we could do – we'd never catch up with her, with the tide against us.'

'We could try signalling her,' Hamish suggested eagerly. The fate of the distant tanker had suddenly become to him a matter of concern.

'What, run a pretty little flag up the masthead and hope she catches sight of it on a night like this? Give me another.'

'Why not try raising her with the Aldis?' Hamish pressed.

'Oh well, off you go if it'll ease your conscience,' the skipper conceded.

Hamish scrambled into his oilskins and went out into the night, while the skipper settled at an untidy table in the corner, on which stood the ship-to-shore radio. 'Just for peace of mind, I'll see if I can have a word with the coast-guards. They're bound to know something.'

He sat down in front of the wireless, tuned it in through much crackling and, picking up the microphone, began to chant his call sign. Soon, through a buzz of static, he was talking to the coastguard station on Orkney.

'Trawler *Andy* of Wick, No. 2787, present position some four miles north of Strathy Head.'

'Come in *Andy*, what is your message?' The voice of the coastguard came through a buzz of static.

'We have to report sighting a large unidentified vessel, probably a tanker, that seems to be heading due south. She's some three or four miles astern of us, and we suspect she may be off course. Over.'

'Thank you, *Andy*. Just a sec.' In the crowded, steamy wheelhouse the two men could hear the coastguard talking to someone in the background. '. . . Hello, *Andy*, are you still there? Over.'

'*Andy* here, over.'

'Well, *Andy*, we have a report of a super-tanker, the *Katherina Vathos*. She passed through Pentland about 17.20 hours. She'd be in your area about now and we've tried to raise her on the radio, but she seems not to be keeping watch. Over.'

'Bloody tankers, they're all the same, think they own the sea,' muttered Mory from the wheel.

'Shut up, Mory,' snapped the skipper; then he bent again towards the wireless.

'If she's off course, we think she may be in some danger, over.'

'Thank you, *Andy*, but we don't think you need worry too much.' The coastguard's disembodied voice sounded vaguely amused. 'The *Katherina Vathos* is under the command of Captain Dougall, a Scot and as good a seaman as yourself, skipper. She's almost brand-new, and we think she's probably run into some radio trouble: in that case, Captain Dougall would be making for the shelter of Loch Eriboll, which makes sense of the course you report.'

'Oh. Ah.' The skipper sounded discomfited. 'We'd no cause to be worrying you, then.'

'You were quite right, *Andy*, and thank you. Over and out.'

The skipper switched off and went to the wheelhouse door. On the narrow bridge, Hamish had braced himself against the rails and had swung the Aldis lamp westwards. Steadily, he was flashing the message dot, dot, dash, dot, dot, dash. U . . . U . . . You are standing into danger.

'You've made fools enough of us, Hamish,' the skipper bellowed, 'let's have an end of your brownie games.'

Away to the west, the *Katherina Vathos* ploughed steadily south.

16

In 1965, the last of the high water springs fell on the night of 22nd/23rd March, a factor crucial to the success of Captain Dougall's plan. As, in the half-hour before midnight, he stood on the bridge of the *Katherina Vathos*, he could feel the flood tide tugging at the bows of the vast vessel, attempting to carry her off course. Already, he had made several trips to his cabin where, behind a locked door, he plotted her exact position with the RDF set in his wardrobe, and the much-folded chart he clutched in his hand showed boldly their putative passage almost due west and out into the Atlantic as well as, with a series of discreet and pencilled dots, the real course south towards the gaunt northern coast of Scotland.

On the bridge it was eerily quiet. Apart from Able Seaman Privas at the wheel, Captain Dougall was alone: the other officers were scattered about the ship, preparing their damage reports for the skipper's conference at twenty-four hundred hours, except for the observant First Officer Manises, conveniently unconscious in the sick bay. The emergency lighting, though adequate, cast deep shadows across the deck, though highlighting the squat grey bulk of the electronic navigational equipment, blistered and buckled after the brief fire and now silent, unchattering.

A hand came panting into the bridge house to report, from the streamed log, the sea-miles covered in the last half-hour. Gravely, the captain made a pencilled note, then, after another adjournment to his cabin to check the RDF, ordered a change of course two degrees to starboard. Stolidly, Privas chanted back the alteration. Momentarily, Dougall wondered what the able seaman made of his captain's frequent disappearances to his cabin: if he thought at all, he probably put it down to the skipper's need for an occasional dram: he would be too loyal – and too unimaginative – to mention such a suspicion later.

Outwardly, the captain appeared his usual disciplined self, the deep lines furrowing from his nose drawing his mouth into a grim downward curve of determination. Inside, however, he was as tense as he had not been since hunting submarines during the war: with the vessel heading straight for the inhospitable Scottish coast, there was by now no turning back; even at five knots, the great ship had enough way on her to make avoiding action impossible. In fact, to alter course now would stand her into greater danger. In any case, he realised, whatever happened in the next few hours until dawn, his career as a master mariner was ended.

There was time, he decided, for a last look outside before his officers began to report to the bridge. He went out onto the wing, grasping the rail as he looked down over the weather deck. There was a low cloud base and the sky was dark, not a star to be seen; with a thin sea mist, the light at the bow, hundreds of feet forward, seemed to flicker like a candle. There was no wind, and little sea running; only the wash of the waters along the tanker's sides and the steady thrumming of her engines disturbed the deep silence of the night. Conditions were perfect for what had to be done.

It was just as well. From the start, Captain Dougall had made it clear that he would not be party to any plan that might imperil his crew: if the weather was not suitable, the plan would be called off and that decision would be his alone. His mouth set more grimly as he remembered his owner's protest at this stipulation, as they sat round the table in the aft saloon of the Vathos yacht.

The order that Captain Dougall report to the *Thermopylae* had come three months ago. The *Katherina Vathos* had just completed her sea trials and was due to be handed over to Ithaki-Hellenic at any time: Dougall assumed he was to

188

receive his final orders for his new command – a matter of routine. He had been surprised, therefore, to find Mme Vathos also present, behind her tray of Turkish coffee: he knew that she did not favour the winter on the Côte d'Azur, so, he concluded, more than routine was on the agenda.

It was. He had gone through the plans in some detail with his owners: most issues were now settled, but one thing remained outstanding. Captain Dougall had reached over into the bookshelf behind Vathos' desk to take out *Reed's Almanac*.

'I see the last of the high water springs in March will be on the night of 22nd/23rd, at 0.44 hours. That gives us the cover of darkness. Would that date suit you, sir?'

The atmosphere between the three of them was so amicable, even social, that Dougall, as he watched Vathos consult his own diary, thought they might have been arranging some future dinner engagement.

'Perfect, Captain,' said Vathos. 'On the 22nd March, my wife is giving a soirée in Paris before a Gala at the Opéra. For some time, she has been pressing me to accompany her and now I can say I shall be delighted to be present. There's sure to be a lot of publicity,' he added as he closed his diary.

'Explain to me, Captain,' said Mme Vathos. 'If the tide is at its highest shortly after midnight, when will it be at its lowest?'

'About a quarter past seven in the morning, Madame.'

'And when does it become light?'

Dougall consulted the *Almanac* again. 'It'll be twilight by 5.22 and the sun comes up just before six.'

'It won't do, Captain, it won't do at all.' Mme Vathos shook her head decisively. 'What you propose is that for five hours of darkness and then a further hour and a half of daylight, the ship would be visible to any passing vessel, or even an aircraft. That is most undesirable.'

'Nonetheless, Madame, that is the way it will be.' Dougall stood over Mme Vathos as he spoke, his voice harsh. 'Otherwise, I'll not do it at all.'

There was a silence as Vathos stared hard at his captain.

'Very well,' he said at last, 'you're in command, Dougall. But at least you might tell us something to allay my wife's doubts.'

'Aye. For a start, at that time of year, we can count on the weather being pretty murky: we don't want a clear, star-lit night with a bit of moon, so if there isn't a good thick cloud base, the operation will be postponed. If we have a sea mist, not too thick, mind, that'd be a bonus.'

'But what about other shipping? The salvage tugs? The coastguards?'

'One at a time, sir, if you please.' With the comfortable feeling that he had established his authority, Dougall sat down again. 'We'll have to keep radio silence. Everyone at sea is used to Greek tankers that don't maintain a proper watch – though that's never been the case on any of my ships – and if another vessel or the coastguards spot us changing course to head south, like as not they'd conclude that we were making for the shelter of Loch Eriboll. And once we're under the lee of Whiten Head, we'll be off the radar screens anyway.'

'That would seem to take care of other eyes,' Vathos agreed, 'but I'm still concerned about the salvage tugs. Don't they often hang around the Orkneys, waiting for a killing?'

'Indeed, sir, they stand by in Scapa Flow. Generally Dutch, they are, blast their greedy eyes. I'd suggest we ought to arrange some kind of diversion that would take them scurrying off in another direction. Perhaps another Ithaki-Hellenic vessel might get into difficulties and send out a distress signal from the Forties?'

Vathos shook his head. 'Not another of my ships – that would be too much of a coincidence. But I think I have the answer. Do you know Captain Velos?'

'I've met him once or twice. But hasn't he left Ithaki-Hellenic?'

'That's right. He now has a command with the Dimitri line: one of their rusty old tramps that plies Scandinavian waters. And Captain Velos, I'm sure, could be persuaded to arrange the diversion you require.'

'Good. I'll advise you later of the exact timing when I've made my detailed plans. And that brings me to my next point: I won't be able to manage this operation on my own: I'll need to have some assistance on board.'

'I have already anticipated that, Captain Dougall. It so happens that I had a private conversation with your chief engineer when he was last in Piraeus. He too is willing to oblige. You may trust him completely and he is ready to assist you in the preparation of your plans.'

'Ulysses Stavros? He's good.' Dougall wondered to himself what price Vathos had proposed for the engineer's cooperation. 'It may be that between us, we could undertake the operation without any of the rest of the crew knowing. None of the hands speak much in the way of English, and as for the other officers, they'll do what I tell 'em.' Dougall had a thought. 'Except Mr Manises. I wish he wasn't my first officer: he's too damned clever by half; he might spot something amiss.'

'In that case, Captain Dougall, you will have to arrange for Mr Manises' absence from the scene of action,' Mme Vathos said, her voice soft. 'Perhaps he might go overboard?'

'Really, Madame!' The captain, rolling his 'r's, was outraged. 'I'll trouble you to remember that – ' He broke off: he had been about to say 'Katherina Vathos', but some delicacy reminded him that the name was the same as that of his owner's wife – 'that the tanker is under my command and I am responsible for the safety of every man on board. Including Mr Manises.'

'I think, my dear,' Vathos interposed, 'that we may safely leave all the details to Captain Dougall and Mr Stavros. In fact, the less we know, the better. Now, Captain, here is a small payment in advance, just to seal our agreement, as it were: it will be paid into your account in Geneva today.'

Dougall glanced at the paper: it was an advice of the transfer of twenty-five thousand dollars, just enough to hook him to the venture. He nodded and tore up the advice.

'And here,' Vathos continued, handing over a fat manila envelope, 'are your orders for the maiden voyage. We need to have an explanation for your presence here on the *Thermopylae* today, and it is my whim to hand you your orders personally.' He stood up.

'From now on, Captain, we are relying on you, both for

191

your skill and your silence. We won't meet again, so it only remains for me to wish you a successful outcome on the night of 22nd March.'

Now that night had come, thought the captain as he stood on the bridge of his ship. The die was cast and the detailed plans hatched in the privacy of his cabin with the chief engineer were already in action. The contrived explosion had done just what was required of it. Manises was disposed of, and it wanted five minutes to midnight, when his officers would convene.

Along the rim of his peaked cap a row of droplets had gathered, moisture from the dank mist. He put up his cuff to wipe them away and as he turned, he glanced in through the glass of the bridge housing. There, standing by Able Seaman Privas, was the second officer: and he was staring down at the binnacle. He seemed to be checking the ship's course and there was on his face an air of puzzled bewilderment. Captain Dougall hurried inside.

17

Captain Dougall faced his complement of officers assembled on the bridge of the *Katherina Vathos*. They were all present, except First Officer Manises, still unconscious in the sick bay, and (as arranged) the chief engineer. The second officer, who had been looking at the binnacle when the captain came in, still wore an air of faint puzzlement, and it was from him that Dougall called for the first of the damage reports. The rest in turn made their reports.

'Well, gentlemen,' Dougall said, after a few moments' thought, 'I think we may conclude from what you have told me that I still have a vessel in a seaworthy condition under my command. The damage has been an inconvenience, but no more; and I feel that my decision to maintain our course westward has been borne out by this.'

'But Captain,' protested the radio officer, whose arm was in a sling, 'surely we cannot proceed while the radio is out of action, the radar useless? Why, there is no knowing where we are!'

'I know exactly where I am: I'd remind you that I've been navigating by dead reckoning all my life at sea, and I've no call on yon new-fangled gadgets to tell *me* my ship's present position. If we can effect the necessary repairs on board and quickly, then we'll make our passage to Nigeria without incurring any delay.' Dougall scowled around the knot of officers, as if defying any to gainsay him.

'I'm sorry, Captain, but it is not as simple as that.' The voice was that of the chief engineer, who had appeared at the top of the companion way, a hand braced on each rail. His face and his overalls were smudged with dirt and grease, his peaked cap awry: he stood his ground as the captain glared across, then swung himself into the bridge house.

'The damage is worse than I thought,' he declared. 'First, I find we cannot hope to repair the main generator ourselves; and, second, the hydraulics are useless. Without hydraulics, we have no pumps; and without pumps, we would be help-less if we had to shift the ballast.'

'So, Chief, what are you suggesting?' Dougall's tone was icy.

'I'm suggesting, sir, that we run for the nearest harbour. This ship is in no condition to remain at sea: we're sailing blind, and in bad conditions we'd be in the greatest danger.'

The chief engineer's statement threw all the other officers into jabbering confusion. Until then, they had relied without question on the judgment of their skipper: with that judg-ment questioned by the chief, they began, loudly and in a mixture of Greek and English, to advance their own ideas of a safe haven for which they should now head. Even Cadet Pissou, his mind still full of the lesson in Scottish geography he had received earlier in the day, joined in.

Captain Dougall moved away from the babel of argument to stand alone in the middle of the bridge, looking forward. To any of the officers who might look over, it would appear that he was deeply concerned at the chief's announcement of their plight; hand on his chin, he frowned out into the black night. In fact, through the soles of his shoes, he could feel a subtle change in the rhythm of the vast ship, a minuscule easing of her movement that told him they had entered the lee of the cliffs of Whiten Head and were now in calmer waters, sheltered by the land from the scend of the long Atlantic rollers.

His eye went up to the chronometer, high on the bulkhead above him: 0.34, it read. Just a few minutes, a very few minutes, and he would know whether his navigation had been accurate, whether he had allowed enough for tidal drift.

194

Or would the *Katherina Vathos* smash without warning into the towering cliffs of this fierce northern coastline? Then again, on either side of the entrance to the Kyle of Pogue there were jagged, half-submerged outcrops of rock, ranged like teeth at the mouth of the estuary: perhaps the vessel would impale herself upon these, with a dreadful, shattering shriek as they tore through the tanker's thin bottom? He shook his head, to dismiss the thought: by now, the fate of his command was beyond his control.

'Sir, sir!' Captain Dougall turned to find Cadet Pissou tugging at his sleeve. 'You remember, sir, you told me about a safe harbour, like a finger into the Scottish mainland? Loch . . . Loch Eri-something?'

'Loch Eriboll? Aye, I'm minded of it. Why?'

'Well, sir, I thought that maybe we might make for that: you said it was an anchorage for the largest ships, and it has a lighthouse too.'

'H'm.' As a master, accustomed to having his orders obeyed without question, in normal circumstances he would never have entertained such a suggestion from the cadet, his most junior officer; but, now, he had to act out the, for him, difficult role of a man in a rare state of indecision: this would serve to throw his officers into further confusion. 'It's an idea,' he conceded: then, hands behind his back and with Cadet Pissou eagerly at his elbow, he rejoined the knot of officers gathered around the helmsman's back.

'Gentlemen!' He reduced the hubbub to silence. 'The chief engineer's report has put a very different complexion on our plight. I now think we have no choice: we must alter course by ninety degrees and run for the nearest safe anchorage where we can summon aid. That means Loch Eriboll which, according to my reckoning, is now sou'sou'east of us. We should make landfall by first light.'

The second officer, whose air of bewilderment had increased as the captain gave out his decision, stepped forward. 'I'm sorry, Captain, but I do not understand. What do you say is our present course?'

'Two-seven-two degrees: almost due west: what of it?' Dougall snapped.

'But, Captain, that is not our course!' The second officer's

195

voice rose into a wail. 'Look, look at the compass: we have been steering one-seven-two degrees – almost due south.'

Captain Dougall strode over to the binnacle and glared down on to the illuminated compass card. 'What in hell's name?' he murmured, adding in little more than a whisper, 'My God Almighty, we must have been heading almost due south ever since the explosion.'

In the bridge house, there was utter silence. On all the officers the realisation was dawning that their captain had made a gross error of navigation, and that their new, vast ship was – and had been for some hours – heading straight for the inhospitable and perilous mainland. Dougall himself was just waiting.

At last it came. High up on the bridge, they all felt the huge length of the ship give a gentle heave: slowly, softly, the bows, away ahead in the blackness of the night, rose up: then came a series of bucking, juddering jolts that caused several officers to miss their footing, while the nearest stumpy derrick tumbled over to fall athwart the weather deck in a mass of tangled stays.

The chief engineer was the first to act. 'Stop the engines!' he cried, leaping to the telegraph to ring down the change. But the order had no effect: driven on by her own momentum, the vast mass of the ship cleaved her way into the sandbank under the surface of the sea with a groaning, grating roar as the plates beneath the water scraped against the shoal.

In the bridge house, all was chaos. While some were still groggily rising to their feet, Cadet Pissou had gone over to a locker, from which he was handing out orange lifejackets, and the second officer stood at the top of the companionway, bawling out an order for All Hands on Deck. The captain remained braced against the binnacle until, after what seemed like an age, the ship's crazy motion came to a stop and she rested still, with a ten-degree list to port.

'In God's name, where are we? What has happened?' It was the third officer who spoke into the quiet, voicing all their thoughts.

'I . . . I don't know.' The captain slowly turned to face his officers. 'It would seem that we have run aground.' He made a show of studying his folded chart and of making calculations. 'It is probable, if our true course was 172°, that

196

we are actually in a sea loch called the Kyle of Pogue. We shan't know, I might add, until first light; if that is our present position, then I consider we have been very lucky. We must wait until dawn.'

'I'm not going to hang around and twiddle my thumbs while the ship sinks beneath us,' declared the second officer, who thought he saw signs that the skipper had lost his nerve.

He took charge, sending men to swing the lead at various points along the deck to determine the depth of water beneath the hull, others to stand as lookouts against the time when visibility should improve, and a third party, under the control of Cadet Pissou, to swing out the boats on the port side, in case they should have to abandon ship. This task took some time, for it had to be done manually, owing to the failure of the hydraulics.

The chief engineer was heading back to the engine room when the second officer stayed him with a call. 'Mr Stavros, one moment: I've been thinking that if we could pump out the forrard tanks and shift the ballast aft, we'd lift the bows further out of the water: perhaps she might free herself with the help of reverse thrust from the engines.'

The chief shook his head. 'Good thinking, boy,' he conceded, 'but we haven't a hope, with all the pumps knocked out of action.'

'We've got to do something,' the second officer said desperately. 'It's past high tide already, and soon it'll be ebbing fast. In a few hours, we'll be high and dry.'

Still fretting against inaction, the second officer launched into a diatribe against the skipper's apparent indifference to their plight: both men looked round, and saw no sign of Dougall. He had left the bridge house.

'Let him be,' said the chief quietly, for the first time speaking in Greek. 'It's a sad time for the master of a vessel when his command comes to grief. The old man will want to be alone: then, you'll see, he'll be himself again when daylight comes.'

Under the chandeliers in the bright-lit salon of their apartment in the *XVIe arrondissement*, M. and Mme Vathos had just returned from the Gala at the Opéra.

'I thought Callas was in fine voice tonight,' Mme Vathos observed, as she perched in a Bergère chair and began to peel off her long gloves.

Vathos did not answer. He was engaged in lighting a cigar. In any case, he had not been interested in the music, and the name of the piece they had just seen escaped him; what gave him satisfaction had been the flashlights of the photographers in the foyer. He knew that in the morning, gossip columns all over Europe would record the presence, among that glittering throng, of the Greek shipowner and his jewel-bedecked wife. He would be conspicuously distanced from any unfortunate events that might be taking place off the north coast of Scotland.

Mme Vathos was now unscrewing her pendant ear-rings: the sapphires clattered as she laid them on a table at her elbow, then her hands went to the cleavage of her ball gown to undo the safety catch of the brooch: the great stone, the Rose of Alexandria, glinted as she placed it carefully alongside the ear-rings.

'I'm glad we didn't have to sell them,' she remarked. 'And I'm glad you insisted that tonight I wore the real thing. After all, Laertes, they were the best present you've ever given me.'

'Of course you had to wear 'em tonight. The *gratin* could tell in a flash if you were trying to get away with paste.'

She settled back in her chair, looking up at her husband as he straddled the Aubusson carpet, his legs apart as if he were at the helm of one of his ships. In his dinner jacket he looked constrained, uncomfortable; and she knew that they were both on edge.

'And so,' she said quietly, 'tonight will see the demise of our super-tanker.'

'If all goes according to plan, yes. Mind you, Captain Dougall can still call the whole operation off, if he's not satisfied about weather conditions.'

She glanced at the lyre-shaped clock on a Boulle *bureau plat* ticking away the minutes. 'By now, it will be too late. Already the die will be cast.'

A silence fell between them, their thoughts stretching to the distant northern coast. The ticking of the clock made

Mme Vathos nervous. One aspect of the plan still troubled her.

'Tell me, Laertes,' she said, 'why must all this take place just off Scotland, so near to land? Surely it would have been more judicious to let the ship go down far out to sea, in deep water?'

'And the crew would have their little suitcases all packed and ready in the lifeboats, I suppose?' Vathos laughed harshly. 'No, my dear, it may be easy enough to open the seacocks and let her go peacefully to the bottom, but it's happened too often before and the finger of suspicion points straight at the owner. What we need – and what I hope we're having – is a genuine shipwreck.'

'You hope?' she echoed. 'Are you not certain?'

'Don't worry, my dear.' He rose, patted her shoulder and then went over to the writing table. 'It's happened before, you see,' he said over his shoulder as he rummaged in a drawer. 'There was a tanker that got into trouble in the approaches to Rotterdam: she beached herself on a shoal and when the tide went down, she broke her back.'

'Was she a total loss?'

'No, that time the salvage tugs reached her in time – and she was fully laden. But let me show you.' He returned with a Cartier pen across which he laid, at right-angles, a long wooden pencil. 'The pen is the sand-bar at the entrance to the sea loch and the pencil is our tanker. Now, our ship is in ballast: she's empty amidships. With her forward tanks filled with sea water, and with the weight of the engines and the top-hamper aft, by low tide she will split in two.' He pressed hard on each end of the pencil, which broke with a sharp crack at the point where it pivoted on the pen beneath.

'That should be satisfactory,' she murmured. It was her turn to fidget; she got up to pace across the parquet, giving the clock an impatient look as she passed.

'How long, do you think, before we have any news?'

'It should come through to the office some time tomorrow morning. It depends how long it takes for the crew to reach the nearest village. And then the office will inform me.' Vathos chuckled. 'Little Masterakis will be scared out of his wits at having to break it to me that my beloved *Katherina Vathos* is a total loss.'

'What will happen next?'

'I shall issue a dignified statement from here in Paris. While expressing my dismay at the loss of such a magnificent new vessel – and one named in honour of my beloved wife – I shall also express my thanks to God that the lives of the crew were spared. And I shall confirm my intention to continue the expansion of Ithaki-Hellenic: which we shall indeed be in a position to pursue.'

'But the money, the insurance money, Laertes: how soon will Lloyd's pay out the claim?'

'It will not do for us to be impatient, my love. The British have their own laborious rituals with which they dignify these things. With any marine loss in British waters, there has to be a Board of Trade inquiry.'

'An inquiry?' Mme Vathos' voice rose. 'Laertes, you never told me! We shall be ruined.'

'Calm yourself, my love. It is not a police examination, not by any means. Of course, Lloyd's themselves will make investigations, but they won't find anything. As for the inquiry, it's rather like an English court of law, very gentlemanly, very smooth – and, I think, quite easy to mislead.'

'You may say that, Laertes, but what if you yourself had to make an appearance? It would be most undignified, and our reputation might be torn to shreds.'

'They will not be able to call me as a witness, for there is nothing material I could tell them. I do not even own the tanker, remember? Ithaki-Hellenic has merely acted as its managing agents. In any case, I am Laertes Vathos, the Greek shipowner: no Board of Trade inspector would expect a personage of my stature to travel all the way to Inverness merely to confirm a few facts that could better be provided by my employees.'

'Who, then, would be called as witnesses?'

'Paul Blackett, for one, in his capacity as the London manager of Ithaki-Hellenic. But since he knows nothing, there's no risk in that.'

'Paul will make a good witness,' Mme Vathos observed. 'He looks so clean and truthful – like an English schoolboy.'

'Exactly, my love, and that will be his role. He'll convince them that Ithaki-Hellenic – and the management of Ithaki-Hellenic – runs in an honourable, straightforward British way. Though he'll have nothing to tell them, for he knows nothing, he'll be a convincing witness.'

'But it won't end with Paul, surely? What, precisely, is the purpose of this Board of Trade inquiry?'

'The inspector – who's rather like an examining magistrate – hears evidence to enable him to determine the causes of and reasons for the loss of the ship. It will be a tedious affair, with a multitude of technical witnesses: Apallson's, for instance, will be represented in order to establish that there was no fault in the construction. But the main witnesses will be Captain Dougall and the chief engineer, Ulysses Stavros: it is here that we will encounter possible danger.'

'They're being paid enough: they'll keep their mouths shut,' said Mme Vathos succinctly.

'But we don't want them to keep their mouths shut.' Vathos looked down crossly at the stub of his cigar, which had gone out: he took another, bit off the end and lit up. 'Their evidence will be crucial. You must understand that in order to disable the ship's radio, radar and all the navigational equipment, Stavros has had to stage an electric fire, enough to knock out communications without disabling the ship.' He glanced at the lyre clock. 'That fire will have occurred several hours ago, and by now he should have had time to clear up, and to remove any indications that the fire might have been deliberate; even so, the inspector will, without doubt, go closely into the matter of the fire. Divers might even be sent down to examine the wreck, and here we must just hope that the rough seas of the Atlantic will have done their worst.'

'Hope?' Mme Vathos cried. 'We cannot rely on hope.'

'Indeed, my love, we cannot. Instead, we rely upon Captain Dougall. It will be the captain's task to divert the attention of the inspector from the fire: he will declare, under oath and with all the weight of his forty years' experience at sea, that the wreck was due solely to an error of navigation. As master of the vessel, he will take complete responsibility for that error; and, in the face of such evidence from a Scottish master mariner, the inspector will find his task made easy.'

'And what will happen then to the captain?' Mme Vathos sounded anxious: she had always had a soft spot for Ben Dougall.

'The inspector's report will censure him severely: he'll be disgraced in the eyes of the Merchant Navy and he'll probably lose his master's ticket.'

'*Mon pauvre capitain*,' Mme Vathos murmured.

'Not so poor,' her husband reminded her. 'Once he's been paid his price, he'll have more than enough to console him in his retirement.'

Mme Vathos rose and went over to the marble chimneypiece: restlessly, she rearranged the ormolu candelabra, its crystal pendants tinkling as she moved it. They were both insulated by inaction: there was nothing they could do, and the long wait until morning stretched ahead intolerably. They couldn't stand around in silence, so she broached a topic that would absorb them both.

'It has never been quite clear to me,' she began, 'exactly how much we will clear from this venture at the end of the day.'

'Let's go through it,' Vathos responded. 'Once our claim is paid, we first discharge our debts to the bankers.'

'Miserable usurers,' said Mme Vathos. 'I shall be relieved to be rid of the burden of Mauser's.'

'Nonetheless, they have been useful to us, and may well be so again. After all, our credit will still be good.'

'Let us hope we will not have to avail ourselves of it,' she said sharply, turning to look across at him.

'There will be no more speculation on the spot market, if that's what you mean,' he answered. 'From now on, I'll stick to shipping.'

'I'm glad to hear it. Well, proceed.' She waved her hand. 'Let us see what resources we will have to devote to the wellbeing of Ithaki-Hellenic.'

'The expenses of the operation are considerable. There's Dougall to be paid off, and Stavros, and a *pourboire* for Captain Velos, not to mention a clerk at Apallson's who's been most obliging in the matter of certification of invoices.'

202

'I know all that.' She tapped her foot impatiently. 'I just want to hear what we net.'

'I would estimate that at the end of the day, we should clear between four and four-and-a-half million.'

'Dollars?'

'Dollars.'

'I consider that most satisfactory.' From her tone, Mme Vathos might have been approving a dress at Givenchy. 'But' – her brow furrowed – 'strictly speaking, the ship – and the insurance money – belongs to the Liechtenstein corporation. Do you propose to further enrich the other shareholders?'

'Not if I can help it. Captain Dougall will be amply rewarded in his retirement: he'll not expect more.'

'And Paul Blackett? Will he be silent?'

'Paul knows nothing. He may suspect a little of what will have happened, but the last of the relevant papers covering the final insurance of the tanker were cleared through the London office while he was kicking his heels in the South of France. He may hear of the final figure from his brother, the broker, but he'll find no documentation to prove a thing.'

'He might still talk,' Mme Vathos warned.

'I fancy he'll keep his mouth shut.' Vathos chuckled. 'He knows better than to cross a Greek shipowner. Yes,' he pursued with confidence, 'we can retain the whole of the profit for ourselves.'

'It is not just for ourselves,' she said, 'it is for the future security of Ithaki-Hellenic.'

Vathos fetched himself a cognac, and his wife a Green Chartreuse; then they settled down, side by side on a sofa, to elaborate their plans for the expansion of their shipping line, with its new fleet of smaller, faster, more profitable vessels sprung from the bones of the vast super-tanker which would, if the events of the night went according to plan, soon be rusting on the rocky floor of the North Atlantic.

Captain Dougall descended from the bridge and picked his way slowly in the dark along the tilting weather deck. There was now no more than a breath of wind and the sounds of the sea came clearly to him: the even, sucking hiss of waves upon a pebbled beach and, further away behind him, a more thunderous roar from ocean rollers breaking over rocks.

It was done, he thought. Everything had gone according to plan, his navigation had been without fault, the ship had run smoothly on to the sandbar and was placed where he had intended. Yet he felt no jubilation, only a sadness as vast as the night sky above him. He felt, deep down in his guts, the stirring of the traitor's worm: he knew he had betrayed the sea, which was his calling and his life, and he was about to betray this fine vessel, the mighty *Katherina Vathos*, a ship he had watched as she was built, had seen launched, had commissioned and which was now entrusted to his command. For this ship, here on her natural element, was his, his alone, and he was about to be her executioner, for the sake of naked avarice.

His hands grasping the rail, he felt the ship twist and shudder as the ebbing tide sucked at her underbelly. Alone on the vast weather deck, he faced the bitter truth: whether it be thirty pieces of silver or six hundred thousand dollars US, the price of betrayal is self-hatred.

Dougall straightened his back: it was too late now for regrets. He had no choice: he must see the operation through. Then he felt his cheek and looked up: the wind, which had been a light sou'westerly, was now backing and becoming fresher by the minute; by morning, it would be blowing from the northeast, straight into the mouth of the Kyle of Pogue. The low cloud cover was beginning to break up, with a few stars showing through the ragged gaps, and as he climbed the companionway back to the bridge he saw for the first time an intermittent flashing light, a regular glow reflected from the sky through the lifting haze. He paused to time it, and nodded with satisfaction.

In the bridge house, the officers were still gathered in a knot. He scowled at them as they jabbered away in Greek, then barked out, 'Gentlemen!' They turned round at once: their captain had reasserted his authority. 'I have now established to my satisfaction that we are indeed aground in the Kyle of Pogue. The lights you may see flashing in the sky to the west come from Loch Eriboll, the next inlet over the mountain.'

'We must send up Very lights,' urged the second officer. 'The men at the lighthouse would see them and get us assistance.'

'No, we'll keep the rockets until we need them. In any case, I doubt that the lighthousemen keep watch all night. Where is Cadet Pissou?' He looked around.

It was explained, by several voices, that the cadet was supervising the preparation of the boats. Able Seaman Privas was despatched to fetch the boy back to the bridge, for Dougall wanted to make sure that the cadet's log was kept up. Then he called for a report on the soundings.

'That's not so good. It would appear,' he explained, 'that the vessel is aground amidships, but both bows and stern are in deeper water. As the tide runs out, she'll be high and dry just about in the middle, in the area of tanks eight, nine and ten. Now, the bow tanks have the ballast, which we cannot pump out, and here at the stern we have the full weight of the engines and the top-hamper. There's a considerable danger that by low tide she may break her back.'

'Then we must free her,' the second officer declared loudly. 'Why don't we put the engines full astern and see if she'll come free under her own power?'

'It wouldn't work,' said the chief, 'the engines are simply not big enough.'

'Besides,' added the captain, 'she's stuck pretty hard: you can tell from the list. Giving the engines full power would only risk pulling the hull apart. Mind you, a couple of strong tugs could do the job, but without our radio, how are we going to whistle them up out of the night?'

'I shall go ashore,' said the second officer. 'Once on land, we should be able to raise the alarm.'

'Good thinking,' Dougall agreed, satisfied that things were going his way. He peered out of the glass. Visibility was improving, already he could see against the clearing sky the black silhouette of the mountains which lay to the east. 'You'll need to see where you're going, but it'll be first light in forty minutes or so. You will take a party ashore then.'

He went on to give more detailed orders. First Officer Manises was to be brought from the sick-bay and placed in

205

the shore-going boat, where he would be joined by the injured radio officer. Blankets and a tarpaulin must be found so that the shore party, as their first task, would erect shelter where the injured men would remain until help came.

Dougall then called the second officer over to the chart table.

'I've no road map to help you so I'll explain the lie of the land.'

He placed his finger on the chart. 'You'll land here, and there are no houses for miles around. There'll be quite a march ahead of you before you can get to a telephone.'

'I'll just take three men with me, sir. A small party will be faster.'

'Aye. But make sure you choose the fittest: and that you all have stout boots. Now, there's a burn – a small river – that runs into the Kyle of Pogue at the head of the bay. There may or may not be some kind of sheep track alongside it, but whatever you find, just follow the burn as near due south as you can manage. Keep away from the hills and the moorland, mind, for you could easily get lost and wander round in a circle if you lose sight of the stream. It will be a difficult march, six or seven miles maybe, and then you'll come to a decent road.'

'That shouldn't take us more than two hours, sir.' The second officer was eager to be on his way.

'You don't know the terrain, laddie; it'll be more like three hours, I'm thinking. It's uphill all the way. And once you reach the road, you turn east – to your left: that will take you over the moors for another three or four miles, and then you drop into the next valley. I seem to remember there's a causeway across the water; then you will have reached Tongue.'

'Is this Tongue a port, sir? Will there be a guard of the coast? Who do we go to for help? Perhaps, Captain, you should come with us, for our English is not good?' The questions came from all round.

'One at a time, please. You won't find much in the way of a port at Tongue, for it's no more than a few cottages and a scattering of crofts. But like as not, there'll be a police station or a Post Office, and they'll put you through to the nearest coastguard station. Once alerted, the coastguard will know what to do.'

'I still think, sir, that you should lead the shore party. It will be difficult for any of the rest of us to make ourselves understood.'

'No. My place is with my ship. But I'll write it all down for you, what you have to say, the ship's position, all the details. As for the rest of the crew, I shall pick six or seven men to stay with me: all the others you will take ashore, and they must remain on the beach with the injured until help arrives.'

'Please, sir,' said the cadet, 'please let me stay with you on board.'

'Very well, Mr Pissou, you may be part of the skeleton crew. And the chief engineer remains on board.' The captain proceeded to more detailed orders, such as the lowering of another boat and the provision of scrambling nets from the rail on the lower side, in case the men left behind should have to abandon ship in a hurry. By this time, in the eastern sky there was a faint glow of yellow, and with the sea mist gone they could see, minute by minute, more of the bay in which their ship was stranded: it was a desolate place, with sombre moorland rolling down to the curving beach: no houses, no trees, nothing but the sound of the sea as it broke upon the shingle.

Captain Dougall chivied his men as they prepared to leave: now dawn had come, he was anxious that they be on their way. Then, without warning, they all froze: from the very bones of the ship there came a long, low groan that boomed echoing through the empty tanks and set up a violent tremor in the high bridge house.

'She's coming under strain, sir,' said the chief. 'If the shore party are to get help in time, they'd better be on their way.'

Captain and chief engineer watched from the wing of the bridge as the boat swung away from the black side of the hull: it was crowded, not only with twenty men and the first officer's stretcher, but with blankets and small cases in which the crew had hastily stowed some of their more treasured personal possessions. Soon the small boat had grounded on the beach, was hauled well up from the water's edge and a bivouac established around a fire of driftwood.

'It's a pity about the fire,' the captain remarked. 'It might just attract the attention of some nosy-parker aircraft.'

'We'll soon be attracting enough attention anyway. That little beacon on the beach will be nothing to the smoke signal I plan to send up.' There was a grim relish in the chief's voice.

'What do you mean?'

'How long do you estimate we have before help arrives?' asked the chief, answering the captain's question with another.

'It'll take 'em four hours to reach Tongue, and after that they have to explain themselves.' The captain gave his sardonic grin, thinking of the confusion that would be caused by the arrival in the grey morning of four Greek seamen at a little local police house: it would be a little time before their dramatic story of a grounded super-tanker made sense. 'It's low tide in about an hour and a half.' Another clanging groan resounded through the vessel. 'The pivot of the hull amidships must be under great pressure already.'

Both men leaned over the rail. Far below, the surface of the sea was changing. With the effect of the on-shore wind against the waning tide, the water was breaking up into random little waves, and over the bar itself it had begun to bubble and swirl, patched with the yellow of the turbulent sand.

'I do not think we can count on the sea completing our task unaided,' said the chief carefully. 'Even after her back is broken, it might be possible to salvage the stern half at least.'

'And so . . . ?'

'And so I am planning to give the sea a little help. You don't need reminding, Captain, of the ever-present danger of fire at sea. Especially in a tanker, and even more in a tanker whose tanks, though empty, might still contain some highly explosive fumes. It can take no more than a spark to set them alight.'

'I trust that this spark will not be traceable to a human hand?'

'You can rely on me for that.' The chief looked slyly

208

sideways at Dougall. 'You've done your bit, and a very neat piece of navigation too. The rest is up to me, and I've got to see that the *Katherina Vathos* is utterly destroyed.'

'You're right: Mr Vathos insists on a total loss.' By now the groans were sounding regularly through the hull: a new noise was the occasional shriek of steel against steel as the plates buckled and the rivets were torn from their seating. Here in the stern the decks were heaving and twisting, not rhythmically with the sea but in uneasy little jerks and trembles, while far ahead they could see that the bows, listing more violently to port, were beginning to droop into the lowering pool of water that lay beyond the bar.

'The tide is doing its work,' Dougall said quietly, adding in a louder voice, for the benefit of the crew, 'you'd best go and check the engine rooms, Chief. And I think it's time we had all hands on deck.'

Stavros took his cue and disappeared below, while the captain joined the rest of the men, huddled in the bridge house in their flaring orange lifejackets. Able Seaman Privas, oddly, still stood at the helm, as if the stranded ship might still answer the commands of the wheel.

'I fear I was right,' Dougall told them, 'the ship is beginning to break her back. But we are in no immediate danger, for the sea is comparatively calm and we are not threatened with a storm.' He kept on talking: he had to occupy their attention while the chief engineer was engaged in his last tasks below, and he had to establish in their minds that up to the end their captain was taking all possible steps for the safety of his ship. 'Even if the stern half breaks away, it will still be buoyant and seaworthy,' he went on. 'Once that happens, we must take a line aboard the boat, and see if we can secure her with her stern anchor.' He was interrupted from further directions by the return of the chief engineer, his face sooted and smudged, his eyes wild.

'Fire, Captain, fire below!' he cried. 'Number One tank is in flames and with so few men, we have no chance of fighting it.' As if to confirm his report, a cloud of black, oily smoke puffed out from one of the hatches on the weather deck and drifted forward.

This was too much for the discipline of the crew: with wild

shouts they made for the rail and began to scramble over the side and down to the waiting boat.

'There's nothing for it, Mr Stavros,' said Captain Dougall, 'we must abandon ship.' He turned to Pissou, still hovering at his elbow. 'Over the side with you, boy,' he commanded, 'and mind you take good care of that log of yours.'

Alone on the bridge, the captain fetched his battered leather attaché case from the chart table and took a last look round, at the binnacle, the wheel and at the charred door of the burned-out radio room; then he too climbed down to the boat and slowly they pulled away from the towering hull to make for the land.

Seen from the beach, the enormous bulk of the tanker filled the bay. Her black bows rose up out of the water like another cliff, her long length ran out to sea as if it was some vast breakwater, hiding the horizon, and where she listed, she showed the red paint of her underbelly. It looked, Dougall thought, in some way obscene. And, seen from the distance of several hundred yards, the signs of the ship's distress were more apparent. The hull had sundered amid-ships and a jagged crack was opening down her flanks. From the hatches forward of the bridge, a twisting column of smoke spiralled into the sky: rich black and glutinous, it formed a pall over the stricken vessel.

The crew had gathered round their captain as he stood on the shore, watching. They were hushed, awe-struck by what was happening out there on the sand-bank: the nightmare of a company of mariners, forced to look on, helpless, at the death of their ship.

Without a word, the captain and the chief engineer detached themselves from the crew and, after climbing a few rocks, found a position on a small promontory above the bay, from which they could look down on the wreck. The fire had a real hold now: orange flames could be seen licking at the smart white paintwork of the superstructure. The gaping crack in the hull was widening by the minute as the tide ebbed faster: soon the forward section gave a violent heave, the bows dipped and slowly it rolled over to lie sideways, awash in the deeper water inside the bar, like the corpse of a stranded whale.

The aft section of the ship, now severed from its own long length, slipped backwards off the sand-bank towards the open sea, where it was caught by the tidal stream. Spun by some freak of the current, it began to twirl round slowly and almost with dignity.

This strange pavane did not last. A muffled boom came across the grey waters of the Kyle of Pogue: the fire had reached the fuel tanks and a glowing fireball erupted from the bowels of the hulk to send flames and sparks high into the air: flying debris fell hissing into the sea all around: for a moment the stern reared up to reveal propellers and rudder: as it hung there, they could see, emblazoned on the stern, the words KATHERINA VATHOS; then with a roar like that of a bull elephant she sank back and the boiling waves closed above her.

EPILOGUE 1968

From the counter of the newsagent's shop, Martin Coley picked up the *Financial Times*. A discreet headline had caught his eye: '1965: WORST EVER YEAR FOR LLOYD'S'. The article contained nothing that he didn't know already, except for the final figure for the total loss across the whole market, which was almost £38 million: this signified, he read on, that each member of every syndicate had suffered an average loss of £6,928, although of course this would vary in each case according to the individuals' premium income limits and their underwriter's policies.

Martin smiled grimly. His own syndicate had fared worse: far worse than the average. It was three years now since he had left Lloyd's; but owing to the requirement of the Corporation that the accounts for each year are not finalised until another two have passed, to allow for the settlement of all likely claims against the year concerned, he had only recently received the final figures from what had been the Murchison box.

The *FT* journalist had made much of the effect of the devastating Hurricane Betsy, which had swept up through the Gulf of Mexico to cause enormous damage along the American southern seaboard in September 1965. The lines which Martin had written in that market were unusually large, and only partly covered by re-insurance: the claims had been enormous. But what had been worse had been the total loss of the Greek super-tanker the *Katherina Vathos*, and here, Martin remembered, he himself had without doubt been derelict. For the loss had occurred just after he had written a large line on the risk; his intention had been to offload a large part of it on the re-insurance market; but then his domestic life had fallen apart, he had not returned to Lloyd's, and by the time his successor was installed on the box, it had been too late.

'Good morning, Mr Coley.' A middle-aged woman in a headscarf broke into his thoughts. 'I'll have twenty Benson, please, as well as my usual.'

Across the counter, he handed over the cigarettes and a *Daily Mirror*, then reached below. 'I've got your *Practical Woodworker* too, Mrs Dixon,' he told her, taking her pound note and ringing up the cash register.

She was followed by several more customers, and then there was a rush of children on their way to school. Later, the pensioners would start to drift in, for their tobacco, their paper and a little chat, and by mid-morning, trade would be slack enough for him to have a cup of coffee. Martin enjoyed running the little shop. He liked the casual contact with his regulars and it pleased him to meet their small needs: both the routine and the occasional surge of enterprise – such as stocking up with greetings cards before St Valentine's Day – gave him a structure to his life and such stimulus as he required, and there was a comforting feeling that each pound in the till was his and his alone.

For his mother had not long survived her collapse. She had lingered on, occasionally conscious, in the Intensive Care Unit, for about ten days. Once, she had come to and recognised her son standing at her feet: urgently, she had begged him not to sell the shops; a good little cash business, she whispered, was a great deal more useful than all his high-falutin' friends in the City. Martin, still feeling guilty at the state to which his neglect had reduced his mother, had made her a promise: in fact, her wish coincided with his own inclinations.

When he first returned to Oaklands Drive, he had known deep down that he could never go back to Lloyd's. Once, he might have loved the Underwriting Room and the bustle of the market place; now he knew that it represented another world, the world of Toby Blackett and his kind, and, recognising that he would never truly belong there, that love had died. As far as Lloyd's was concerned, a shutter rang down in his mind.

Keeping on Mrs Coley's business had been a battle. With five shops on good leases in West London, her estate had been surprisingly large, considerable enough for estate duty to bite hard. At all costs, Martin determined to hang on to the original corner shop that had been his grandfather's; and he would have hated to lose the semi-detached house in Oaklands Drive, the home that had welcomed him back from the West End. But it had not been easy. Despite his resignation, both as underwriter and from membership of Lloyd's, neither the Corporation nor his former employers would let go easily. Since Martin had not been a member long enough to build up any substantial reserves, the authorities at Lloyd's looked to his deposits to cover his underwriting losses: they would all be needed, and more. But Martin's financial position was made worse by the fact that when he first became a member of Lloyd's, Ivor Murchison's agency had advanced him most of his deposits.

The agency was now in the charge of Toby Blackett; and Toby felt under no obligation to be generous or even charitable to Martin. In his view, Martin had run away from his duty, had left Toby in the lurch and, what was more, had, with his misjudgment over underwriting and his failure to reduce the risk on the Greek tanker, put all the members of his syndicate in a very difficult position. Some names, admittedly, like Gasper Grieve, had built up reserves so ample that they hardly felt the effect of the losses at all; but the new members had to face a demand for more money. Toby himself had had to stump up rather over £7,000, and he resented it.

All this, and more, Toby had said when finally he made the effort to go to see his former friend. Martin had been busy in the shop, and they were continually interrupted while customers were attended to; but Toby's suggestion that the shop be closed and that they adjourn to a nearby pub to talk privately was turned down with a gentle shake of the head. 'I can't leave my shop unattended,' Martin said quietly. 'It would be very bad for trade and my regulars wouldn't like it at all.'

In the face of Toby's anger at his own losses, Martin had merely smiled, as if it were news as remote from him as a small earthquake in Chile, then glanced through the shop window. Toby had arrived in a black Daimler, and the uniformed chauffeur, decidedly out of place in the busy Ealing shopping street, was standing to attention by the door. Toby's protestations of poverty, he felt, were not very convincing.

Martin hadn't seen Toby again. But with all the daily papers spread around, he couldn't help but read about him from time to time. In the financial pages, Toby Blackett was talked of as a coming man; the Draycott Group was a favourite of the tipsters and the shares had climbed spectacularly during the years of the Bleach-Blackett management. There was some speculation that Toby would soon be elected to the Committee of Lloyd's; he also made frequent mention in the gossip columns, especially after his purchase of a famous Lutyens house in South Oxfordshire, with a thousand Chiltern acres around it. Even so far removed, Martin had known that Toby could not have afforded that from what he might be making at Draycott's, and it puzzled him for some days, until he remembered hearing of Toby's involvement in Bay Street & Global, the offshore re-insurance outfit which Martin had always considered faintly dubious: it must have survived Hurricane Betsy and be prospering mightily, he had concluded, for Toby to have embarked on so ambitious a purchase.

As for his mentor, the shadowy figure of Trevor Bleach seldom reached print. Occasionally, his name appeared as being behind some mammoth takeover, not just in London but in New York, Sydney and Hong Kong, but he remained behind the scenes; the only time he was exposed to the limelight was after a dinner party at Downing Street: the following day, his name appeared well down the list of prominent businessmen and City figures who had been entertained by the Prime Minister, and for a day or two speculation ran that he might have been recruited to the ranks of Mr Wilson's advisers.

Oddly enough, it was to Trevor Bleach that Martin owed his continuing ownership of the newsagency. After Toby left the shop in a rage, Bleach had instructed the new underwriter, another of his clever, avid young men by the name of Parnell, to visit Martin Coley and to resolve all outstanding matters that lay between them. He had also told Parnell not to be too severe: it wouldn't look good for Lloyd's to appear vindictive, and if possible Coley should come out with his home and at least part of his business intact.

Parnell had told Martin this: he didn't like his task and he added savagely that if he and Toby had had their way, Martin would have been stripped of all he possessed, down to his last shirt-button. Unlimited liability should mean just that.

The legend was growing in the Underwriting Room – and fostered by Parnell – that Martin Coley was responsible for the syndicate's exceptional losses, and much was made of his involvement in the *Katherina Vathos* disaster. The implication was that poor Coley had suffered some kind of breakdown.

He had given notice in March 1965, but had continued as an underwriting name until the end of that year. His losses, added to the existing debt to the agency, amounted to over £24,000. While Parnell went through the figures, Martin just sat back, indifferent, as if none of it was his concern; in the end, Parnell devised a scheme whereby, after selling two more shops and taking out a mortgage on the house at Oaklands Drive, Martin would avoid bankruptcy. Martin agreed, and signed every paper presented to him without even reading it.

Martin received nothing from the sale of Adelaide Place, his one-time matrimonial home. Since some of the original purchase price had come from Lucinda's family, she insisted that any profit from the sale was hers too. Martin didn't care; nor did he want any share of the furniture, or any reminder of the marriage that was now as dead as his passion for his wife. On only one point was he stubborn: he insisted, much to Ursula Murchison's distress, that Lucinda should be the defendant in divorce proceedings and that Sir Woodbine Bulkely-Grieve be named as co-respondent. Even so, Gasper Grieve, with an upper-class indifference to the implications of adultery, refused to leave his own wife to make an honest woman of Lucinda; she, dropping the name Coley and

216

reverting to Murchison, had been passed around the fortune hunters of Chelsea without, so far, nailing any of them to the desk of the Registrar's office.

The shop was quieter now, and Martin felt it was time for his morning coffee. He went to the rack at the door to fetch the *Daily Mail* which it was his habit to browse through; and, on an inside page, he was given another reminder of his former life. It was a short report, no more than a paragraph, under the heading 'Echoes of Tanker Disaster?', and it stated that the body had been recovered, in the waters between Hong Kong and Macau, of a man believed to be Captain B. Dougall, formerly of the British Merchant Navy. Hong Kong Police believed that the man had gone overboard from one of the harbour ferries, and the story concluded with a reminder to its readers that it was Captain Dougall who had commanded the ill-fated super-tanker *Katherina Vathos*, wrecked off the north coast of Scotland some three years previously. At the subsequent inquiry, the loss had been blamed on a navigational error on the part of the captain.

Martin grinned wryly. The implication was clear: that Captain Dougall had drowned himself in a fit of remorse. He was not surprised; he had always felt suspicious of the circumstances surrounding the loss and, being so closely associated with it, he had followed in some detail the reports of the Board of Trade Inquiry. The proceedings had been very dignified, very civilised: Vathos himself had not made an appearance, nor was he even represented; but expensive and learned counsel had been retained on behalf of Ithaki-Hellenic, who had been the vessel's managing agents, and of the Liechtenstein corporation who were the owners. The underwriters, too, had been represented, but in view of the captain's evidence under oath that he had made a mistake which he had subsequently failed to rectify as to the ship's course, and the confirmation of exactly how and when that mistake had occurred, from the personal log of some cadet who had been on the bridge at the time, the inspector had laid the blame squarely on the captain's shoulders. Dougall had been severely censured, and suffered the loss of his master's ticket; but the underwriters had perforce to meet the claim.

217

It was ironic, Martin thought, that the loss had had such a beneficent effect on the fortunes of Ithaki-Hellenic. With the claim settled, they had been ideally placed to move into the new era of oil freight, and during the 1967 war in the Middle East, Vathos' fleet of smaller, faster vessels had made him yet another fortune.

The bell at the shop door rang with a loud clang. The customer in a headscarf had come back. She looked around to see that the shop was empty and then leaned confidentially across the counter.

'Mr Coley,' she hissed, 'I've got a little problem with my insurance. My late husband, Mr Dixon that was, he used to deal with all that and I don't know what to do for the best. They tell me you used to be an insurance man, Mr Coley: would you be very kind and look at the papers for me?'

'I'm sorry, Mrs Dixon,' Martin answered with a gentle smile, 'I'm afraid I can't be of assistance. I'm only a news-agent: I know nothing about insurance.'